Praise for Pam Binder's
M[illegible]es

"Featurin[illegible]ne as fiery as her bri[illegible], this crisply written romance is lighthearted yet engaging."

—*Publishers Weekly*

"[An] intelligent, innovative approach to time travel. . . . With *The Quest,* Ms. Binder establishes herself as a powerful and inventive voice in paranormal romance. . . . Her brilliance and cleverness shine out of each and every page of this unforgettable book. . . . Let yourself be swept away by a brilliant new talent." —*Romantic Times*

The Inscription

"Readers will be drawn in by Pam Binder's magic touch for blending the natural with the supernatural and creating a spellbinding tale with many subplots, wonderful historical backdrop and color, and the added attraction of the Highlander immortal. This is truly a love story for the ages."

—*Romantic Times*

"Magical. A timeless love story."

—Stella Cameron, author of *Bride*

Books by Pam Binder

The Quest
The Inscription
A Season in the Highlands (anthology)
The Enchantment

Published by POCKET BOOKS

PAM BINDER

THE ENCHANTMENT

SONNET BOOKS
New York London Toronto Sydney Singapore

For information regarding special discounts for bulk purchases, please contact Simon & Schuster Special Sales at 1-800-456-6798 or business@simonandschuster.com

An *Original* Publication of POCKET BOOKS

A Sonnet Book published by
POCKET BOOKS, a division of Simon & Schuster, Inc.
1230 Avenue of the Americas, New York, NY 10020

ISBN: 0-7434-1794-1

First Sonnet Books printing September 2001

10 9 8 7 6 5 4 3 2 1

Front cover illustration by Richard Bober

Printed in the U.S.A.

To Jim,
my husband and best friend,
and the person who adds sunshine to my life.

Prologue

It was the end of all his dreams. Conor MacCloud stood with his wounded men and looked toward the mist-shrouded town of Inverness, Scotland. He was defeated. His castle and lands were in the control of his uncle, Simon. All was lost. He would not ask his men to fight again. The price was too high. He must find another way.

Death clung to the air as he eased his friend, Douglas, gently to the ground. "Fear not. At your request, Rowan has gone to fetch the healer, Magdah."

Douglas lay in a pool of his own blood. A glazed expression covered his eyes. Conor had seen that look before on the battlefields. He clenched his jaw. This was his uncle Simon's doing.

Douglas clasped Conor's arm. "I will not survive this day. It is for future generations of MacClouds that I ask for your pledge." He shut his eyes. Blood formed on his lips. He opened them and gazed in

Conor's direction once again. "Force alone will not defeat Simon. Magdah will know what to do."

Conor felt warm blood ooze from the wound on Douglas's head. "Rest easy, friend. We have sent for the woman ye speak of for her healing arts alone. I have told ye before we do not need a witch's magic. We failed to reclaim the castle today, but I know we can defeat my uncle. We need an army as great as his. When ye have recovered . . ."

Douglas's voice trembled. "I will not."

Conor swallowed, knowing the truth of the words his friend spoke.

A cool afternoon breeze rustled through the birch trees that bordered the clearing. Douglas shivered and his teeth clattered together. His face was the color of the storm clouds overhead. Conor knew the end was near.

The ground trembled from the force of horses' hooves. Conor looked toward the crest of the hill. His brother Rowan and the woman Magdah approached. He hoped she would at least have a potion that would ease his friend's passing.

Rowan reined in his horse next to Douglas and helped the old woman to the ground. Her waist-length gray hair blew around her weathered face as she hobbled toward them.

She withdrew a leather pouch strapped to her waist and sprinkled a translucent blue powder over Douglas's mouth.

Rowan knelt beside Conor. His shirt was torn, exposing fresh wounds on his chest and arms from the battle with Simon. "Brother, how fares he?"

Conor lowered his voice. "Dying."

Rowan nodded. "Have ye reconsidered Douglas's request to seek the Peacemaker?"

" 'Tis a legend, nothing more."

Rowan clasped him on the shoulder. "Perhaps not. Magdah believes there is such a woman. She may be our only hope."

Conor looked past his brother to the men who waited in silence beside their mounts. Each man nursed wounds received in their fight to regain the Castle MacCloud. There were six left from the hundred valiant men who had accompanied him on the Crusades over the past eight years. The price of death was too high. They had returned to discover that Simon had seized their lands.

His brother had suffered as well. His leg was broken in the battle at the mouth of the Nile River and had healed poorly after their capture. The Crusades had hardened Rowan's features until he resembled a man much older than his twenty-five years. But thankfully it had not blackened his heart. Nay, that gift the Crusades had saved for Conor MacCloud. He was older than Rowan by only five years, but felt as though it were more like ten.

Today Conor thought he would reclaim his

birthright. He had spent years fighting in the Crusades, and then after the siege of Damietta, in the year of our Lord thirteen hundred and ten, wasted even more in the hellhole of a prison in Egypt. He had returned home and learned that his father had died and the people lived in terror of the bloodthirsty Simon. There had not been time to grieve the loss of his father. There was only time to attack.

Douglas coughed and grasped Conor's hand. "Promise me."

The woman Magdah stood and leaned toward him. She whispered. "Your friend is beyond my power. I have given him something to ease his pain." She paused and pressed a gold ring in the palm of his hand. "If a Peacemaker still exists in any of the six realms, this band and the power of the Ring of Time will bring ye to her. I have consulted with the cards and the time is right. But ye must go today, on the eve of the full moon."

She straightened and walked over to the standing stone behind him. No one knew its age. It had been on the hill overlooking Inverness for as long as any could remember. Magdah circled it slowly. Conor wished he had not agreed to bring her here. It was common knowledge she was a witch and mad as well. He should have let his friend die in peace.

Douglas tightened his grip. Conor was surprised by the strength his friend still possessed.

His friend gasped for breath. "Promise me ye will seek the Peacemaker."

Conor sensed the life force ebbing from his friend's body. Time was running out. What Douglas asked went against all Conor believed. To keep such a promise would mean he would have to associate himself with a woman who practiced the forbidden beliefs. He had fought in the Crusades against such people.

Douglas's voice was little more than a whisper. "Promise."

Magdah began to chant in a language Conor did not understand. It floated on the wind toward him, easing his pain. His heart ached from those who had died on the battlefield. There must be another way to find peace.

Conor looked down at the ring he held. His eyes brimmed with unshed tears as he held his friend close and bid him farewell. "I promise, Douglas, I will find the Peacemaker."

1

The Present

Eilan Dougan unlocked the door to the antiques shop. She drew in a breath of crisp autumn air and smiled. The silver mist of morning wrapped around Seattle's Pioneer Square like an enchanted cloak. Surrounded by concrete buildings that blocked out the sun, this tree-lined oasis was home to Eilan and her parents' antiques shop named A Dance Through Time. Pale light filtered through the windows of the store and cast a haze over the assortment of antique mahogany tables and chairs. Inside, a grandfather clock stood next to the door like a palace guard. It seemed out of place on the same wall where a collection of medieval two-handed swords, crossbows and shields were displayed.

However, Eilan liked the clock right where it was and so that is where it stayed. It was one of the few items in the shop that was not for sale. The last time she remembered hearing it chime was on June 6, the day she graduated from Seattle University. That was also the day she'd decided to take control of her life.

She remembered the comment her dad had made in the days that followed. He told her it was as though the clock had stopped working the day her life as an adult began. It was also the day the headaches and the ringing in her ears had begun. That was five and a half years ago.

Eilan pulled a dust rag from the pocket of her jeans and wiped the glass that covered the face of the clock. The day she graduated from college was a nightmare. There were so many people. Normally she was able to keep her distance, but that had not been the case on June 6.

She shivered, remembering, the waves of thoughts and emotions flooding her mind. They surrounded her in a suffocating embrace. She couldn't breathe. She had run from the reception hall in panic.

Eilan was an empath.

Her mother said it was a gift. Eilan believed it came under the heading of a curse. The blasted ability to read people's minds only occurred when they touched her. If her gift stopped there she might have been all right, but it did not. It seemed as though everyone on graduation day wanted to either shake her hand or give her a congratulatory hug.

She glanced in the reflection of the clock's glass as she pulled her dark hair into a ponytail. A few strands of snow-white hair framed her face. They were another reminder of the reason she had chosen the life of a recluse.

She took a deep breath. Moving to the isolation of the backcountry of Colorado had been the right decision. She'd thought she'd successfully convinced her mother she was okay living alone. That was, until Eilan received the phone call bringing her back to Seattle.

The opportunity came at a time when she had wanted to check out her headaches at Swedish Hospital. The pain had grown worse over the last few years and Eilan was concerned. Her worst fears were realized, but there was no reason to worry her parents. There would be time enough to tell them when they returned from their trip.

Her mother and father had asked Eilan to help with the antiques store while they were on vacation in Great Britain. Eilan hadn't needed to read her mother's mind to decipher the real meaning of why she'd been called home. Her mother felt Eilan had withdrawn too much into an emotionless world. Eilan shrugged. Well, what if it were true? It was her decision, wasn't it?

Eilan shook free of her thoughts and concentrated on the business at hand. It was good to be home. She had missed the store. She had grown up in this neighborhood. Eilan glanced around the room. There were so many memories. Her mother had once compared the attraction to certain types of antiques to falling in love. A person couldn't explain why they felt drawn to a mahogany shelf clock constructed around the early eighteen hundreds or feel compelled to collect fine antique porcelain. The only thing that mattered was that the George I side chair they had just bought was perfect for them.

Love was like that as well, her mother would say. Because, when you met the right person, logic took flight. Eilan was still waiting for her first flying lesson.

After years spent in the wide-open spaces of Colorado, the close quarters of the shop felt stuffy. She walked over and opened the door. The bell chimed its welcome. A warm autumn breeze and a calico cat entered the antiques shop at the same time. The animal padded over to her and rubbed against her leg.

Eilan knelt down and scratched the fur ball behind its ear, wishing that her empathic abilities extended to animals. It would be fun to see what these creatures really thought about the human race. "Well, Cally, I haven't seen you in a while. Your milk is over there against the window."

Eilan stood and watched the cat pad silently toward her breakfast. The menagerie of stray animals she and her mother had befriended over the years was another memory she treasured.

She took a deep breath. How she had let her father talk her into watching over the shop, she would never know. It had seemed like a good idea at the time. September in Colorado was the start of the down time for river rafting and rock climbing. And of course she had just broken it off with ol' what's his name. Her parents said the timing was perfect for her to be away from her tour business. It was hard to argue with flawless logic. However, if Eilan had stayed in Colorado, she might never have found out about the inoperable tumor.

Eilan gathered an armful of Battenberg lace tablecloths and doilies and shoved them into a cupboard behind the counter. It felt good to keep busy rearranging some of the antiques. Her mother considered each item in the shop to be a valuable treasure to be displayed, not hidden or thrown away. Eilan smiled. She was beginning to think this was only one of the similarities she shared with her mother.

Eilan dusted off her hands and turned her attention to the Art Deco jewelry in the curio cabinet by the front door. Time to get to work.

The bell over the door chimed.

Dede Rogers, Eilan's roommate in college and best friend, breezed past her toward the counter at the back of the shop. She was carrying a paper cup in each hand. The rich aroma of coffee, laced with chocolate, floated into the store.

Dede set the drinks on the counter. She removed her green leather jacket and tossed it over the arm of a red velvet wing chair. "Found any magic lamps today?"

Eilan laughed and shook her head. The standing joke had started after they'd spent all night studying for a history exam. They'd celebrated their newfound knowledge with a bag of Hershey's kisses and watching reruns of *I Dream of Jeannie*.

Eilan walked over to the counter and reached for the latte. "This is great." She paused. "I wish I had found a magic lantern. I would ask the genie to help me sort through all these things. Are you still under a deadline at your job?"

"Afraid so. The head of Architects R Us," Dede frowned, "I still hate that name, has us all working overtime on his pet project. Maybe I can help you this weekend." Dede sank down in an overstuffed chair covered with giant blue roses that were splashed all over the fabric. She smiled. "Too bad about that lantern, though. It might help our failing love life. I'd wish for a tall, dark and rich."

Eilan laughed, put her coffee down and turned her attention to a table littered with clocks of varying sizes and shapes. "You don't mean that. You're as much of a romantic as I am. Besides, I thought you liked David. He's been asking you out every day for the past two weeks."

Dede sipped her drink. "True, he is persistent and I like that quality in a man. But our dates always end in arguments over politics. I think he wrote the book on conservative."

Eilan polished the brass trim on one of the

clocks. "Aside from his political views, what do you think of the man?"

Dede took another swallow of her coffee. "Okay, you've made your point. You know I'm nuts for him." She smiled. "It's just like it was in college. You were always trying to keep the peace and find someone a date. What did we all call you?" She tapped her fingernail on the cup. "Now I remember. It was the Peacemaker. You couldn't stand to see anyone unhappy. I think your mom was really the one who first started using that name. It fit. You're pretty good in the matchmaking department as well." She smiled. "How about finding a Mr. Right for yourself?"

Eilan rearranged the clocks on the table in even rows. "I'm not looking. My last adventure into romance was a disaster. Or have you forgotten?"

Dede took another sip of her latte and set the cup down on a nearby table. "No, I haven't. The guy was a real dud. However, save the comment that you're not interested in the valiant knight fantasy for your parents. I know you. You're still holding out for a warrior prince type. Gary Parker just didn't measure up to your specifications."

"That's an understatement. And as far as the fantasy about the valiant knight is concerned, haven't you heard, they're on the endangered species list."

Dede wrinkled her nose. "What a cynic. As I said before, we really need you to find that magic lamp, and fast."

Eilan laughed. Maybe visiting Seattle wasn't so bad after all. She had forgotten how much fun it was being around Dede. She was the only one of her friends who had not thought her empathic ability strange. However, she wasn't ready to tell her friend about her illness, at least not yet.

Eilan reached for one of the clocks on the table. "Good grief, what am I going to do with all of these? None of them work."

Dede pointed to one that was gilded and decorated with silver cherubs and rosebuds. "Your mother always did like these. Sometimes I think she liked them better if they didn't work. You're like her in that regard."

Eilan picked up the one Dede had referred to and smiled. "It's eighteenth century, and one of my favorites. And to respond to your comment, my mother and I may be alike in some things, but not where time is concerned."

Dede raised an eyebrow. "Really? Then explain why you never wear a watch, are always late . . . "

"Okay, okay, you've made your point." She set it back on the table and walked over to the grandfather clock. She climbed up on a stool and straightened one of the shields on the wall. It had an image of a golden sword thrust through flames painted on its wooden surface. It was her father's favorite.

Dede glanced at her wristwatch. "Well, it's time for me to get to work. My boss is expecting me to come up with a new concept that will revitalize the Capital Hill area."

Eilan stepped down from the stool. "Any ideas?"

"Not yet, but I still have half an hour." Dede smiled. "Promise me if any interesting male prospects do come in, you won't read their minds and scare them away like you did Gary Parker. He was so freaked out he hopped on a plane headed for the East Coast."

Eilan folded her arms across her chest. "It's not something I can turn off and on. He kissed me and I was flooded with his thoughts. Besides, it served Gary right. His fantasy about me involved chains and leather and . . ."

Dede shuddered. "Well, aside from anything you're not comfortable with, just promise me you'll make sure the person has actually spoken before you blurt something out."

Until Gary Parker, Eilan had felt confident that there was no situation she couldn't handle. But the man only thought of women in one way; as objects for his pleasure. She knew all men were not like Gary, but the search seemed never-ending. Eilan took a deep breath. "I'll try."

"Well, I guess that's all I can ask." She turned toward the door and waved good-bye. "Don't work too hard. Call me and we'll meet for lunch."

Eilan watched her friend leave. As usual, Dede was right. But reading minds was not like trying to give up smoking or biting your fingernails. It was not that simple. The only way to avoid reading a person's thoughts was to make sure there was no touching involved. It was not the best solution if you were trying to start a relationship. Sometimes a person's thoughts were so strong it seemed as though they'd spoken them out loud.

For a long time she thought she could handle her unusual ability and even managed to live a pretty normal life. She'd run cross-country in high school, mountain biked every trail she could find in the state of Washington and even found paths that weren't on the maps. She'd planned on becoming a history teacher, but that involved potential contact with a lot of people. During her college graduation she'd realized she needed to get away for a while. At times, she wondered if she had really made the right decision.

Eilan went over to the shelf that contained the collection of Victorian lace collars and gathered them in her arms. Many were used to adorn wedding dresses at the turn of the century.

The grandfather clock bonged.

Startled, Eilan dropped the lace. They floated to the wood floor. That was odd. It hadn't worked in years. Maybe she'd only thought she'd heard it ring. She looked around the room. Morning sunlight streamed through the window and cast a golden haze over the shop. It reminded her of the brown photos in her grandmother's album. Everything was in its place. She must have imagined the sound or maybe the noise was coming from next door.

It bonged again. The sound vibrated through the room. Eilan clenched her hands at her sides. It had been over five years since she had heard that sound. An alarm clock on the table buzzed. It skittered around the table, knocking into the others. The one decorated with the cherubs and rosebuds chimed. Eilan felt a chill chase up her spine.

What was going on? The deafening sound ranged from shrill persistent rings to deep-throated bongs. There was probably a scientific explanation, perhaps an earthquake or an electrical storm, or maybe Mount St. Helens had erupted again. However, she hadn't felt the floor move. She glanced toward the window. No ash-covered streets, no rain soaked sidewalks, and it was a beautiful clear autumn day. Well, so much for that theory.

Eilan walked slowly over to the table. She picked up one of the clocks that buzzed and looked at the back to see how it was powered. This one was electric. She sucked in her breath. The only problem was that it was not plugged in to an outlet. She dropped it back onto the table as though it were a glowing ember.

She took a calming breath and ordered herself to think logically. There had to be an explanation. The electrical storm idea was out, and she assumed so was the volcano and earthquake theories, so the next assumption was that Dede was playing a practical joke. Maybe one of her computer friends had rigged them all to go off at the same time.

A small self-winding clock, shaped like a cat, buzzed and skittered off the side of the table. One framed with brass suffered the same fate. Yes, Dede must be at the bottom of this mess. Eilan rubbed the back of her neck. The noise was getting to her. She'd never known Dede to play practical jokes, but there was always a first time.

Eilan heard a crash and then a string of colorful oaths.

What now? Maybe it was the person responsible. Good. Whoever it was hadn't managed to make a clean getaway. After she persuaded him to shut off the racket, she'd find out who was behind this joke. Usually she liked the sound of a clock bonging the hour, but thirty or forty going off at the same time was another matter.

She headed toward the sound and wove her way around an oak hall tree and a table covered with vintage baseball cards.

Eilan stopped abruptly. Her heart slammed against her chest.

A man wearing a bloodstained kilt stood before her.

He was well over six feet tall and looked strong enough to wield the antique claymore in the locked glass case by the cash register. He had a full beard, dark shoulder-length hair and piercing blue eyes.

He dropped a canvas bag, let out a battle cry, reached behind his back and drew the longest sword she'd ever seen. He kicked over a small table in front of him and advanced toward her. "Are ye the woman I seek?"

His voice seemed to bounce off the walls of the shop.

She stumbled into a curio cabinet and a table with antique silver-plated letter openers. "Who are you?"

The glass plates and porcelain cups in the cabinet rattled from the contact. She tried to control her erratic breathing and the growing panic in the pit of her stomach. Pioneer Square was noted for its unusually dressed occupants, but this was extreme even for downtown Seattle. The man in front of her did not look like he was trying out a costume for Halloween; rather he looked as though he had just stepped off a battlefield in the Highlands of Scotland.

She swallowed. Bloodstains covered his clothes and his body. She clenched her hands at her sides to stop them from trembling. *This can't be real,* she said silently, over and over like some ancient Gregorian chant.

He stood before her, like a demon conjured from the depths of hell. He looked in the direction of the clocks. His eyes widened as he brushed past her toward the cluttered table. With one swift movement of his sword he swept the clocks off the table. They clattered to the ground, but the noise persisted. He yelled and turned his attention once more to her.

His voice rose above the deafening sound of the clocks. "Did ye not hear my demand?"

She backed against the curio cabinet and table once again. The plates rattled and broke against the leaded glass door. The letter openers clattered to the floor.

She had nowhere to go. The phone on the counter seemed a million miles away. The shop wouldn't be officially open for another half hour. She tried to remember if she had heard of any kilt-wearing serial killers in the area. Why couldn't he have backed her up against the wall with the medieval weapons instead of a table and china closet? She doubted he would feel threatened if she held a broken Wedgwood plate in her hand.

His voice was a deep monotone, devoid of emotion. "If ye are not the one, show her to me. At once."

Her voice shook. "I have no idea who you're talking about. Maybe if I knew her name?"

Eilan's heart seemed to stop. He had a thick Scottish burr, and it was hard to understand exactly what he was saying. However, there was no mystery in the tone of his voice. His demands seemed scripted from a serial killer's manual. She was going to die. She had to remain calm.

She reached behind her and her hand touched metal. Her pulse rate went into high gear. A letter opener still remained on the table. She wound her fingers around the blade. She would not make it easy for him.

She couldn't tell what he was thinking. She would have to touch him in order for that to happen, and under the circumstances, getting closer to him didn't seem like the smartest path to take. He looked strong enough to break her in two. She shut her eyes and wished she hadn't thought of that particular visual.

The Scotsman gripped the sword with both hands. His eyes narrowed. "I dinna have much time." He clenched his jaw. "I seek the Peacemaker. Do ye know if she exists?"

Eilan's mouth snapped open. She shivered as though someone had opened a window and let an icy winter gust into the room. She remembered Dede's conversation. Eilan's nickname in college was the "Peacemaker." She took a deep breath. This couldn't be happening. It was just some weird coincidence.

The clocks stopped ringing as though someone had turned off a switch. She glanced in the Scotsman's direction. He seemed frozen to the wood floor, as immovable as a bronze statue. A muscle twitched on the side of his face as though he had clenched his jaw.

Conor looked toward her and felt the blood surge through his veins. He was frightening one of the most beautiful women he had ever seen in all his travels. Magdah said she would be fair, but there were no words worthy of her. However, she also said her hair would be white. Perhaps she was not the one he sought.

He clenched his jaw again. The sound of buzzing still rang in his ears. Magdah said his task would be simple, and the woman he first saw when he arrived would be the Peacemaker. Magdah told him that he need only ask the woman for help and she would agree. It was her duty. However, things had not gone as planned. The incessant noise had disoriented him. His head throbbed and he couldn't think clearly. And the woman was afraid of him. Nay, things had not gone well at all.

He sheathed his blade, admonishing himself. Frightening her had not been his intent. He wanted her to trust him, now more than ever. Perhaps arriving in these strange surroundings had been the cause of him instinctively drawing his weapon. It mattered not. He would have to be more cautious. There was much at stake.

The words Magdah had said still rang in his ears. "She must come to ye willingly." He watched as the woman palmed the small silver knife in her hand. He admired her courage. Her weapon was no match against him, yet she armed herself nonetheless.

The silence wove around the cluttered room. He must be in some storage chamber containing pieces of plate and furniture. It mattered not. He would not remain here long. He rested his hand on the hilt of his knife. Magdah had assured him the woman he would encounter would be the Peacemaker, but he wanted to be certain. He did not trust Magdah; after all, she was a witch.

He walked slowly toward the woman. He did not want her to flee, but he had to know the truth. He lowered his voice. "Are ye the one they call the Peacemaker?"

The woman closed her hand around the silver blade. "Leave my store at once."

He squared his shoulders. What manner of woman was this who would defy his command? "I willna leave without ye. My land is torn apart in war and vengeance. My castle in Inverness is in the hands of my enemy. Ye are to come with me."

"I don't think so."

He looked into her eyes. They were a deep emerald green and the fear he had noted moments before had been replaced by smoldering rage. He wondered at the change. He had little doubt her wish was to shove her knife into his flesh. Magdah had chosen well.

Out of the corner of his eye he saw a brown, white and orange cat pad silently toward him. The animal bounded softly to the arm of a carved wood chair and then leapt to the ground at his feet, where it wound itself around his leg. It reminded him of a cat that used to live around Dragon's Lair Castle when he was a lad.

The cat leapt once more to the chair and then in one fluid motion, it sprang into his arms. It nuzzled against his chest and purred. It had been a long time since he had held an animal such as this. Much had happened in his journey from boy to man.

"Cally, what are you doing?" The woman's voice was high-pitched and laced with panic.

The cat turned toward her, twitched its nose and then settled back into Conor's arms. Did the woman believe he would harm such a creature? In a short span of time she had concluded he was a monster. The battles he fought in the Crusades tore through his mind in dark procession, each memory more bloody than the last.

He shuddered. The cat meowed loudly and leapt from his arms. Perhaps the woman was correct if she thought him to be a monster. This was not going well. He should have brought a gift to show his respect for who she was. He paused. Or at least taken the advice of his brother and bathed.

2

The door opened and a woman entered. Her blond hair was cropped close to her head. She wore black legging type garments and a matching tunic. Conor wondered if all the women in this land dressed like men?

Her eyes widened as she approached. Her words came out slowly. "I forgot my jacket." She hesitated. "Eilan, what's going on?"

The person, who Conor hoped was the Peacemaker, tightened her grip on the knife. "Dede, call 911."

Conor watched as the woman with short hair walked to the back of the shop. She reached for a small white object attached to the wall. She poked it with her finger and then held it up to the side of her face and talked to it. What manner of place had he come to? Magdah said he would encounter strange and wondrous things, but so far he had not seen the wonder; just the strange.

Dede returned the object to the wall and turned toward him. "Stay right where you are. The police will be here in a matter of seconds."

He understood only a part of what she was saying, and combined with the tone of her voice, it could mean only one thing; these two women were going to have him forcibly removed. Magdah had said he should go slowly when explaining his intent, but that had never been his strength.

He glanced toward Eilan. Her eyes were kind, despite the weapon she wielded; he hoped she also understood he would not harm her. "I believe the legend is real."

Her voice was even. She rubbed her forehead. "You said you had come for a person called the Peacemaker."

"Aye."

The other woman gasped.

Eilan glanced in the direction of the door and then back toward him. "Why do you need this person?"

He clenched his jaw. This woman was bothersome. She asked too many questions. "The reason is unimportant. Ye must come with me. Now."

She folded her arms across her chest. "I don't think so. Why don't you tell me why it's so important?"

She was testing his patience. It would be a simple matter to fling her over his shoulder. He paused.

Magdah had warned against using force. He would tell her only what she needed to know in order to make a decision. The rest she would learn as time passed.

He took a deep breath. "When I returned from the Crusades I discovered my father had died and my uncle had taken possession of my ancestral castle. Simon has driven my people from their lands. They have resorted to stealing to survive."

Dede leaned toward Eilan. "Good grief, his accent is thick. He's hard to understand. Did he mention the Crusades?" She shook her head. "Something is very odd here."

Eilan rubbed her forehead. "Exactly where is your castle?"

"Inverness, Scotland." He paused. "Ye dinna look as though ye feel well. Magdah mentioned to me that if ye have not used your powers ye might be in pain. Does your head trouble ye?"

There was a knock on the door.

Dede rushed over and opened it. She pointed toward him. "That's the man. Arrest him. He's as crazy as they come."

This did not bode well. Two men, dressed in blue, close-fitting clothes drew iron rods from their belts and turned their attention toward him.

The taller of the two shouted, "Hands on your head."

The men were yelling at him. The way they brandished the objects they held, he suspected they were weapons.

The stout man moved toward him cautiously. "Take it easy, big guy, and no one will get hurt."

Conor withdrew his sword. "Aye. 'Tis time. Take your leave. I have important matters to tend to this day."

Conor heard a clicking sound as the two men aimed the rod they held toward him.

The stout man nodded to his comrade. "The woman who called was right. We have a nutcase on our hands. Better call for backup. He sure acts the part, right down to the Scottish burr, sword, and the kilt."

The tall man's eyes narrowed as he withdrew a long metal box and talked into it. "We have a bad situation here. This guy's swinging around a serious-looking sword. He's also covered in blood. I'll be willing to lay odds its not his own."

Time ticked by so slowly, Conor felt he could measure it with the beating of his heart. The men who stood before him were as still as the marble statues he had seen in Greece.

The door burst open and a half-dozen men rushed toward him.

They pinned him to the ground and wrenched the sword from his hands. His hands were manacled together. He knew the feel of iron on his skin. He had felt it before when he was a prisoner in Turkey.

He clenched his jaw and silently cursed Magdah. The witch should have warned him. He could not help his people if he was locked away.

The icy breeze stirred the crimson leaves along the sidewalk in front of the antiques shop. Eilan blew on her hands to keep them warm and watched the policeman guide the Scotsman into the patrol car.

She flinched as the door shut. The Scotsman looked toward her through the car window. He leaned against the backseat and his expression was lost in the shadows. Eilan shivered. He was looking for someone he referred to as the Peacemaker. It must be just a bizarre coincidence. But why had he talked to her about her headaches? She shivered and stuffed her hands into the pockets of her jeans.

Eilan watched the police car edge away from the curb and inch its way through the morning rush-hour traffic. The Scotsman was out of her life as dramatically as he had entered. She should feel relieved; instead, uneasiness had settled in around her. The car turned right at the intersection and disappeared from sight.

Eilan walked back into the shop. She was justified in asking Dede to call the police, she repeated over and over in her mind. After all, it was obvious the man was a raving lunatic.

Dede plopped down on the arm of the chair.

"Well, that was a close call. You must have been scared witless. He was dark and dangerous looking, but I'll bet his thoughts were even scarier."

"I wouldn't know."

Dede arched her eyebrow. "I would have guessed you would've tried to get an idea about what he was thinking the first chance you had."

"Everything happened too fast."

That wasn't true. Eilan hadn't wanted to find out. The man was not what he seemed and for some reason that made her even more fearful of getting too close.

He wore a bloodstained kilt, and looked like he could have easily defeated the policemen. Yet, he went with them peacefully. But even before the police had arrived she thought she'd had him figured out and then he had held Cally.

The cat never allowed anyone to hold her. Dede had tried and was rewarded with scratches on her hands and arms.

Dede frowned. "Can I get you anything? You don't look well."

Eilan shook her head. "I'm fine." She paused. "Dede, do you think we did the right thing by calling the police?"

Dede's eyes widened. "Are you nuts? The guy announced he had come for you."

"He didn't really say it was me he was coming for."

Dede drummed her fingernails on the arm of the chair. "Really? Who else in this neighborhood do you know of who was nicknamed the Peacemaker?"

"Point taken. However, I haven't been called that since college."

"Okay, lets just say we shelve that stranger than fiction coincidence away for a while. There's all the other stuff to deal with." Dede took a deep breath. "I admit the guy has a certain Neanderthal appeal, if you like the bulging muscles and dark brooding expression type, but Eilan, the guy talked about fighting in the Crusades. I think they died out in the fourteenth, or was it the fifteenth century?" She paused. "Anyway, it was a long time ago. This is just too weird."

Eilan forced a smile. "I thought you were the one who believed in little green men?"

Dede raised her eyebrows. "Very funny. You're changing the subject. Besides, that was just a phase I was going through in college. Actually, I think it was more because the guy I was dating thought he'd been abducted by aliens."

Eilan picked up one of the clocks that the Scotsman had thrown to the floor and replaced it on the table. "You know, my mom called last night and said she and Dad had had a great time in Scotland and mentioned they'd be staying in Edinburgh for a few days. She's a real expert when it comes to legends. Maybe I should call her."

Cally leapt to the table and nuzzled Eilan's hand. She picked up the cat and scratched the animal behind its ear and tried to find comfort in the purring sound.

She turned to Dede. "Cally wasn't afraid of the Scotsman."

Dede rolled her eyes. "Didn't Hitler have a cat?"

Eilan grimaced. "I was just trying—"

"I know what you were trying to say." Dede leaned against the chair and folded her hands in her lap. "And just for the record, you're hopeless. Sometimes I think you'd welcome every stray that crossed your path."

Eilan let the cat down gently to the floor. Her friend made perfect sense. The streets of Pioneer Square were filled with lost souls of all ages and the Scotsman was just one more. It was one thing to give a saucer of milk to a cat and quite another to let a stranger into your home. Eilan had to try and take her mind off the Scotsman.

She walked behind the counter and reached under the glass cabinet to straighten a collection of knives that dated back to the fourteenth century. The leather strips that wrapped around the hilt of the blades were brittle and the steel of the blades was dark gray and pitted with age. Her fingers traced along the surface. This knife resembled the one the Scotsman had. Except that his was highly polished and gleamed in the light. His had looked new.

She straightened. A new sword did not prove his story. His weapons were probably just first-class replicas.

Maybe the Scotsman was someone who performed at medieval reenactments, and somewhere along the way he had started believing the part he played was real.

Dede leaned across the counter and waved her hand in front of Eilan's face. "Hello, Eilan? Have you heard a word I've said?"

Eilan looked at her friend and smiled. "I'm sorry. What were you saying?"

"Only that I think it's a good idea to talk to your mom. She'll be able to convince you that what the Scotsman called you was only a coincidence."

Eilan took a deep breath. "I hope so."

"Me too, because I know that unless you resolve this problem, you won't be able to think of anything else. And most likely you'll end up baking chocolate chip cookies for this guy and bringing them to his jail cell."

Eilan smiled. "Nope, he looks more like the oatmeal-raisin type."

Dede frowned. "I'm serious."

"Unfortunately, so am I. Okay, you've convinced me. I'll call her." Eilan walked to the phone and punched in her parents' number. She looked over at Dede. "Good grief. I didn't think of the time change. Do you have any idea what time it is in Edinburgh?"

Dede shook her head. "Not a clue."

The line connected and someone picked up the phone. It was her mother.

"Mom, this is Eilan. How are you and Dad?"

Eilan could hear her mother yawn. "We're great. It's nice to hear your voice. We're a little tired. We've spent the day touring Holyroodhouse Palace." She paused. "How are you, sweetheart? Is everything all right?"

"I'm fine." Eilan could hear her father in the background asking if everything was okay with their only child. She smiled, amused that her parents continued to worry about her even though she was an adult of twenty-six. She wondered if she would be the same way with her own children, that is, if she ever had a family. Her dream seemed to grow more unattainable every day.

She cleared the lump in her throat. "Mom, I called because I need to ask you a question. Do you remember a legend called the Peacemaker?"

Her mother yawned. "Celtic?"

"Yes, I think so."

"Why do you need to know?"

Eilan covered up the phone with the palm of her hand. "She wants to know why. I can't tell her there was a sword wielding man in here. She and Dad will freak."

Dede scrunched down in the overstuffed chair. "Smart people."

Eilan frowned. "You're no help."

There was no easy way to tell her mother and lying wasn't an option. She removed her hand from the receiver. She sighed and blurted out the story.

Dede tapped Eilan on the shoulder. "What's she saying?"

Eilan shook her head. "She's talking to my dad. I can't hear them. It's too muffled."

"Is your mother upset?"

Eilan leaned against the counter. "It's hard to tell."

Dede stood and buttoned her coat. "Okay, this may take a while. I'll go buy us another latte and you can fill me in when I return."

Eilan cradled the receiver against her shoulder. "I thought you had to get back to work."

Dede smiled. "I'm taking the day off to help a friend. Be sure to send your mom and dad my love."

She heard her mother's voice through the receiver. It no longer sounded tired. Her words tumbled out in a rush. "You did the right thing. Now, just get some sleep and we'll talk to you in the morning."

Eilan knew her mother well enough to recognize an evasive maneuver. "Mom, it's ten in the morning. And I'm not so sure I did the right thing by having the guy arrested. That's the reason I called you. Do you think there's anything to his Peacemaker story?"

"Well . . . there was something, but . . . you know these legends, they've no basis in fact."

Eilan felt a shiver race over her body. Her mother was trying to keep something from her. "Whatever you know will be helpful."

Her mother cleared her throat. "Your dad said he heard something about a Peacemaker legend the other day. We had split up. I wanted to visit the woolen shops and your dad was intrigued by the brass rubbings in St. Giles church." She paused. "Your dad said he overheard an old woman on the sidewalk retelling a tale about an old Highland legend. He was interested in the story because it described a woman who had the ability to read minds."

Eilan tightened her grip on the phone. "Go on."

The silence on the other end of the phone was so thick Eilan could feel the weight of it come through the phone. Even her father had stopped talking. She could hear her mother's even breathing through the receiver.

Her mother's voice was barely above a whisper. "That was all there was to the legend. It is just a silly myth, really. You know the Scots, they love to make up stories."

Eilan listened as her mother told her again that she was glad the Scotsman was arrested. And each time her mother told her that the legend had no basis in fact, Eilan's uneasiness grew. Her mother was afraid of something. Eilan said her good-byes and hung up the phone. Why was her mother in full protest mode? Eilan glanced in the direction she had first seen the Scotsman.

Out of the corner of her eye she saw a leather sack. She walked over to it and remembered that he'd dropped it to the floor. She knelt down beside the sack, opened the loosely tied leather thongs and pulled out what looked to be women's clothes. Eilan sat back on her heels and examined the garments. They were all hand-sewn. Not a zipper or machine buttonhole in sight. The questions kept building and she knew of only one person who knew the answers. The Scotsman.

3

Gray stone and red-brick buildings sped past Conor as he rode in the strange horseless carriage along the crowded road. He felt beads of sweat form on his forehead. Conor clenched his teeth and willed a calmness he did not feel. He could not explain how the vehicle was able to move through the streets on its own. It must be under a spell. He shuddered. He should not be surprised. After all, this was Magdah's doing. His heart thundered in his chest. The witch should have prepared him. He shut his eyes and tried to clear his thoughts. He had a more serious problem than trying to puzzle the wonders he had seen thus far. He felt the steel restraints cut into his flesh around his wrists. He was shackled and no doubt was being taken to prison.

He pulled against them. The chain connecting the circles of metal clinked as he tested its strength again. It would take a mighty blade to break his bonds. His own weapon had been taken from him. He must find a way to retrieve it if he was to escape.

The two men who sat in front of him talked about something they called the Mariners and hitting a ball out of a park. It made little sense to him. He shuddered, remembering the guards in the prison in Egypt. They ignored him as though he offered little threat. Conor had worked that to his advantage. He hoped he could repeat the opportunity here.

He shut his eyes, trying to block out the memories of his imprisonment. The thoughts came without permission. Men, wearing long flowing robes and wielding curved swords chained him and his brother to a stone wall. Conor had not understood the language or the customs of that world, either. He had lived through the imprisonment and the torture by building walls around himself. He hoped he had the strength to do it a second time.

The horseless carriage lurched to a stop. The door was flung open and Conor was pulled to his feet. A man with red hair and a bushy mustache that covered his upper lip led him into a brown stone building.

The hallway was as bright as daylight. Men stared in his direction, some pointed, while others laughed and whispered to one another. Aye, this was just as before.

The man with the red hair stopped in front of a door and turned toward him. He unlocked the metal restraints with a key. "Do you know where you are?"

"Aye. Ye have taken me to your prison."

The man scratched his head and turned to someone behind him. "Hey, I have a funny feeling about this one. Has he been read his rights?"

The person who had shoved him into the horseless carriage raised his voice. "Twice, but he hasn't said a word, so we don't know if he heard or even understood what was said."

The man with the mustache shook his head. "Great. Nothing was ever easy." He turned to Conor. "What's your name?"

"Conor MacCloud."

"Well, that fits. Okay, MacCloud, let's get you settled in for the night. I'll let the lawyers battle this one out."

Conor knew how to behave in prison. You had a better chance of surviving if you said as little as possible and did what you were told. He closed his fingers in a fist as the screams that came from his nightmares intruded into his thoughts. The guards in his last prison liked it when you screamed. He had not given them what they wanted then; he would not now. He allowed himself to be pushed down a narrow, dimly lit corridor. Yes, this was just as before.

It had been a long day. Eilan stretched her back as she climbed the narrow staircase to her parents' apartment. Now she would have the time to try to solve the mystery surrounding the man who had appeared out of thin air. She could still hear the sound of the clocks. It was one more odd thing to add to the list. Dede had taken the day off from work and stayed to help Eilan clean the shop. They'd worked through dinner and just finished a veggie pizza. She knew her friend had left feeling Eilan had forgotten all about the Scotsman.

Eilan paused on the landing. She wished it were that easy.

She opened the door. A blast of cold air greeted her. She shivered and flipped on the switch. Lights, reset into the ceiling, illuminated the clutter. Books lined the floor-to-ceiling shelves and were stacked in piles around the perimeter of the room. An overstuffed sofa with a blue-and-gold tapestry fabric was positioned against the window. Dede had described Eilan's home as organized chaos. Most people noticed the clutter, but to Eilan everything here had a story to tell. It was like being surrounded by old friends.

She turned the thermostat to seventy and felt a twinge of guilt prickle her skin. Her parents liked their apartment at a freezing sixty-five degrees. Of course, they had each other, whereas, she was very alone. Oh perfect, now she was indulging in self-pity. That was intelligent.

She blew on her hands and an image of the Scotsman, huddled in a cold dark cell, popped into her mind. She shook her head. This was ridiculous. In the first place, the Seattle jail was brand new, state of the art. It probably had a better heating and cooling system then her parents' building. It was not some medieval dungeon, complete with dripping water and pet rats. She was allowing her imagination to sprout wings and take flight. She looked down the hall toward the bathroom. A hot steam bath, scented candles and an even steamier novel seemed just the right medicine to clear her head. She paused, knowing full well she could not rest until she solved the mystery.

The answer had to be here somewhere. Her mother had collected enough books to stock a small library. Once Eilan had asked why her mother didn't use the public library for her research. The answer was accompanied by a smile. Her mother said that in the beginning she had checked books out at the city library, but usually forgot to return them. At times the fines equaled the cost of the book. In the end her mother said it was easier just to buy the book.

Eilan suspected it was also because her mother just loved them. Well, right now she was glad of her mother's eccentric behavior. She particularly liked the myths of Great Britain. If there was a story about a Peacemaker, there was probably a record of it somewhere within her mother's remarkable collection.

She scanned the titles. Over half of the library was comprised of books on myths and legends. She had everything from the Big Foot of the Northwest to Nessie of the Loch Ness monster fame. The remainder of the books ranged in scope from a collection of poetry by Robert Burns to a book on Tutankhamen, the boy king. There was even a copy of *The Malleus Malleficarum*, or *The Witch's Hammer*. It was a manual on how to legally try and convict a person of witchcraft and even suggested the most effective methods of torture. Eilan shivered. She had never understood how people could be so cruel to one another. She swept the dark thoughts away and concentrated on her search.

She put her hands on her hips. Where had she seen that book on Scottish folklore? She scanned the shelves and then remembered. Eilan walked over to the hall closet and opened the door. Stacks of books were jammed into the small space. She searched down the titles until she saw the one she was looking for and pulled it out of the pile. Dust clung to the spine. She blew it clean, brought it over to the sofa and sat down. A clock on the white brick mantel over the fireplace chimed the hour. It was seven o'clock. It reminded her of the cacophony of bongs and buzzes that had filled the air when the Scotsman arrived this morning. There had to be an explanation for that as well.

She thumbed through the contents of the books, more determined than ever to find an answer. One chapter was devoted to the pink ghost at Stirling Castle, and the green lady ghost seen in Ashintully, while other chapters mentioned Scottish elves, fairies, pixies and kelpies. There was no mention of a Peacemaker legend. This was not going to be as easy as she first thought. She leaned back on the sofa and gazed over at the tall bookshelf by the window.

She said the words out loud. "Maybe I'm looking in the wrong place."

The book entitled *The Witch's Hammer* caught her attention again. Beside it there were a number of volumes on the history of witchcraft in Europe. Witches were often linked with magic, spells, and enchantments. I wonder. She stood and walked over to the bookcase beside the window. Wedged in between the larger books was a thin paperback. It was frayed and worn around the corners of the pages. She pulled out the blue book, entitled *Witch's Almanac*. There was an image of a rabbit, a raven, a lion and a whale etched into each corner of the cover.

She sat on the window ledge. There was a ribbon marking one of the chapters. It was entitled The Enchantment of Inverness. She thought she remembered the Scotsman telling her he was from there. She turned the page.

When the beast of fear and of vengeance,
Runs free in the Highlands of Scotland,
And no one is safe from its reach,
Seek through time the woman known as the
Peacemaker,
She alone knows a man's thoughts before he
speaks them,
And has the power to restore love to a war-torn
land.

Eilan shuddered and a dark foreboding washed over her as she glanced toward the window. A gentle mist washed against the panes of glass. Her pulse quickened as one of the phrases from the poem wove through her. *Seek through time the woman known as the Peacemaker.*

Was the poem referring to her?

She leaned her head against the cool panes of glass and the contact seemed to ease her headache. This had to be a wild series of coincidences. She pushed away from the windowsill and sat down on the plush carpet. Finding a poem was not enough proof. A person did not just zip through time as though going to the store for a carton of milk. She rubbed her forehead. What was happening to her? She had read one silly poem and was ready to abandon all reason. This was all wrong. However, if he was who he said he was, then the rest might be true as well.

Impossible.

Eilan pulled her knees against her chest. There must be a concrete, surefire way to prove the Scotsman was stark raving mad. She glanced over at the shelves. Mixed in among the history books were those on archaeology digs. The scientific community used carbon dating to prove if a piece of cloth was made yesterday or five hundred years ago. It should be simple enough to clip a piece of the Scotsman's kilt and sneak it over to a lab for testing. Minor detail: She had no idea where to find such a facility, or if Seattle even had such a thing. She wondered if it was listed in the phone book.

She stood and stretched. If she could find such a place, the results would prove who he was once and for all. And then she could forget him and his crazy quest and get on with her life. She rubbed the back of her neck and glanced in the direction of the bathroom. The tub seemed to beckon her. She glanced toward the clock on the mantel over the fireplace. It was eight o'clock. There would be time for a long indulgent soak before collapsing into bed.

Eilan took a deep breath. Or she could visit the Scotsman and ask him what he knew about the poem. Better still, if she could touch his arm there was a good chance she would learn the truth without having to deal with the whole carbon dating process thing. She nodded. Yes, that might be the best plan after all.

She grabbed her coat and headed for the door. She

felt better than she had all day. After she'd learned the truth from the Scotsman, she would reward herself with that bath, maybe even pick up a one-pound box of dark chocolates with cream centers.

She opened the door and walked down the stairs. The minute her parents returned, she was moving back to Colorado. It was much simpler there. She doubted there had ever been a report of a time-traveling Scotsman. Yes, that confirmed it; the first chance she had, she was moving back to a saner and safer life.

The hours had folded into one another as Conor was led to his cell. He did not know how late it was. There were no windows in this prison with which to track the path of the sun. The iron bars closed behind Conor. The sound vibrated through him. Although this prison was cleaner than others he had been in and he had been fairly treated, the end result was the same. He was here against his will and was thus prevented from accomplishing his mission. Time was critical. With each day that passed, more of his people were being driven from their land by Simon and his men.

Conor passed back and forth in front of the bars. Three men stood huddled in the far corner talking to one another. Good. He had no intention of getting to know them. He would not be here that long.

The image of Eilan appeared in his thoughts. She

had been lovelier than any woman he had ever seen, her features made even more appealing by the strength of will he had seen reflected in her eyes. He did not blame her for her actions, 'twas his fault alone. He had behaved badly. He had frightened her into believing her life was in danger. She followed the only course open to her.

Shouts erupted in the cell.

Two men shoved a third against the iron bars. The one being attacked screamed for help. His mouth was stuffed with a strip of white cloth. The larger of the two assailants had an image of a snake etched down the length of his arm, and the other assailant's head was shaved.

Conor clenched his fists at his side. He ground out his words. "Ignorant fools." They would bring the wrath of the guards down on them all. The last thing he needed was to give the guards an excuse to detain him further.

Conor walked over and grabbed the bearded man and spun him around. "Ye willna fight this man. Leave him be."

The bald man laughed. "Well, what have we here? Never could understand why a grown man would wear a skirt. You're a long way from Scotland."

"Aye, that I am."

The man with the snake painted on his arm doubled up his fists. "You even have the accent. This is none of your business. I don't know how it is where you come from, but here we stay out of each other's way."

Conor looked over the bald man's shoulder to the person who cowered against the bars. His eyes were filled with terror. Conor had seen that expression too often. He nodded to the frightened man. "Dinna fear. These men willna harm ye."

The bald man laughed again. "It's not for you to say. Now go back to your corner and behave yourself. A man dressed with a skirt had better keep to himself. If you know what I mean."

Conor did.

He reached for the man's throat and pinned him against the wall.

The man's eyes bulged and his face turned red. "What're you doing? Are you mad?"

Conor's voice was even. "Some have called me thus, others worse. Ye willna harm this man."

"All right, all right. Put me down. I can't breathe. Fred, don't just stand there. Help me."

Conor narrowed his gaze and glanced over to the man called Fred.

He backed away with his hands raised, palms up. "Roger, this guy's as crazy as they come. Let's just leave it alone."

Conor released Roger. The man grabbed his neck and rushed over to Fred. The two men muttered to themselves as they hugged the far wall of the cell.

The man against the bars pushed away and nodded. "Thanks." He held out his hand. "Name's Steve, what's yours?"

"Conor MacCloud."

Steve reached for Conor's hand and pumped it up and down. "Your coming here was my lucky day. Yes indeedy, MacCloud. This is my lucky day. Anything I can do for you, just you say the word." He lowered his voice. "Got a lawyer? You know, someone who can spring you from this place?"

Conor looked toward the man he had rescued with renewed interest. He was reed thin. Dark whiskers shadowed his face and his eyes bugged out of their sockets. Steve's words interested him. When Conor was chained to the wall in the Egyptian prison the man next to him had claimed to be a lawyer for the Spanish Inquisition. The man would ramble on and on about his cases. He claimed to have won them all.

Conor rubbed the back of his neck. "Can a lawyer ask them to release me?"

Steve shrugged. "Sure. Just give your guy a call," he snapped his fingers, "and poof, you're a free man." He scratched his chin. "What did they say you did?"

Conor turned to face the corridor. "I think it was breaking into a house with a weapon."

Steve winced. "Ugh, that's a tough one. Still, you saved my neck." He reached into the pocket of his shirt and pulled out something white. Steve shoved it toward him. "The name of my lawyer and his phone number are listed on this card. I'm not saying he'll take your case, but . . ."

The buzzer sounded and a guard came from around the corner and headed in Conor's direction. The man paused at his cell. The sound of metal on metal echoed around him as the door slid open.

The guard grinned. "Well, Scotsman, it seems you have a visitor. Hurry along, visiting hours are almost over."

Conor tucked the card Steve had given him in between his belt and his plaid and followed the man down the corridor. When he returned he would ask Steve how to contact the lawyer. He only hoped too much time had not been lost already.

4

It was 8:45 P.M. Visiting hours in the jail were almost over as Eilan emerged from the elevator. There wasn't much time left, but she couldn't wait until tomorrow. She wanted to settle the matter of who the Scotsman was, once and for all. She held the book that contained the disturbing legend against her chest. It had posed more questions than it answered.

Eilan stopped abruptly. She stared at the floor-to-ceiling glass wall that separated her from the prisoners. She pulled the book closer. She had not considered that there would be a barrier. How would she know the Scotsman's thoughts if she could not touch him? This would be a waste of time. Someone should have told her. She took a deep breath. Maybe she should tell the guard she had changed her mind about wanting to speak to the Scotsman.

Eilan heard a buzzer sound and then a click as a

door opened. The Scotsman came from around the corner and headed in her direction. His dark eyes stared at her. His shoulder length hair was tied at the nape of his neck with a leather thong. He seemed taller than she remembered and his shoulders broader. Her heart raced. It was easy to envision him on a battlefield in the Highlands of Scotland. She swallowed. There was no turning back now. He was here.

She eased down on the metal chair inside the enclosed blue cubicle and waited. Glass windows gave her a clear view of him as he came closer. Tonight, she and a woman with sad eyes and clothes that hung loosely over her body were the only visitors.

He entered the booth and sat down opposite her. Glass and green painted steel separated them. He folded his hands on the counter in front of him and waited.

The palm of her hand felt sweaty as she picked up the phone attached to the wall to her right. She decided to come right to the point. She didn't know any other way to do it. She'd heard that a person's eyes dilated when he was lying, or was it that their nostrils flared? She shook her head. Without being able to touch him she would have no way of verifying either theory. She cleared her throat and held the book up to the window. "Have you ever seen this book before?"

He shrugged his shoulders and shook his head.

Maybe he hadn't heard her. She raised her voice and repeated her question.

His reaction was the same.

The woman in the cubicle next to her leaned over and pointed to the phone attached to the prisoner's side of the wall.

Eilan nodded. Of course, he couldn't hear her. She motioned to the phone on his side of the glass panel. His eyebrows scrunched together. She could tell he had no idea what she was trying to say. She pointed to the phone she held and then to the one in his cubicle.

He picked it up and tentatively held it against his ear.

She cleared her throat. "I need to ask you a few questions."

His eyes widened. He yanked the phone away from his ear and stared at it. He dropped it as though it had suddenly caught on fire.

"Oh no, don't do that." She stood. "Scotsman, you have to pick up the phone."

He stared in her direction as though she had sprouted another head.

She pointed to the phone dangling from the cord on the wall. He backed away.

The buzzer sounded. Visiting hours were over.

He glanced quickly toward the guard and then at her. He pulled a card from between his belt and his kilt and placed it against the glass window. It was a lawyer's business card.

The buzzer sounded again. This time it seemed more insistent.

The door to the Scotsman's cubicle opened and as quickly as he appeared he vanished into the bleak corridors of the jail.

She sank down in her chair. What a disaster. This had been a total waste of time. The man had not said one word and was behaving as though he had never seen a phone before. She remembered his reaction to the clocks and the police car. She felt a shiver run up her spine. Was he telling the truth and she was in massive denial or was he just a master at staying in character?

She stood and walked to the elevator. Thinking, even for one moment, that this guy was for real was a stupid idea. She blamed her indecision on her mother's belief that legends were based in fact. The notion must be imbedded in her mother's DNA and thus passed down to her only daughter.

The elevator door opened and she and the woman entered silently.

The woman smiled. "Not the best place to talk to your man, is it, honey?"

Eilan nodded and watched the numbers over the elevator door click downward from nine. She thought about telling the woman he wasn't her man, but didn't see the point. She had nothing in common with this person.

The woman tugged at the frayed cuff of her

dress. "Sometimes they're like that. Not much to say. It'll be better when he's released. You wait and see if it's not. What did his lawyer have to say?"

The door to the elevator creaked open. The woman didn't wait for an answer. She shuffled into the corridor and headed toward the exit. Sadness and despair seemed to envelop her like a heavy cloak. Eilan shivered. She didn't like being in this place. Her own world was safe and full of joy in comparison. It was far removed from the people who dwelt here.

Eilan stepped out of the elevator and paused in the artificial light, surrounded by pale gray marble walls. They seemed to press in on her. It was not her fault the Scotsman was in jail. She had done the right thing by having him arrested. He was delusional and possibly dangerous. If anything, she was making the world a safer place. She should feel proud of herself. These types of people deserved to be behind bars. She should take Dede's advice and just let it go.

She headed down the corridor toward the flashing exit sign. The guard, seated at a desk, waved good-bye to her as though she were a regular visitor. She resented his smile. She did not belong here.

A pregnant woman rushed through the metal detector archway toward the guard. A young child of about three or four, wearing a floppy purple knit hat and matching sweater ran beside her. Tears streaked the woman's face as she gripped the desk. "You have to let me see my husband."

The guard patted the woman's hand. "Visiting hours are over, madam. You'll have to come back tomorrow."

The child broke away from her mother and raced toward the elevators. She screamed, "I want my daddy!" as she plowed into Eilan.

Eilan was knocked off-balance and landed on the floor. The book flew out of her grip. The little girl was sprawled on top of her. An image from the child's thoughts flashed through Eilan. The little girl was sitting at a child's-size table and chair set. She was having a tea party with her teddy bear. Sitting opposite her was a man with a broad smile. He was laughing as he took a sip of imaginary tea. Eilan knew the man was the little girl's daddy.

The child scrambled to her feet and raced over to the panel and punched numbers.

The door opened.

The pregnant woman screamed and the guard ordered the child to stop. Of course the little girl marched straight into the elevator.

Eilan scrambled to her feet and blocked the door. It shuddered open. Eilan reached for her. "Take my hand."

The child folded her arms across her chest, clamped her lips shut, and backed to the corner of the elevator. She shook her head. "I want my daddy."

The pregnant woman and the guard reached the elevator at the same time. The woman swept past Eilan and gathered the child in her arms.

As quickly as the event had occurred it was resolved. The guard ushered the sobbing pair out the door. He sighed deeply and took his place at the desk. Order was restored.

Eilan stood as still as the marble walls and felt as cold. She had lumped everyone who came here into the same pile. She didn't feel very good about herself right now. In her quest to protect herself, she had cut herself off as effectively as the rules of the jail separated the people from those they loved.

The love the child had for the man she called her daddy was evident. Eilan sensed the man's feeling for his daughter was just as real. Whatever crime he had committed, it had not diminished the love he had for his daughter. How many more of these stories were there? Eilan was protected in her comfortable cocoon world. As long as she kept her distance from people she would be free of their pain, and free of their love.

Eilan walked over and picked up the book, wiping imaginary dust off the cover. An uneasiness swirled around her. She pressed it against her, headed for the exit again, and walked out into the crisp autumn air. She buttoned her raincoat and cinched her belt.

A horn sounded and someone leaned out a car

window and shook his fist at the person in the car behind him. Once Seattle was known for its polite drivers, but times had changed. Although authorities tried to regulate road rage, it was accepted as a by-product of a crowded and stressed-filled city. Like the people behind bars, and homeless along the street corners, it was easy to look the other way or step over them. Ignorance is bliss was a timeless excuse.

She held the book tighter and knew she was guilty. An image of the Scotsman behind the glass barrier floated through her mind. She could not dismiss him like she had so many other things in her life. Especially since she knew there was an easy way to find out if he were telling the truth. Her method was foolproof. Much better than truth serum or a lie detector test. Her original plan was sound. She could touch him and find out if he were telling the truth.

The business card the Scotsman had shown her had the name of the Carlton, Taggart and Nelson law firm sprawled in gold English script across a black background. If she were the sort of person who believed in signs, that one would be flashing neon yellow. She smiled to herself, thinking of the Scotsman. For someone who claimed to be from the Middle Ages, it hadn't taken him long to figure out that he needed a lawyer. She didn't want him released. She just wanted a chance to talk to him. It shouldn't take long, and her conscience would be eased.

Eilan wondered if the law firm of Carlton, Taggart and Nelson had a twenty-four-hour answering service. She turned down James Street and headed in the direction of Pioneer Square and her antiques shop. For some reason she felt as though there was an invisible clock ticking away the precious time. With any luck she would return tomorrow with a lawyer and end this drama.

She quickened her step. Yes, by this time tomorrow she and Dede would be laughing over the evidence. She took a breath of the crisp air feeling more relieved than she had all day. Soon it would all be over.

Her luck was holding. Eilan sat on a wooden bench in the courthouse and rubbed her eyes. This morning the law firm of Carlton, Taggart and Nelson had come to her rescue like a white knight straight out of a romance novel. She only hoped the rest would be as simple. A clock against the courthouse wall ticked away the seconds and echoed down the deserted corridors. The blue-gray tile floor seemed to blend into the color of the painted woodwork. Eilan had not slept well last night and there had not been time for a latte. She laced her fingers together in her lap to keep them from drumming on the bench. This had to work. Eilan leaned against the wall and closed her eyes.

The sound of footsteps clip-clopped over the tile floors. Eilan straightened and opened her eyes. A well-dressed man in his early thirties approached her. His head was shaved and he was wearing a dark suit and a white linen shirt and yellow tie. She guessed it was John Carlton from the description he had given her over the phone.

The man walked over to her and reached out to shake her hand. "Eilan Dougan, I presume. My name is John Carlton."

She nodded, grateful he was all business. At the prices his law firm was charging she didn't want to waste time with small talk.

He withdrew a folder from his briefcase. "I'll get right to the point. I explained to the judge your position in this case and that you now realize the Scotsman was on his way to one of those reenactment fairs in Carnation."

"But how will you explain his appearance in my parents' antiques shop?"

John nodded. "Good question. Fortunately there is an espresso shop right next to the antiques store. I explained that he went into your place by mistake." He paused. "By the way, the Scotsman's name is Conor MacCloud."

Eilan repeated the name to herself. One of the psychics her mother knew claimed it was possible to tell the character of a person by their name. If that were true it would certainly make life easier.

Eilan's name dated so far back in history that it had stumped her mother's friend. She shook the thoughts away and focused on the problem at hand. If she could meet with Mr. MacCloud, she wouldn't have to worry about what his name meant.

It would all be over soon and she could go on about her life. She would read Conor MacCloud's thoughts and determine he was stark raving mad. That he was living in a fantasy world and needed strong medication. She would be commended for seeing to it that he had found the help he needed.

She didn't want anything to prevent the meeting between them. "What about the weapons he carried?"

John shrugged. "If Mr. MacCloud had drawn his sword he would have been guilty of a gross misdemeanor. However, no one could be sure if that had occurred." He put the folder back into his briefcase.

She took a deep breath. "How long will I be able to meet with Mr. MacCloud?"

John paused. "You have as much time as you like. As you requested, the charges have been dropped."

Eilan clutched the book to her chest. "You can't be serious. That's not what I wanted."

John held his briefcase in front of him. His voice held that singsong quality that signaled a person was being patronizing. "Your instructions were clear. You asked to have the man released."

Eilan said her words evenly. "I just wanted him released long enough for me to . . . talk to him."

He leaned forward. "Those were not your instructions. You clearly stated the word released."

A swinging door at the far end of the room opened. It creaked back and forth on its hinges. Eilan held her breath. Conor MacCloud paused and scanned the room. He turned and seemed to walk in slow motion toward her. His muscles flexed beneath the kilt he wore.

His expression was devoid of emotion as he approached. "I thank ye for my release."

The seconds blended into minutes as she looked into his eyes. She let out her breath in a rush of air as he came closer. It was now or never. She reached out and put her hand on his shoulder. His thoughts became her own. Beside a teal blue sea he fought a man with a curved sword. On the ground was a shield with a crest she recognized as belonging to the Knights Templar.

Conor put his hand over hers and the image faltered. His thoughts were blurred as though a dark velvet curtain had been drawn across them. Eilan straightened and stared at her hand. She still touched him and yet she could not read his thoughts. This had never happened to her. She gazed into his eyes. They were as guarded as his mind.

John cleared his throat. "What have you decided? Do you want the Scotsman released or not?"

Eilan turned slowly toward the lawyer, trying to

focus on his question. She reviewed Conor's thoughts before he had mysteriously blocked them. The man he fought resembled a picture of a Moslem warrior she'd seen in the books her mother owned. The shield was ancient and common during the Crusades. She swallowed. John still waited for her to answer his question.

She could deny what she had seen and tell John to lock up the Scotsman and throw away the key. She'd never look back. Eilan held her hand against her stomach, to try to quiet the giant butterflies. God help her, she knew only one choice was open to her.

"I want Conor MacCloud to go free."

5

On a scale of one to ten her brilliant plan at the Seattle jail was a minus twenty. Eilan tucked her book under her arm and jammed the key into the lock in the door of her parents' apartment. She looked over her shoulder. The Scotsman was still behind her as stoic as ever. She had no choice but to bring him here. Where else would a man from the fourteenth century go?

The door didn't open. She had the wrong key.

Her fingers trembled as she chose another.

Except for a brief moment in the courthouse, she had only been able to get a glimpse of his thoughts. That had never happened to her before. For some reason his mind was blocked. Great. The timing couldn't have been worse. Many times in the past she had longed to be like everyone else. Knowing a person's thoughts, while they held you in their embrace, did tend to dampen the romantic mood. At least with the dim bulbs she had dated.

She shoved the door open and locked her memories safely away as she walked into the room.

Conor MacCloud followed her inside, and headed toward the window. He stared in the direction of the street in silence. The brief image she was able to see of his thoughts confirmed what he had told her was true, at least the part of being from the past. If possible, he looked even more menacing than he had in the courthouse. His unkempt hair and beard made any sane person want to run for cover. She rubbed her forehead. Even knowing his thoughts she should have turned her back on him. She was out of her depth.

He must feel as though he had dropped into the land of the Wizard of Oz. She wondered how it would feel to be in a different time and place. She shoved the thoughts out of her mind. It didn't make any difference how it felt, as she had no intention of returning with him.

Conor glanced in her direction. His only reaction to her was the muscles in his jaw tightened as though he were grinding his teeth. It might give him a headache. She should tell him. She paused. No, on second thought, why should she be the only one with a building migraine?

She flicked on the switch. His eyes widened as he looked toward the recessed lights in the ceiling.

She cleared her throat, willing a calmness in her voice she didn't feel. "I just turned on the lights."

She demonstrated and flipped the switch off and then on. "It's a lot easier than lighting a torch, don't you think?"

He raised the eyebrow over his right eye, but his expression remained stone still. He was either a lot more disturbed by his surroundings than he appeared, or he lacked a sense of humor. It was probably the latter. She really knew how to attract them.

The silence hung in the air so thick she could hear the clock over the mantel tick off the seconds. His gaze was relentless. It was as though he were trying to read her thoughts. She shivered. Good grief, wouldn't that be a twist. She didn't like that idea at all. Maybe she should try again. She needed to find a way to send him back and the answer might be locked in the recesses of his mind.

Eilan walked over to him. As she grew closer, she noticed a pungent odor. It had been present in the courthouse, but she had thought nothing of it. However, it was hard to ignore in the close quarters of the apartment.

She inhaled and coughed. It was the Scotsman. The man wouldn't have to worry about frightening his enemies away with his appearance. All they had to do was to get a whiff of him and they'd scatter to the four winds.

She took a shallow breath and regretted even that feeble attempt to breathe. However, she was determined to try again. She reached out to him.

His eyes narrowed, but he did not move away. She touched his arm. It was warm and she felt the muscles tighten under her touch.

Nothing, nada, zilch.

She put her hands on her hips. Something was wrong. This couldn't be happening. She poked him in the chest. Nothing.

"Why do ye stab at me as though I were a straw dummy?"

She wasn't going to touch that with a ten-foot pole.

Eilan turned toward the window. Rain drizzled over the glass panes. The gray day fit her mood. She felt disconnected, as though a part of her had malfunctioned. She crossed her arms over her chest. She had never told anyone about her empathic ability. Some guessed and ran screaming from her, while others, like Dede, accepted it as though it were a talent like painting or opera singing. She should tell him. With any luck, he would become so freaked that he would will himself back to his own time.

She turned toward him, deciding she'd just blurt out the truth. "The reason I was poking you is because I can read minds if I touch the person." She paused, watching for his response.

A muscle on the side of his jaw clenched. "Then there is no need for words between us. Ye know my thoughts."

"Well, not exactly. For some reason your thoughts are blocked to me."

Eilan leaned against the windowsill and thought she saw a smile flicker across his lips.

That did it. She pushed away from the windowsill. "Look, I'm just trying to help here. And when you block your thoughts, I can't find out the truth."

His voice lowered. "I told ye the truth. I have traveled to your world to find ye. The legend is clear. Ye alone have the power to bring peace to my land. There was no need to work your evil witch's magic."

"I am not a witch."

"Ye said yourself ye can read the thoughts of others. 'Tis not an everyday occurrence."

She put her hands on her hips and ground out her words. "Well, since I possess this 'evil' habit of reading people's minds, maybe I'm not the person for the job. Why don't you just go back to wherever it is that you came from and start again?"

He folded his arms across his chest. "I canna return without ye."

She felt as though the floor had dropped from beneath her feet. "Are you telling me that you are stuck in this century unless you take me back with you?"

"Aye."

She rubbed the back of her neck. "And you would be willing to settle for a witch?"

"Aye."

She didn't feel very good. Of course she wouldn't have to go with him. She could find him a job. Teach him a skill. Her headache was back with a vengeance. She wondered where her mother kept the aspirin.

"Are you hungry?" Maybe if she kept herself busy, she would think of a plan.

His eyes narrowed. "I was given nourishment while I was in your prison."

Eilan ignored him. She had never heard of a man yet who would turn down the offer of food. He was probably just being polite. Besides, a good meal was sure to take him off guard. Of course what he needed more was a hot shower.

She pushed away from the wall and headed toward the compact kitchen opposite the living room. The raised panel cabinets were painted a glossy white and the tile counters were sea foam green. Seashell magnets covered the refrigerator and a framed picture of the San Juan Islands hung on the wall. Her mother loved the ocean and believed in surrounding herself with the things she treasured. Eilan's small apartment in Colorado had little more than the bare necessities. Even her walls were vacant. She alternately told herself that she didn't have time to decorate or that it was a waste of time.

Eilan ran her fingers over the ceramic flour canister. A picture of a mermaid sunning herself on a rock was painted across the surface. Eilan smiled. The apartment might be cluttered by some people's standards, but there was warmth about it that folded you in its arms. She had missed that.

Eilan opened the refrigerator more forcibly than she had intended. Bottles of catsup and mustard rattled in the side compartment. A carton of soymilk and a bunch of wilted celery took center stage on the rack. She closed the door and turned toward the cupboards. She knew they would be as bare. Her mother had told Eilan to stock up on whatever she wanted. However, cooking for one had never been a favorite pastime of hers. Especially when great restaurants were only a few steps away.

She turned and opened the cupboard over the refrigerator and reached for the bottle of aspirin. It was empty.

Eilan took a deep breath and turned back to the Scotsman. "I don't have any food." She had the sudden urge to run. She needed to get away from him for a while to sort out her thoughts. If he wasn't here when she returned, so much the better. "I have to go to the store."

He nodded.

A man of few words, well, at least that hadn't changed over the centuries. She wondered how long it would be before he discovered the hypnotic appeal of sports. She walked over and motioned for him to follow her. This would be the perfect time to introduce him to water.

She walked down the narrow hallway and opened the door to the bathroom. She made a sweeping gesture with her arm. "This is called a bathroom. Spend some time here. Get to know the place." She stepped inside, turned the handles over the sink on, flushed the toilet and turned on the shower.

"What is it ye wish me to do?"

"Wash."

She was confident she had covered all the bases. She had been tempted to tell him he smelled. He deserved it after calling her a witch. However, seeing the look of bewilderment on his face was reward enough.

Steam slowly filled the room.

"This is called a shower." She opened the cupboard under the sink and took out soap and towels and handed them to him. "You might feel better if you wash and have clean clothes to wear."

He arched one eyebrow. "I am not feeling ill. There is no need to go to the trouble."

She had never realized how small her bathroom was. He was standing so close to her she could almost hear his heart beat. Too bad she also had to hold her breath. The pungent order that surrounded him was suffocating. She needed to have time away from him to clear her head.

"Let me put it another way. You are covered in blood. I would appreciate it if you would take a shower. You can take off your clothes and set them outside the door. We can talk about your problem after I've returned."

"Aye." He unbuckled his belt. The fabric of the kilt loosened around his waist.

Her face warmed. There was that imagination again, running amok.

She closed the door behind her before she saw more than she bargained for. The Scotsman had traveled seven hundred plus years into the future, she figured he could handle figuring out a simple thing like a shower by himself.

Eilan looked at her watch as she hurried down the stairs and through the shop. She should have enough time to make it back before the Scotsman finished his shower. She opened the door and headed toward the Pike Place Market. The afternoon was crisp and the sun had peeked out from behind the gray clouds. It sparkled on Puget Sound and she could see a ferryboat making its rounds to Bainbridge Island.

A produce delivery truck stacked with crates of fresh lettuce, corn, tomatoes and carrots blocked her path. She veered around it and dodged a man on a bicycle. She jumped over a small puddle of water, a reminder of last night's rainstorm, and walked over the tile floors, past the fish market toward the butcher shop.

The smell of fresh seafood and sourdough bread mingled and wove around her. She smiled. She loved it here. It made her feel as though she had stepped back in time to a place where open-air markets were the norm, instead of a curiosity.

Eilan reached the butcher's counter and looked through the glass cases at the assortment of steaks, pork chops, chicken and ground veal.

Angus peered over the counter. "Looking for something special, Eilan?"

She laughed. "How did you guess?"

He folded his meaty arms over his round belly. "Not that hard to figure. You only come here if you have a guy over for dinner. Otherwise, its seafood." He wrinkled his nose. "Or that tofu stuff that looks like white gelatin cubes."

Eilan took a deep breath. She should have anticipated the questions. Except for the last five years, she had lived here all her life. These people were her family. She didn't mind that they were interested in what she did, only that she was so predictable.

She shook her head. "You know me too well."

He laughed. "True enough. Now let's get to work planning your main course." He rested his hands on the glass case. "So who's this guy?"

"Just a friend. Well, not exactly a friend, more

like an acquaintance." She hesitated trying to define the relationship.

He raised his eyebrow. "And you're going to cook for an acquaintance?"

"Of course."

Angus opened the case and reached for a New York steak. He slapped it on a piece of brown paper and handed it to Eilan. "This will be easy. Fry it, grill it, or bake it. Serve it with bread and a salad and your meal will be a success." He smiled. "Even with an 'acquaintance.' "

Eilan ignored the comment. "Actually, I was looking for something else. This guy is from Scotland. What do you suggest?"

He grinned. "Haggis. No one but the Scots like the stuff. Have you landed yourself a Highlander?"

She counted to ten. Six years ago when she turned twenty, it was humorous that everyone who lived and worked around Pioneer Square and the Pike Place Market tried to get her married off. And that every man she met was a potential husband.

Eilan kept her voice even. "Haggis sounds perfect, but I have not 'landed' anyone. I just thought it would be nice if I made him something he would be familiar with."

Angus winked. "I understand, and you are as right as rain. Haggis is the right choice. Remember to pick up some whisky. I'm not sure if they drink the stuff because it's good or because it kills the taste of haggis. Don't forget to bring the lad by soon. I'd like to meet him."

Angus turned and headed toward the back of the shop. She sighed and looked at her watch. This was taking longer than she thought it would. She looked around. She would purchase the haggis, sourdough bread, makings for a salad, a few more essentials, and flowers. Yes, a big bunch of roses would cheer up her place.

She heard Angus close the freezer door. No wonder he was so curious about Conor. It had been a long time since she had taken the time to prepare a meal for a man. She took the package Angus offered and put it on her account. Thankfully Angus was silent. She didn't blame him. He would naturally assume that if she was cooking for a man it meant something.

Eilan put the haggis in a shopping bag Angus had given her and headed toward the flower stand. She did not believe in love at first sight, the power of pheromones, or chemistry. She'd experienced all those methods with disastrous results. Her empathic ability was like a bucket of cold water. Every time she believed she knew someone well enough to entertain the idea of romance, she would be kissing him and *poof;* his thoughts would invade her mind. Knowing what a man was thinking while you were held in his embrace was not good. At times they were actually imagining you were someone else, or perhaps interested in you only as long as the relationship ended in the bedroom.

Her parents said not all men were like the few she had dated. Eilan was becoming tired of looking.

She picked out a bouquet of yellow roses and inhaled the heady fragrance. The next time she'd get involved with a man it would be after she'd learned everything there was to know about him, starting with the brand of toothpaste he used and ending with a detailed accounting of his entire life. She hoped that would make the difference.

Eilan paid for the roses and shifted her bundles. She still had to purchase clothes. She glanced at her watch. It was three o'clock. She had been gone longer than she had wanted. She wondered if he would be there when she returned. She hastened her steps and then paused. Wait a minute. Wasn't that what you wanted, to have him out of your life? She resumed her walk, forcing herself to a more leisurely pace. If he returned to his own time, your life would be back to normal.

Her pace quickened.

6

Conor was trapped in the small room. While fighting in the Mediterranean, he and his men had visited a Roman bath. In that place, the water had flowed from hollow metal rods, much as it did in Eilan's room, into large heated, tile-lined pools. However, the chambers he visited were capable of accommodating hundreds of men and women. This room was barely large enough to accommodate his frame. Behind the marble walls in the Roman baths anything was possible. He and his men paid for their indulgence in such luxuries of the mind and body. That night they were attacked in their sleep.

He heard Eilan humming in the corridor. He did not recognize the melody, but the tune was like a balm to his troubled spirits. Conor had never met anyone like her in all his travels. Her gentle features were pleasing to him, but it was her voice that quieted his soul. He gripped the smooth surface of the white counter. He must remain strong and fight to resist her.

He had failed on all fronts. Not only was she not willing to return with him, but he was falling under her spell instead of the other way around. Magdah should have sent Rowan in his stead.

He heard footsteps on the wood floor and then the door clicked shut. She was leaving to purchase food. His stomach growled in response. He clenched his teeth and resolved to refuse anything made from her hand. It was common knowledge, in his village, that witches placed magic potions in the food in order to control unsuspecting men. He must be wary. He could not afford to lose more of himself than he already had.

The room was filling up with steam. He reached over and turned off the faucets in the white tub and caught a glimpse of himself in the reflecting glass. His image was blurred. He wiped it clean with his sleeve.

Conor stepped back and slammed against the wall. He did not recognize the man who stood before him. His beard was matted with blood. His hair was snarled and knotted and hung past his shoulders. His eyes reflected a depth of tiredness that no amount of sleep would cure. He now understood the fear he had seen in Eilan. No wonder she felt the need to ask for aid. Perhaps that was the reason she was still reluctant to journey with him.

He glanced toward the water. She had meant for him to bathe, but he had never done so standing up.

How was a man to clean himself? The soap would slide off his body.

However, Eilan had insisted and for now the fear that he had seen in her eyes was gone. He would bathe if that was her wish. He unsheathed his blade and set it on the side of the tub. He would also remove his beard.

Conor removed his weapons and then his clothes and stepped into the tub. He turned on the water. The spray felt hot against his skin. He stepped back. He had never encountered water so hot, even in the Roman bath. He let the water cascade down his chest. It felt good on his bare skin. This world was too noisy and crowded, but this was a wonder he could enjoy.

He put his head under the running water and let it pound against his forehead and over his shoulders and chest. The water washed away the blood that had caked his bare skin.

He reached for the blade and began removing his beard. He threw the hunks of hair on the tile floor. It had taken years to grow it and only moments to remove it. He felt the years fall away with each cut.

His reaction to her must be the work of a spell. That she was a witch, there was little doubt. Eilan had as much admitted it when she stated she could read his thoughts. He felt a sense of relief when she told him that his mind was closed to her. That was fortunate, for at that moment he was wondering how her lips would taste against his mouth. He shook his head.

But, a witch would soon find a solution and his mind would be opened to her. When he first traveled to this time, he believed he would be immune to her charms. After all, he was here on a noble quest. Magdah had said the Peacemaker would ask a price and that Conor must give it. The price would be Conor himself. However, he was determined to bring her back to help his people, nothing more. At least that was his goal in the beginning.

Finished with the task of removing his beard, he set the knife on the ledge. The water washed over him into a drain at his feet, ridding his body of the remnants of the battles he had fought. He put his hands on the cool white tiles on the wall and wished his dark memories were as easily discarded.

He closed his eyes and the dream that plagued him both night and day crept into his thoughts.

Black smoke funneled from a hundred fires and traveled toward the night sky. The air was still and smelled of death and rotting flesh. Conor warmed his hands over the fire and stared into the flames until he could see the shifting colors of blood red and charred flesh. He had won the battle this morning against the Saracens with their fast horses and curved sabers, but the price was too high.

The Muslim's flaming arrows had scorched flesh;

swords had severed limbs and pierced hearts. How much longer could they survive?

Clouds of billowing dust rose over the horizon. He stood slowly as his worst nightmare unfolded. A wall of horses emerged. The riders held sabers above their heads and wore armor made from small iron plates laced together. Conor felt the blood drain from his body. He recognized the new terror.

They were slaves recruited by the Muslims, who had transformed them into an elite body of troops called the Mamluks. Death was the only escape from their attack.

He unsheathed his sword. He would not make it easy for them.

Eilan stirred the simmering beef broth on the stove. The rich aroma of the ingredients of haggis; nutmeg, onions, toasted oatmeal and lamb, blended together with the cock-a-leekie soup mixture of parsley, thyme and bay leaf. The smell was making her hungry, and almost worth the effort it had taken to reproduce an authentic Scottish meal. She wiped her forehead with the back of her hand. She hoped Conor appreciated all the work.

She glanced at her watch. The Scotsman had been in the bathroom over an hour and a half. The shower had been going since she had retuned from shopping. He had probably drained her water tank dry. Among other things, she'd have to give him a lesson on conservation.

Eilan dipped a clean spoon into the broth. She wanted to taste her masterpiece. She heard a crash and dropped the spoon. It clattered to the floor.

The sound came from the direction of the bathroom. Had he slipped and fallen? Good grief. She should have warned him about how slippery the tub could become when it was wet.

Eilan sprinted down the hallway and opened the door.

The Scotsman was sprawled in the tub. He looked unconscious. His right arm was sprawled over the side and his head was slumped forward. The white lace shower curtain and chrome rod lay on top of him. She blinked. He had shaved.

Her pulse raced. He must have slipped and hit his head. She blamed herself. The man had never seen a shower before. She was an idiot. Eilan rushed over to him. She held her breath as she knelt down beside him and felt for a pulse. He was breathing. She gulped for air. Good.

Her mind raced with different options. She had to get him out of the tub. No, she shouldn't move him. What if he'd damaged his back, his neck? She couldn't do this alone. She needed help. She'd call 911.

The Scotsman's eyes snapped open and he grabbed her arm. "Ye willna break me."

Eilan knew at once he was dreaming. His grip was

like an iron vise. The pressure increased. She felt her bones might be crushed, but she didn't try to pull away. His eyes were wide and glazed over. It was not she he saw, but someone from the depths of his nightmare. She could feel the waves of his mental torment crash against her. His pain became her own. The need to help and protect him overwhelmed her.

Since he first arrived, she had referred to him only as the Scotsman. It was as though by not using his name he was not real. Tears welled in her eyes as she felt another wave of his thoughts swell toward her. He held a dying comrade in his arms on a blood-soaked battlefield. Her heart was heaving as a tear journeyed down her cheek.

Her voice trembled as she whispered against his ear. "Conor, you are safe here with me."

His eyelids drooped and his breathing increased, but still he held on.

She shook him gently. "Conor. No one can hurt you." She brushed wet hair off his forehead. "Conor, please wake up."

His erratic breathing calmed and his eyes closed slowly. He loosened his grip and slumped back in the tub. Eilan leaned closer to him and put her fingers against the pulse at his neck. He was breathing easier now. His facial muscles were more relaxed. Maybe she should still call 911. Yes, that would be the smart thing to do. She glanced toward him.

With his beard shaved, she realized he looked much younger than she first thought. He was probably in his early thirties. His features were chiseled, and his jawline square. The muscles on his shoulders and arms were well defined and his chest looked like it was flat all the way . . . She cleared her throat. He was drop dead gorgeous.

He opened his eyes.

She couldn't move.

Conor reached out toward her and placed his hand on the back of her neck. He drew her gently toward him. His lips molded against her mouth. Giant butterflies fluttered in her stomach. Emotions flooded her senses, but they were all her own.

She pulled away and scrambled to her feet. She put her fingers against her mouth. She could still feel the warmth of his lips. She should have been bombarded with his thoughts. What was happening to her?

Her pulse raced as though she'd just finished a triple shot of espresso mixed in with a grande mocha latte.

Conor rose from the tub. The shower curtain crumbled to the floor.

Eilan swallowed. "You're naked."

She stumbled out of the bathroom and slammed the door shut. Eilan clenched her fists at her sides and spoke out loud as she headed toward the kitchen. "That was smooth. You acted as though you'd never seen a naked man before."

She paused at the counter, reminding herself that Greek statues in art books didn't count. Well, that wasn't her fault. She'd had plenty of opportunities, but whenever a man kissed her she read his mind. Their thoughts were not about the kiss, but about how fast they could get her undressed and into bed. Until now, that is. When Conor had kissed her it was as though a curtain had been drawn across his thoughts. It was unnerving. She touched her mouth. She could still feel Conor's lips on hers.

She took a deep breath and counted to ten. She needed to keep busy. She was behaving as crazy as she had once accused him of being.

She turned back to the preparation of the meal that had become a major production. This would be just the project to keep her distracted.

What had ever possessed her to try to fix an authentic Scottish meal?

The door to her bathroom creaked open. Conor stood framed in the doorway. A white bath towel was wound loosely around his waist. It looked as though it could fall off at any minute. She bit down on her lip to stop the impulse to give the towel a tug. He was clean-shaven. His dark wet hair hung to his shoulders. His muscles flexed over his broad shoulders, chest and arms. She gulped.

The broth bubbled over, hissing as it landed on

the burner and spilled on the stove. Eilan grabbed a cloth and sopped up the mess, thankful for the distraction. She heard his footsteps on the wood floor and looked toward him.

A muscle alongside Conor's cheek line twitched as he walked toward her. "Forgive me. I dinna mean to kiss ye. It willna happen again."

Eilan rubbed harder with the cloth. Darn.

His eyes narrowed as he drew nearer. "I must warn ye, I have no intent of eating any of your witch's brew. I am accustomed to going days without nourishment."

"Witch's brew? What are you talking about?"

"Although ye are fair of face and body, 'tis plain ye are a witch."

Amazing. They had just shared a heart-stopping kiss, at least from her perspective, and he'd managed to pay her a compliment by saying she was fair. However, in the next breath had taken it all away by calling her a witch. What a jerk.

She put her hands on her hips, happy to express a little righteous indignation. It helped to get her mind off his bare chest. "Why, exactly, do you think I'm a witch? Do you see any warts on my nose? Maybe you've found a black hat in the closet."

"I dinna know the significance of warts or hats, I only know a witch's magic brought me to your world and witches are beings that are feared."

"That is why so many were burned at the stake."

"Aye."

She clenched her fists at her sides. The Middle Ages and early Renaissance was laced through with such dark logic. It was a time of world awareness, alongside black superstition and fear. It was a confusing time, but it was over. This was the twenty-first century.

"You don't want to eat the food I have cooked because you think I might have cast a spell over it? Are you saying a witch's sole purpose in life is to poison people?"

"Nay, of course not. It is a well-known fact their real purpose is to have power over mortals. Only when that path is not open to them will they resort to poison."

Eilan wished at that moment that she really did possess the power of witchcraft. She would use it to turn Conor into a toad. She tapped her foot on the floor. "A well-known fact?"

"Aye."

"If I'm such an evil person, why are you asking for my help?"

"I made a promise to a dying man that I would seek the Peacemaker."

"And do you always keep your promise?"

"Aye, that I do."

"That must have really bothered you, having to make a deal with someone like me."

"I will do what must be done to save my people from the tyrant that rules over Castle MacCloud."

"Even if it means making deals with a witch?"

"Aye, even that."

Eilan picked up the roses on the table. In her haste to prepare the meal, she'd not had a chance to put them in water. That was a good thing. She had another purpose in mind. She took a butcher knife, laid the flowers on the cutting board and whacked off the blooms. She then placed the stems in the water vase and threw the flowers away. She'd seen Morticia Adams do that in the movie, *The Addams Family*. If Conor thought she was a witch, she might as well act the part.

She looked over at him to see if her dramatics had made an impression. He backed toward the window. Maybe if she were lucky, he would jump. She picked up the glass vase and tried to figure out the best place to display the little reminder of just how odd she really was.

A horn blast and yelling came from the street below. Conor glanced toward the sound. It must be something in a man's DNA, as regardless of the century, automobiles seemed to hold a fascination for the male of the species.

He turned toward the window. Crisscrossed over his bare back were thick red scars. They covered him from shoulder to waist.

She gasped. The vase slipped from Eilan's hands

and crashed to the tile floor. Shards of glass sprayed around her feet. He turned toward her and looked at the disaster on the floor.

She whispered. "Your back."

He shrugged. A shadow crossed over his face. "It was a lifetime ago."

Tears choked her voice. She could not stand to see someone hurt. "Who?"

"I would rather not talk of it."

The memory of the pain she had seen in Conor's thoughts moments before wove through her. There was a great deal about this man she didn't know. All she knew about life in the Middle Ages she had read in history books, but he had lived in those times. And from the angry scars on his back, it had not been an easy life.

Eilan stepped over the broken glass and turned off the flame under the steaming pot of soup. If he distrusted her cooking, he probably had a good reason. She opened a narrow closet alongside the refrigerator and retrieved a dustpan and broom.

"I'll clean up the mess. Why don't you get dressed and we'll go out to eat." She bent down and swept the glass into the pan and smiled. "I'll bet we can even ask someone to taste the food for you, if you're worried there might be a spell on it as well." She thought about the bloodstained kilt. "Maybe we'll go shopping for clothes for you before we eat."

He stood before her, his bare feet inches from the glass. "I dinna need clothes nor food. Each day I am gone, more of my people die, or are driven from their homes. Ye must go back with me."

She focused on her task and tried to ignore the half-naked man who stood before her. It took all the willpower she possessed. His problem was not hers. She repeated the phrase over and over in her thoughts. She was only one person. How could she succeed where he had failed? There was nothing she could do to save his people.

Eilan swept the last remnants of the glass and flower stems into the dustpan and stood. "I'm not going with you. I thought I made that clear. The way I see it you have two choices. You can stay here or return to your own time." She turned and dumped the glass into the wastebasket under the sink and put the dustpan and broom away. She rubbed her forehead. If possible her headache seemed worse tonight. "It makes no difference to me what you decide." She couldn't look at him when she made this last declaration.

He reached over and turned her toward him. "I know the reason ye are in pain."

She swallowed. He was too close. "Yes, I remember. Something about not using my powers."

He nodded. "Aye. But 'tis more than that. Magdah said the strain could kill ye."

She felt her breathing increase. If what he said

was true, that would explain the tumor. She shook her head. What was happening to her? She was starting to think like the Scotsman. She took a deep breath. "As I said before, I can't go with you."

"And I canna leave without ye." He paused. "Do I displease ye?"

"What did you say?" She backed toward the refrigerator. "No, don't repeat it. What has how I feel about you have anything to do with anything?"

He leaned against the counter and folded his arms across his chest. " 'Tis said that the Peacemaker must be pleased with the warrior who has come for her."

"Who said? I didn't read that in the legend. And why should that have any bearing on my . . . that is to say, the Peacemaker's decision?"

He shrugged. "The wisewoman of the village told me it was an essential part of the success or failure of the mission." He straightened. "I mentioned to her that my brother would make the better choice, but Magdah disagreed."

The phone rang. Eilan flinched and fumbled for the receiver on the wall. "Hello?" Her voice sounded strained.

It was Dede.

"Eilan, you feeling okay? I stopped by the shop earlier, but it was closed. Want to go out for dinner?"

Eilan glanced toward Conor. The towel had dropped lower on his hips. Good grief, what was she doing? She hadn't told her friend about dropping the charges at the police station or about having Conor released. Dede would throw a fit if she learned Conor was in Eilan's kitchen. She couldn't tell her friend until she sorted this out for herself. The last thing she needed was more advice.

"Eilan, are you still there?"

Eilan cleared her throat. "Yes, I'm here. I can't meet you for lunch tomorrow. I'm working on a project. Why don't I call you?"

There was a long pause on the other end of the phone. "What project?"

Conor turned and headed in the direction of the bathroom. Now what was he up to?

Eilan spoke into the receiver. "It's a long story."

"Is it a man?"

For someone who was not an empath, her friend was extremely psychic. "Dede, it has to do with researching a legend." That was a true statement. It just wasn't the whole story. "Don't worry, Dede, I'll call you."

Dede laughed. "You're becoming more like your mom every day. She was always reading about some new myth she'd discovered. Just remember, unlike you, she took the time for romance."

Eilan ignored the statement. There was a big difference between her and her mom. In fact there was a big difference between her and the rest of the female population. Being an empath put a serious damper on moments of passion. She took a deep breath. However, there was no need to remind her friend of the obvious.

"I'll talk to you tomorrow. I promise."

As she hung up the phone, Conor appeared.

He walked toward her, fully dressed. His long hair was tied at the nape of his neck with a leather thong. And it looked as though he had tried to spot clean the bloodstains on his kilt and shirt. The stains blended into the green and blue wool plaid fabric. A sword was strapped to his back and a knife at his belt. She thought if he put clothes on her pulse rate would return to normal. She was wrong.

Her heart skipped a beat. Eilan had heard the expression once that there was nothing sexier than a man in a kilt. She couldn't have agreed more. She let out her breath slowly and swallowed back the word "wow."

He nodded. "I am ready."

"Excuse me?"

"Ye mentioned food."

"Oh, yes, sure, we can go right away." Terrific, she was stuttering again. She headed for the hall tree by the entry and grabbed her coat and slung the strap of her purse over her shoulder. "What changed your mind about the food?"

He leaned closer to her. "I am hungry."

"And?"

"It will give me more time to convince ye to return with me to my world."

She nodded. "Fair enough. But I must warn you. I'm pretty stubborn."

"As am I."

She smothered a smile. "Okay, but you have to leave your weapons here. In this century people don't walk around with swords and knives." She decided to refrain from mentioning that instead, people carried guns.

He narrowed his eyes as though she had just asked him to walk naked out into the world. However, after a long pause, he removed his weapons and laid them on the sofa.

She nodded, opened the door and headed down the stairs. Dede would think she was crazy to be walking around with this man and her mother would have called for the men in white jackets. The weird thing about this was she wasn't afraid. In fact, she had never felt safer with anyone else in her life. She hesitated at the bottom of the stairs and looked over her shoulder. Dede was right. She was nuts.

7

Eilan blew on her hands to warm them as she watched the sun peek out from behind the gray clouds outside her shop. It shone on the large uneven cobblestone meridian that preserved a section of Seattle's past. A bronze statue of Chief Seattle took a prominent place near the thirty-foot high totem pole. Normally the sight of all this history quieted Eilan, but not when she felt so disconnected. Even the sight of the wooden park benches that lined the sidewalk and the turn of the century lampposts had little effect.

The memory of Conor's kiss disturbed her. She knew how it had affected her, but didn't have a clue as to what he thought. She didn't like that one bit. Her empathic ability was as much a part of her as her sight and hearing. Without it she felt as though she were blind. So this was how it felt when someone kissed you. No wonder the uncertainty of love drove people nuts.

And to make matters even more challenging, she'd invited a kilt-clad Scotsman to walk with her along the streets of Seattle. She was inviting trouble. After all, she'd seen the movie *Braveheart.* The Scots were known for their love of fighting. Thank heavens she had asked Conor to leave his weapons behind. It occurred to her that he had not put up much of a fight. She wondered why. She shrugged. As usual, she was overthinking the situation. He probably realized he wouldn't need them.

Eilan blew on her hands again. Conor had stayed behind to examine the medieval weapons that hung on the brick wall alongside the door. She knew her father would have enjoyed discussing them with Conor. She smiled. Her mother believed the only reason her dad had held on to the store for so long was an excuse to purchase additional antique swords and shields.

The aroma of pizza dough baking in the nearby restaurant floated in the air, reminding her that the only thing she had eaten all day was a latte and a raspberry scone. She glanced at her watch. It was almost five o'clock. She hoped Conor would hurry. She was starving.

As though on cue, the chime over the door rang out and Conor stepped into the crisp air and walked toward her. His expression was emotionless as though his features were frozen. It occurred to her that she had never seen him smile. She remembered the brief glimpse she had of his dark thoughts while he lay unconscious in the bathtub. She wished she knew a way to bring the sunshine back into his life.

He stood beside her with his arms crossed over his chest. His voice was as impassive as his expression. "Your collection is impressive. My father displayed our weaponry in much the same way." He paused. "There is a date underneath one of the shields. Does that indicate the year it was made?"

Eilan suppressed a smile. He was the most serious man she'd ever met. She doubted he had ever had a frivolous thought in his life. Her dad's weapons collection was the last thing she wanted to talk about. She wanted to learn more about Conor MacCloud. She wondered if it was because she couldn't read his mind with any sort of consistent pattern.

"My dad personally researched and marked the date the weapons were made. It's one of his passions."

"It was an interest to my father as well. However, the shield with a sword slicing through a wall of flames is dated incorrectly. I have seen its like in my time."

"Really? It's older than the fifteen hundreds? That's great. My dad thought so, but the man he purchased it from was insistent."

She stuffed her hands into the pockets of her coat, wishing Conor and her dad could meet. However, Conor would be long gone before her parents returned from Europe. She was surprised by the regret she felt.

A couple of teenagers jostled Eilan and Conor, separating them. It was rush hour and the sidewalk was almost as crowded as the streets as everyone headed home from work.

Men and women dressed in gray suits and starched white shirts, wove around an old woman pushing a shopping cart filled with cardboard boxes, old shoes and threadbare blankets. Giggling teenagers and a couple wearing red leather pants and matching coats sped past her. Twenty-first century Seattle embraced a wide assortment of people.

No one had paid any attention to the kilt-clad Scotsman as he walked over and examined the totem pole on the far side of the meridian.

A man wearing a ripped gray cloth jacket and patched overalls shouted incoherently as he walked past her on the sidewalk. The man stood on the corner mumbling as he waited for the light to change. He was only a short distance from her. She knew she could reach him before he crossed the street. If she knew what was bothering him, perhaps she could make a difference somehow.

A crisp breeze rustled through the limbs of the trees and burnished gold leaves fluttered to the ground. It had been a long time since she'd entertained thoughts of helping someone. For a brief moment she wondered what troubled him, but doubted he would welcome her interference. Seattleites liked to keep to themselves. She'd learned that lesson the hard way.

The sound of a jackhammer brought her back to reality. Less than fifty feet from where she stood some big developer was restoring one of the old brick buildings on Yesler. High-priced condominiums would replace the low-rent apartments. That was progress. The man crossed the street. It was just as well. He would probably resent her help.

Brakes squealed. Eilan turned toward the sound and saw a car screeching to a stop on Cherry Street. A red Volvo slammed into a blue Dodge. The owners of both cars bolted from their vehicles, inspecting the damage.

The two men yelled at each other as a crowd gathered around them. Each driver accused the other of negligence.

Conor strolled over to her. He glanced in the direction of the crowd and then nodded as he turned toward her. " 'Tis not unlike my world."

Eilan stared at Conor and then the two men. Their voices could be heard over the construction sounds and the steady hum of traffic. It was a heated argument, but Eilan couldn't understand what Conor meant.

She turned back to him. "I'm not sure I know what you mean. The men are just arguing."

"Aye, and soon they will draw their weapons."

Eilan shook her head. "No, it's not like that in this century. We don't settle every argument with the point of a sword. We're civilized."

She wasn't sure if Conor was aware of the last words she'd spoken. He bolted toward the center of the crowd. Now what was he doing? The last thing to do was to become involved in someone's business. It was like trying to separate two rabid dogs.

Eilan raised her voice and shouted for Conor to stop, but he either hadn't heard her or was ignoring her.

He reached the driver of the red Volvo just as the man was pulling something from his shirt jacket.

A shot rang out.

Eilan jumped. Her heartbeat raced. The crowd bumped into one another as they scattered for cover. She couldn't move. The man who owned the red car held a gun in his hand. Smoke curled from the barrel. Conor wrestled him to the ground and wrenched the weapon from out of the man's grasp. The driver of the Dodge weaved on his feet, holding his hand against his shoulder. Blood oozed from the wound.

The air was so still it seemed to crackle as the minutes ticked by. Eilan felt frozen to the ground. She watched as Conor yanked the man who had held the gun to his feet.

Sirens broke through the silence. Three police cars, their lights flashing, converged on the scene. Before you could say "front page news" the gunman was handcuffed and shoved into one of the patrol cars. An aid car screeched to a stop and medics rushed to the injured man. Soon everything would be back to normal. Her legs didn't feel strong enough to hold her. She sank down on a nearby wooden bench.

The air grew chillier as the minutes crept by. This wasn't Conor's world, yet he had stepped in while she had done nothing. She pulled up the collar of her coat and waited. She didn't like the person she had become.

She'd run away to Colorado because she was overwhelmed with emotions. Right now she would welcome them back. It was what made a person feel alive, and want to help others.

Conor nodded toward the policeman, turned and jogged back to her. He slid down next to her and shook his head. He stared back to the area where the man had been shot. "How is that possible? The weapon has the power of a cannon, yet it is small enough a man can hold it in the palm of his hand." He turned toward her. "Do ye have such a weapon?"

"You saved that man's life. And of course I don't have a gun." She paused and took a deep breath. He was safe. She was surprised how relieved she felt. "That was so dangerous. Why did you risk your life to save someone you don't even know?"

He shrugged. "I couldna stand by, knowing I could prevent it."

She ignored the words of self-confidence. He obviously was a man who was used to winning. However, that didn't explain how he knew what would happen. "But how did you know the man would draw a gun?"

He shrugged. "I recognized the look in his eyes. He had finished talking."

Conor made it sound so simple. Eilan laced her hands in her lap. "You know, this doesn't happen all the time. Seattle is a safe city. It's just that," she paused, "some people still don't know how to control their anger. I believe fear drives them to it."

" 'Tis the same in my world."

Eilan felt the silence swirl around her. The traffic and drum of the jackhammer blended together. She had heard the pain in his voice. He had journeyed to this time with the hope of finding this legendary person whom he believed would help his people. It was unfortunate he had pinned all his hopes on her.

Her shoulders slumped forward as though someone had piled weights on her back. She needed to think of something else.

"Conor, are you still hungry?"

His expression brightened. "Aye."

There was a pizza parlor right next to the antiques shop. Eilan didn't feel much like going too far from home, despite her declaration on the safety of Seattle. She stood and led him toward the deserted restaurant. Everyone had vacated the place and joined with the crowd of policemen, media and reporters that had gathered on the street. Her quiet section of the city would be on the six o'clock news tonight.

The aroma of cheese and baking pizza crust wove through the air again blocking out the violence of a few moments before. The wood planks on the floor creaked as she entered. She reached over and touched Conor on the arm, thinking she'd catch him off guard. She could feel the muscles beneath his arm flex, but there was no flood of memories, thoughts or images. She wondered if maybe she had short-circuited her empathic ability somehow. She'd test it on someone else.

A man with a navy blue T-shirt, jeans and a white apron with pizza sauce splattered across the front walked up to the counter. It was John, the owner of the restaurant.

"Nice to see ya, Eilan. Do you want your usual vegetarian pizza?"

She smiled and shook her head. "No, how about the works. I'd like everything from anchovies to pepperoni."

John was the perfect candidate to test her theory. She reached out and touched John's arm. She saw an image of John fighting with his girlfriend, Mary. Eilan pulled back, not wanting to intrude further into his life. Okay, so her empathic ability was still in place. She was okay; it was just Conor who was the problem.

She glanced in his direction. He had picked up a large bottle of Tabasco from the counter. He shook the contents on his tongue.

Conor's eyes grew so wide Eilan thought they would bug out of their sockets.

John roared with laughter and handed Conor a pitcher of water.

Conor tilted his head back and dumped the water into his mouth and over his face.

Eilan reached for Conor's arm and motioned for him to follow her over to a table next to the wall. She smiled. "Why did you do that?"

John brought two glasses, another pitcher of water and plates over to the table. He was laughing so hard he had developed the hiccups. "Your pizza will be ready right away."

Conor downed a glass of water. He set it down and took a deep breath. "I was thirsty and it looked like the bottles of wine I had in Spain." He poured himself another. "What was that?"

"Tabasco. It is very hot and spicy."

His shook his head slowly. "I thought you promised to have someone taste the food for me. That . . . Tabasco nearly killed me."

Eilan laughed. "That's nothing. Wait until you taste the pizza."

He cocked an eyebrow.

She smiled. "I'm just kidding. It's perfectly safe."

Conor leaned back in his chair. "What is this food that you have ordered?"

Eilan leaned forward. "Well, first you take a round thin crust, smear it with a tomato sauce, heap two or three kinds of grated cheese in the middle, add ground sausage, onions, mushrooms, anchovies, shrimp, green peppers . . ."

Conor grimaced. "All of those ingredients are combined together?"

Eilan nodded.

"And 'tis safe to eat?"

"It's yummy."

John brought the pizza over and set it down on the table. "Enjoy." He smiled as he pulled a bottle of Tabasco out of the pocket of his apron. He laughed. "Just in case you want to heat up the pizza."

Eilan smiled and picked up a slice. "Thanks, John." She paused, remembering the image she had seen in his thoughts of the woman John loved. "You know, John, I haven't seen Mary in a while. How is she?"

He rolled his eyes to the ceiling. "Still mad at me."

"Why don't you call her?"

"Ah, she wouldn't want to talk to me."

Eilan put the slice on her plate. "How do you know unless you try?"

John nodded. "Okay, I guess I've nothing to lose. Thanks. Enjoy your meal."

Eilan took a generous bite of her pizza. She watched John walk behind the counter and reach for the phone. She knew it wouldn't be easy for them, but at least John had made the first step. It had been a long time since she had used her empathic ability in this way. It felt good. As long as she kept it simple, it might be okay.

She turned her attention to her pizza. "Delicious. Conor, your turn."

He shrugged. "I thought I would wait awhile."

Eilan picked off a mushroom and popped it into her mouth. "Why do you want to wait? It's the best when it's warm."

He nodded. "If you survive the next few moments the pizza should be safe for me to eat."

She laughed. "And here I thought you were the type that liked to live dangerously. I dare you to take a bite."

"How can I refuse such a challenge?" Conor scooped up a generous slice and brought it to his mouth. He bit off a large mouthful and chewed. He swallowed and shook his head. "This is wonderful. If I die tonight, it will be worth it." He looked at the pizza on the metal tray. "Is this all there is?"

She smiled. "We'll order more."

He nodded, finished off his piece and reached for another.

Eilan thought she saw the faintest hint of a smile crinkled around his eyes as he glanced in her direction. The butterflies that had taken flight when he'd kissed her earlier today awakened once more. She liked the feeling. If this was how he reacted to pizza, Eilan decided that tomorrow she'd introduce him to chocolate.

Eilan had lost track of the time.

She stood beside Conor on the sidewalk outside the antiques shop in silence. It felt good just to share a moment with him. The moon shone through the limbs of the trees and cast a silver glow over the lampposts. All the remnants of this afternoon's drama had been swept away. Even the traffic seemed lighter than normal.

Conor balanced a narrow box filled with a fresh pepperoni and olive pizza on the palm of his hand. A snack in case he became hungry later tonight, had been his explanation.

She reached for the door handle.

"Eilan." It was Dede's voice.

Her friend walked straight toward her, carrying a brown paper sack in her arms. Eilan was not prepared to explain Conor, but then maybe the direct approach was best.

Dede paused, out of breath. "I took a chance you'd be looking for company. Did you see what happened just a short distance from here? It was all over the news. A man in a kilt broke up a fight. He looked a lot like that guy we had arrested the other day, except without the beard." Dede's eyes widened. "It's him."

Eilan wondered what the chances were that Dede was referring to the cat they had named Cally. Probably slim and none. Particularly since Cally was a she. She nodded toward Conor. "Dede, I want you to meet Conor MacCloud."

Dede screeched. "The Scotsman?"

"Aye."

Dede set the sack down, fumbled through her purse and pulled out her cell phone. "We have to call the police."

Eilan reached for the phone and snatched it out of Dede's hand. "No, we do not. Conor is okay."

Dede folded her hands across her chest. "So now it's Conor. Are you out of your mind?"

Eilan looked toward Conor. "Quite possibly. Dede, come on inside. I'll explain it all to you over a cup of tea."

"Since when did you start drinking tea?"

Eilan opened the door and flipped on the light switch. "Since I ran out of coffee. Would you prefer hot chocolate?"

Dede picked up her sack of groceries and waltzed into the shop. "What I want is an explanation."

Eilan motioned for her entourage to follow her up the stairs. This night was going to be a long one. She doubted she'd be able to convince Dede to leave.

Dede followed Eilan and Conor into the apartment. "I guess it's too late to give you the lecture about letting strays into your life?"

Dede didn't wait for an answer, but sailed into the kitchen and set the groceries on the counter.

Eilan turned toward Conor. "I'm going to need to talk to Dede and try to clear up a few things." Eilan picked up the remote and whisked the tapestry-style tablecloth she used to cover the TV off the console. She motioned for Conor to sit on the sofa and gave him a brief explanation on how to operate the twentieth-century invention.

The set buzzed to life. Eilan flicked through a few channels until she landed on the one she thought would hold his interest.

She pointed the remote at the screen. "I think you'll like this. It's called football. It involves a leather ball, goalposts at either end of the field and a lot of running and tackling. The guys with the gold helmets are trying to score against the men with the crimson. Whoever has the most points at the end wins."

Eilan handed him the remote and returned to Dede.

Dede smiled and rummaged around in the sack and pulled out a roll of chocolate chip cookie dough.

Eilan smiled. "How did you know I was having a sugar craving?"

"When have you not?" Dede brought the dough

over to the counter and pulled out the wood chopping block and a knife. "We're friends. So we know things about each other. Like that there is always time for chocolate." Dede whacked off the end of the roll with a knife and turned toward Eilan. "And friends tell each other stuff. Remember?"

"Point taken. Just hold that thought and I'll be right back."

Dede glanced over in Conor's direction. "Is he dangerous?"

"Does he look dangerous?"

Dede winked. "Absolutely, especially now since he's clean shaven." She hopped up on the counter and smiled. "Okay, brought the dough, you grab the spoons."

"Don't you want to cook it first?"

Dede shrugged. "Since when?"

Eilan laughed, pulled two spoons out of the top drawer and leaned against the counter. "Thank you."

Dede smiled. "You're welcome." She scooped a generous spoonful of dough and popped it into her mouth.

Eilan followed Dede's example. There might be at least a hundred rules against eating raw cookie dough, but it was just what she needed right now.

Dede paused. "I assume you dropped the charges?"

Eilan nodded and licked the spoon.

Dede shook her head. "I grant you the Scotsman doesn't look so scary now that he has shaved off that beard, but why did you do it? I mean, the guy claims to be from the fourteenth century. The last time I checked, the airlines weren't able to book a flight that far back in time."

"Very funny."

"I'm perfectly serious."

Eilan put down the spoon and walked over to the bookshelf near the door. She retrieved the legend and brought it over to Dede. Eilan opened the book to the page she had marked. "I found this the other day."

Dede kept her spoon in her mouth and read the passage silently. She waved the spoon in Eilan's direction. "This is a big coincidence, nothing more."

"I don't believe in coincidences, you know that."

Dede made a *humph* sound. "Well, maybe it's time for you to start. So, are you telling me you buy his story about time travel and being this Peacemaker person?"

Eilan took another scoop of dough. "That used to be my nickname in college, or have you forgotten?"

"Of course not, but we used to call Freddy Dunlap 'spaceship' because he was always moving through the halls at the speed of light. That didn't mean he had the ability to actually fly one."

Eilan took a deep breath. "I'm not going anywhere. I just think the coincidence is interesting."

Dede scooped out another spoonful. "Okay, lets just say, for the sake of discussion, that the Scotsman is telling the truth and he's from a zillion years back in time."

"It's more like six or seven hundred."

"Whatever. Anyway, you hop in his time machine, and presto chango you're back in the fourteenth century. Have you given it much thought that if he is telling the truth, you'd be stuck there, like forever?" She shrugged. "It might mean, however, that I can no longer tease you about being my least adventurous friend, but I'll take the risk."

Eilan rinsed off her spoon in the sink. She'd had enough. "You worry over nothing. I'm not going anywhere. Do you want pizza?"

Dede shook her head. "No, but can I use your bathroom?"

"Sure."

Eilan glanced over at Conor. He was asleep on the sofa. His large frame was scrunched in a *V* position to accommodate his length. She wondered how much he had slept over the past few days. Probably not much.

She walked over and reached for the multicolored afghan her mother had made. Eilan unfolded it and spread it over Conor. The memory of him preventing the gunman from killing the driver of the Dodge swept over her. She sat on the coffee table in front of the sofa and watched Conor's slow, even breathing. He had never given any thought to his own welfare, only that someone was in danger.

She reached out and pulled the blanket around his shoulders, resisting the urge to lean over and kiss him on the cheek. She didn't know what was happening to her. Maybe she just needed a good night's sleep. Tomorrow everything would look clearer and she would tell him he was wasting his time. There was no way she could go back with him.

Eilan took a deep breath. Her decision was made. She felt better already.

8

The morning air smelled crisp and clean after last night's rainstorm. Eilan waited in line at the Ivar's Acres of Claims outdoor restaurant and watched the sea gulls and pigeons. They combined forces in their search for food on the sidewalk that spanned the length of the waterfront. The streets looked as though they had been scrubbed.

It was a new day. She glanced over at the terminal. Conor stood at the stone railing and gazed in the direction of the Bainbridge Island ferry. Cars and passengers were being loaded on board for one of the first runs of the day. She was glad he had wanted to come with her. He was good company.

Last night, before Dede had left to go home, she had hugged her and told her to be careful. In the past, when Dede had used the phrase, it could be interchangeable with either "have a great day" or "don't forget to carry an umbrella." This time was different. Eilan knew exactly what her friend meant. Dede's thoughts were clear. She had cautioned Eilan on everything from falling in love to making sure she took an extra sweater when she traveled back in time.

Eilan smiled. She didn't know why her friend was so worried. Eilan wasn't going anywhere. As far as love was concerned, well, that was actually a more farfetched idea than time travel.

She inched closer in line and turned her thoughts to food. She never really considered fish and chips a breakfast-type meal, but Conor had finished off the cold pizza when he woke up and she figured a berry scone wouldn't do. Besides, she didn't know how long he was going to stay and she wanted to pack in as many sights, smells and tastes as possible. Maybe later they could take a ride on the monorail and then the elevator to the Space Needle.

Eilan was one person away from the counter. Evidently she was not the only one who had different ideas about breakfast. She glanced in Conor's direction. If someone was going to psychoanalyze her right now, she knew what they would say. She was avoiding the subject, by trying to keep as busy as possible.

"May I help you?" The freckled face young woman at the counter had her pad and pencil ready.

Eilan nodded, wishing that everything in life would be as simple as choosing whether or not you wanted two pieces of fried halibut or three.

* * *

Conor leaned against the railing by the ferry dock and sipped the drink Eilan had bought for him. It was bitter, but the aroma was pleasing. Eilan's world offered a varied assortment of tastes. He suspected the types of pleasure available were equally as appetizing. In one of the cities he had passed by on his way to fight in the Crusades, he had seen the same fascination with indulgence in the mind and spirit that he saw here. He preferred his life in the Highlands. He finished his coffee in one long gulp.

Salt water leaped against the wood pilings and a sea gull took flight near where Conor stood. It winged its way to a far pier. He envied the bird. Its wants and needs were simple.

A vessel pulled out from the dock. Eilan had called it a ferryboat. Conor had never seen its like. Sails powered the vessels he had seen off the shores of Spain. They also did not contain the number of passengers he had seen board these ships. The great ship edged clear of the wharf as it headed toward a series of tree-covered islands on the horizon. He wondered if they were as crowded as Eilan's city. He hoped not. It would please him if there were still breathing space left for a person to dwell.

Conor dropped the empty coffee container into a nearby receptacle and finished the last of the thin strips of potato Eilan had called French fries. He licked his fingers of the remaining salt. She had insisted he would love the food. It, and the cold pizza he had eaten this morning, had stayed his hunger, but he was not sure how he felt about the meals. However, the salt taste was familiar. Much of the food he had brought with him on the Crusades was preserved in salt. It kept a man from starving, but it was like the Tabasco he accidentally tried last night. So far, much of the food in this world was too spicy for his taste.

A group of brightly dressed men and women walked along the sidewalk. Eilan had called the black and silver boxes slung on a strap around their necks cameras, and christened these people as tourists. She had also described their purpose in her city. He understood her explanation. In Conor's time they were called "pilgrims." He gazed over the water once again. He had witnessed many miracles in this century, but the people remained unchanged.

The gray clouds moved over the sun, and a light rain fell around him. He tilted his head to the sky and felt the moisture against his face. He closed his eyes. The sensation of rain on his skin and the drone of the tourists' conversation were familiar. When he fought on foreign soil, he had not thought it possible so many people could enjoy living in close quarters with one another. He preferred the open spaces of the Highlands. He clenched his fists together and tried to draw strength from within. However, it was becoming more difficult with each day that passed. He felt as though he were being suffocated.

He knew the fault did not lie in this place, but through his experiences on the battlefield. He had long feared that his soul was drained of life. It was in large measure the reason he agreed to this journey. Not only would he fulfill his promise to his friend, but he also hoped the Peacemaker could succeed where he had failed. He had abandoned his people to seek adventure in the Crusades. In return, they had suffered and lost their homes.

He looked out over the horizon. Islands folded into one another, framing the water in shades of green. They reminded him of the Highlands that surrounded Loch Ness near his home in Inverness. He put his hand over his heart to stop the ache. He swallowed. He had never felt so lost. Even in the prison in Turkey, he had always known the direction home. All he had to do was break his bonds and he would be free. Here he must rely on someone else if he were to return and heal his land.

He could not go back without her.

A person riding on a steel frame that rode on two large wheels sped toward him. Conor sidestepped out of the way. His heart raced as though it was he, and not the rider, who had passed him. He gripped the stone railing that separated him from the water and felt the coarse stones cut into his flesh. A sea gull squawked and dove toward the murky green waters. The sound grated against his skin. A ferryboat's horn blasted through the rain-soaked air. He clung to the side as though it were a lifeline to his sanity as wave after wave of new experiences bombarded his senses. He must hold on just a little while longer.

Two young adults walked past him arm in arm. One had green hair that stood like sticks all over the person's head, while the other's head was bald. Jewelry was attached to various parts of their faces. Before Conor had left to fight in the Crusades, a sight such as this one would have seemed odd indeed. Now it was only a curiosity.

He saw Eilan walk toward him, carrying a brown sack. She wore a long straight gown in pale blue. Her hair flowed free beyond her shoulders in dark waves. He decided he preferred it unbound. Her eyes were the color of the sea, changing from deep sky blue to meadow green as suited her mood. Salt air floated on the cool breeze and caressed the loose hair around her face. Her skin was moist from the soft wind and rain and her lips were parted in a smile. Her tongue licked the corners of her mouth as though she tasted the salt sea air on her lips.

Blood surged through his veins as he remembered the pressure of her mouth on his. Conor clenched his jaw, longing to feel her against him. A woman had never affected him in this manner. It gave him hope that he was not dead inside.

She walked over and stood beside him. A flock of gulls flew overhead. The sound of their wings merged with the pounding surf. There was comfort in nature's ability to remain unchanged through the centuries. He would hold on to that thought.

"The seagulls don't seem to mind the weather." She smiled. "And neither do I. I love the rain. It washes away all the dust and grime."

She leaned closer to him. She smelled like the Highlands after a soft rain. It was like coming home. He inhaled and fought the temptation to gather her in his arms.

Eilan shoved a container that resembled rolled parchment toward him. She dumped a portion of its contents in the palm of her hand. "It's called popcorn. I couldn't resist. I bought it along with the fish and chips. You'll love it." She stuffed a few of the yellow morsels in her mouth.

He reached out and examined the fluffy white objects. "Does it taste like the French fries?"

She reached for another handful. "No, but in its own way it's even better."

He returned the popcorn to the container she held and dusted off his hands. His stomach was just recovering from his last adventure with food from this century; he decided to give his body a rest. "I am no longer hungry."

She smiled. "Well, you will be after you try the fish and chips, or maybe you would like steak and potatoes."

Eilan did not wait for him to answer, but pointed

excitedly in the direction of the water a short distance from them. "Did you see that? I think it was a seal."

Ripples in the steel gray water circled toward him. And then he saw it. A seal popped out of the water, stared in his direction, and then disappeared from sight. Conor nodded. " 'Tis a good omen if a lone seal allows his form to be seen by a human."

She leaned against the railing. "I think I've heard that legend before. Is it true?"

"Aye, 'tis true."

She laughed. "Well, then, this is indeed a good day."

Her excitement was infectious. It had been a long time since he had experienced the luxury of a day filled with idle pleasures. If it were possible, it would be an easy matter to stay here in this time with Eilan. The guilt of such thoughts weighed him down.

She ate another kernel of popcorn and stared in the direction she had pointed to moments before. "Why don't you stay here with me?"

An uneasiness washed over him. Had she read his thoughts?

Conor rubbed the back of his neck. He hated himself for the thoughts that danced around in his mind. For a brief span of time he had considered her proposal. Right now her eyes were the same clear blue as a lake in the springtime. Conor could easily lose himself in their depths.

He pushed away from the railing. He must not allow his own desire to pull him from his path. He would not abandon the people who needed him. He had put himself first before; he would not do it again. He must convince her to return with him. He would not even consider the possibility of failure.

Eilan watched as Conor drowned his fish and chips in a sea of catsup. He had told her he was not hungry, and true to his word he had not eaten very much. She had found the perfect table alongside the water. Of course they had to fight off a half dozen seagulls, but that was part of the charm of the area. It was secluded and she thought it would give them a chance to talk. Her plan had failed. He hadn't said one word since they'd sat down.

She had lost her appetite as well. Maybe this meal had not been the best choice for breakfast. She leaned toward him. "Is something wrong. You haven't said a word in the last half an hour. Is it the food?"

He shook his head, set the bottle of catsup down and glanced toward the water. "There is a matter I have to discuss with ye."

"I'm listening." She felt uneasy and wondered if it would've been better if she had not asked him what was wrong? It was too late for regrets. She had asked him what was bothering him and she had a feeling he was about to tell her.

He turned toward her. His eyes were dark and intense as though he were trying to read her thoughts or reactions. "Do ye now believe me when I tell ye I am from the past?"

"Yes, as strange as it sounds, I do believe you. I'm not sure how it happened, yet, but maybe it's something that will never be explained." Okay, so far this was old territory and nothing to worry about.

"Ye know also that I come in search of the Peacemaker."

She nodded. This was getting too close.

He twisted the gold ring on his finger. "I also know how I was able to travel to your time. However, first I want to tell ye why I am here."

A seagull swooped down and perched on the wood railing next to their table. It craned its neck as though looking around for something to eat. She welcomed the distraction of feeding the birds except for one little detail. There were signs plastered all over the waterfront prohibiting such actions. She had a feeling that the way her luck was running she would get caught before she threw the first French-fry.

"Are ye not interested in why I have journeyed to your world?"

"Absolutely." That was a lie.

He settled back against the metal chair. "I must start at the beginning."

Conor took a deep breath and told of his life as a young warrior, and of the responsibilities of being the eldest. He had a younger brother named Rowan and a sister named Rebecca. When there was a call to arms for able-bodied knights to fight against the Turks, his father encouraged his two sons to join in the Holy War. With the force the king was sending, all believed they would return before the next snowfall. Conor and his brother would see eight winters before their return home. Life as Conor knew it had changed. His father and sister were dead and his uncle, Simon MacCloud, had taken control. It was believed that Simon was mad, but as long as Conor's father was alive he had been able to control his brother.

Conor paused and leaned forward. A cloud passed over his features as he rubbed his forehead.

Eilan reached toward him and touched his arm. She no longer believed she would be able to read his thoughts, and she suspected the deep internal pain he had suffered was the reason his mind was blocked to her. Still, the human touch could comfort, and that was what she wanted to offer Conor.

She took a deep breath. "I'm sorry. What about the knights who were with you in the Crusades? Couldn't they help you win back your home?"

He stood and walked to the railing. "Only six of us survived. The townspeople fear my uncle. It seems Simon has been waging his own personal war against evil. All those who speak against him are branded as witches and tortured. Their lands are confiscated, and their families put to the sword."

An icy chill rustled over the water. Eilan remembered the book she had found while searching for the legend. It was called *The Witch's Hammer*. It was a manual on how to torture and kill.

She shivered and rubbed her arms. "Can't he be stopped?"

Conor turned toward her. "My men and I tried to lay siege to the castle. We failed and more died." He sank down in his chair. "It was then I met the witch, Magdah. It was she who sent me to ye. The legend tells us that a Peacemaker can heal our land." Eilan shivered again. She wanted to help, but this was way beyond anything she had ever imagined. Even considering such a foolhardy task was crazy.

"Conor, you need to understand. I don't know if I can do what you're asking." She paused. "I used to think just by knowing a person's thoughts, I could solve all their troubles. I can enter a person's mind and find an incident in their memory where they had a positive experience and pull it to the forefront. However, it only works if they have very small problems to overcome. This is way beyond my ability. I'm sorry, there must be someone else. Perhaps you can return and Magdah can try again."

He leaned back in the chair and shook his head.

"Magdah said there was no one else. Ye are the last." He stared in her direction. "And I canna return without ye."

"You will have to."

He shook his head. "Ye dinna understand. I can only return with ye by my side."

Eilan felt as though someone had hit her in the stomach. "You can't be serious?"

"Aye, but I am."

He reached for a leather string from around his neck and pulled it over his head. A gold band was attached. " 'Tis the mate to mine and brings forth the power of the Ring of Time. The moment ye slip it on your finger, and our hands touch, ye will accompany me back to my world."

Eilan swallowed. "Are you telling me that you are stuck here unless I return with you?"

"Aye."

"Would that be so bad?"

"I canna abandon my people as my uncle doesna value life. However, there is something else ye must know."

His words sounded ominous.

He cleared his throat. "According to Magdah, a Peacemaker has snow white hair."

She brightened. "That's great news, mine is dark."

Conor leaned forward and shook his head. "It only means that ye have not used your gift in the way it was intended." He paused. "Does your mind cause ye pain?"

"If you mean, do I have headaches, the answer is yes. Why do you ask?" She had a bad feeling she wasn't going to like his answer.

"Magdah said that if a Peacemaker doesna use their powers, they would die."

She felt as though all the air was gone. She couldn't breathe. The doctors had told her that the reason she suffered from so many headaches was because of the growth of an inoperable tumor. What Conor was talking about must be some weird coincidence. But even as she tried to rationalize it, she knew the words he spoke rang true.

Eilan stood and looked out over the water. There was a storm brewing over the horizon. It fit her troubled mood. She felt as though she was backed into a corner. She thought of the book, *The Witch's Hammer,* and the people who lived in terror under Simon's rule.

Eilan shuddered. She had no idea what she should do and she doubted her mother had a book on the subject. However, she had always been able to do her best thinking back at her parent's apartment. Perhaps she would discover a solution out of this problem. She took a deep breath and motioned for him to follow her. There were only two choices open to her. She could go with him to a world filled with superstition and hate or she could remain, and die. Tears welled in her eyes as she decided to give in to her emotions and feel sorry for herself. In reality, there really was only one choice.

Sheets of rain pelted against the windowpanes and a flash of lightning split the night sky. Eilan leaned her forehead against the cool glass and tightened her resolve. She had to make a decision. She'd spent the afternoon alternating between cleaning her parents' apartment and pacing. So much for the grand tour she had planned of Seattle.

She glanced over at Conor. He sat on the sofa with the remote. She turned toward him and leaned against the windowpane. Right now he was watching the news and had spent the day trying to stay out of her way. He had not spoken to her about traveling back to his century since they had returned this morning from breakfast. And she admitted to herself that she had been afraid of asking any more questions. It had taken the afternoon and a good part of the evening to build up her courage to broach the subject again.

Much was at stake, for both of them.

She pushed away from the windowsill and joined Conor on the sofa. He immediately clicked off the remote and turned toward her. Eilan smiled and guessed he hadn't really been watching TV, but was as lost in his own thoughts as she was. She took a deep breath. "You are sure that my headaches and this Peacemaker thing are connected?"

He nodded.

"And that you can't go back without me."

"Aye. Magdah made that very clear. There is a standing stone on the hill overlooking Inverness. It is very old and Magdah tells of an energy that surrounds it. The symbol of a circle is carved on its surface. When I placed the ring on my finger it brought me to you. The only way for me to return is with you by my side. But I will abide by your decision."

She hated it when men did that. Why hadn't he just played the caveman, grabbed her by the hair and said "we go"? Because if he had, she would have told him to go suck an egg.

She stood. Her decision was made. She walked over to the hall closet and opened the door.

Conor rubbed the back of his neck. "Eilan, what is it that ye are doing?"

"Looking for a suitcase." She reached up on the top shelf and brought down a black leather satchel. "This should be just about the right size." She smiled at him. "This won't take long."

He watched as she walked down the hall and into the bathroom. She opened a mirror cabinet door and shoved the contents of the shelves into the leather bag. She then opened the doors under the sink and emptied the shelf. She turned toward him.

"I know I'm forgetting something. How long do you think we'll be gone?"

"Ye will return at the end of one full cycle of the moon. Ye may use the clothes I brought."

Eilan rubbed her forehead. "There is no way I can pack for such a trip."

She headed toward the room where she slept. She looked over her shoulder in his direction. "What's the weather like?" She didn't wait for an answer as she opened a drawer and pulled out articles of clothing, stuffing them into her satchel.

Conor looked toward the window. The distrust and hatred that plagued his homeland had taken generations to develop. He hoped it would not be too late.

He watched as Eilan walked toward a shelf in the hallway and reached for a book. He had noticed it before. It was a history of the events that took place in England and Scotland from the eleventh to the seventeenth century. There were others whose topics ranged from life in medieval times to the clan system of Scotland. He doubted any writer was able to capture the true essence of a time period. However, at least Eilan was trying to absorb all the knowledge she could. He admired her for the effort. There was also a book titled, *Romantic Love in the Middle Ages*. Conor doubted it existed. Where did these authors obtain such notions? Certainly it was not from firsthand information.

He glanced out the window and saw the full moon shine as bright as the artificial lamps along the sidewalk on the street below. It was almost as light as a summer day outside. Tomorrow the moon would start its cycle once again. If they were to accomplish their goal of returning to the past, it would have to be tonight. Magdah stated that travel could only occur when the moon was full.

"Eilan, we must leave soon."

She closed the book. "I know." She paused. "I'm trying to learn as much as I can about your century before we leave. I guess I've run out of time."

He nodded. "There are only a few more hours before sunset. We must leave at once."

Eilan walked back into her room to gather her belongings. He was glad she had not found a book on the cruelties of his century. It may have discouraged her from the journey and his land needed the Peacemaker. He paused and realized something more. He needed her.

9

1310, Inverness

Dark amber flames leapt around the wood in the stone hearth. Its warmth spread over the one room cottage. A lone candle flickered in the shadows of the night and cast a circle of light over the mantel.

Rowan MacCloud warmed his hands over the fire. He had not been able to sleep. Too many thoughts plagued his mind. He made the same plea he did at this time each night since Conor had journeyed to find the Peacemaker. He prayed for his brother's safe return.

He glanced toward the window. It would be dawn soon and another day to survive, another day to try to find food for the growing number of people who sought to escape from his uncle, Simon. He turned from the hearth. He did not know if he was equal to the task. It was not just trying to feed all those who arrived here begging for help, but settling the disputes and fights that were a larger threat than the hunger.

Rowan shuddered and stared at the flames once more until his vision blurred. He feared his brother was dead. Rowan was not a stranger to death. He had seen it often on the battlefield, but the uncertainty was what plagued his mind and kept him awake at night.

In the beginning Rowan had believed the legend of the Peacemaker to be true. But too many days had passed. He wondered if he believed it only because it seemed their last chance. However, if his brother lived, he should have returned by now.

The door opened, letting in a cold blast of air and the witch, Magdah. Her gray hair framed her face, but her expression was lost in the shadows of the night.

Dried leaves blew in from the outside and swirled around the dirt floor. The candle flickered and the fire hissed and crackled as an ember spit out onto the dirt floor.

Rowan stared at the old woman. She tested fate. It was as though she offered a challenge to people to brand her a witch. While other women of her age dressed in earth tones, she wore clothes dyed in shades of red and yellow. Her hair was unbound and she preferred the night to the day.

And it was her fault his brother had disappeared to some unknown realm. He clenched his hands at his sides. He regretted the day he had asked for her help.

Magdah closed the door. It creaked shut. She turned toward him and hobbled over to the fire. "Fine night."

"If ye like wild winds and rivers of rain."

She chuckled and warmed her hands over the flames. "Aye, that I do. It brings out only the strong of heart and mind. Ye should try it sometime, lad. Especially when ye take a turn with that young lady of yours."

Rowan turned from the fire. When would the witch stop her meddling? The only woman he desired was lost to him. He did not blame her. He had left her to fight in the Crusades without any thought to how she would survive. He had told himself he would not be gone long, but eight years had passed. Rowan knew she hated him and he shared her opinion of himself.

He straightened. "There is no one in Inverness to my liking."

She shook her head. "Ye canna keep the truth from me. I can see it in your eyes. But no matter, things will right themselves again, and soon."

Rowan paced in front of the hearth. For the last three days he had refrained from asking Magdah the one question that worried him the most. He must know. If Conor was dead . . . He cleared his throat. "Will Conor be returning?"

Magdah removed her yellow shawl and draped it over a wood chair. "Fear not, lad, all will reveal itself in due course."

Rowan's voice was even. He could no longer hold back his temper. "Is he dead?"

"Fairy dust and brownies' wings, what an imagination ye have. Of course Connor isna dead. He is safe with the Peacemaker. Did I not promise ye?"

"Then bring him back."

She shrugged. "Be patient. He will return when he has learned what is needed."

Rowan clenched his fists. His anger rose to the surface and threatened to strangle him. He had asked a simple question and she had answered in riddles. He needed a distraction and knew where to find as many as he needed. He turned and walked toward the door. Soon the sun would be rising over the horizon and the people would be awake. He wondered how long it would take before a full-fledged fight broke out among them. Today he would welcome them. It would distract his mind from thoughts of Conor and of the cruelty of his uncle, Simon MacCloud.

Torchlight burned through the smoke-filled dungeon in Castle MacCloud. Chains rattled against the stone floor, followed by a whimper. Simon held an iron poker in his hand. The tip glowed a blue red in the darkness. He had thought this one would give him the answers he needed, but the woman he held prisoner was like all the others.

The woman had once been a beauty; fair of form, with long red hair. She was also most willing in his bed.

The chains that bound her rattled as she slumped forward onto the blood-soaked ground. It was her fault alone that he had resorted to such measures. He was so close. He would not give up now. He knew she could be persuaded.

Simon shoved the poker back into the white-hot coals and turned it slowly. If this method did not loosen her tongue, he could use the iron maiden. Few could resist it. The door to the dungeon creaked open. It was Finnegan. The man's size reflected his love of venison pie and brown bread. Finnegan had served MacCloud and his father before him. The man was not the quickest wit, but Simon felt that was an attribute. Finnegan always did what was asked of him and never questioned the motives.

Finnegan bowed his head and wrung his hands together. "Sorry, lord, riders come from the north."

Simon shoved the poker deeper into the coals of the fire. "Their raids become troublesome." He glanced toward the woman. He would have to deal with her later.

Finnegan nodded toward the woman. "Be she dead?"

"Nay, but close to it. See you do a better job this time keeping this one alive."

Finnegan's voice trembled. " 'Tis little I can do if the angel of death comes for them."

Simon knew Finnegan felt it a bad omen to witness the death of a witch, but watched over these women out of loyalty to him. It was a trait Simon admired. He did not want to lose such a devoted servant.

Simon put his hand on Finnegan's shoulder. "Do your best, old friend."

Finnegan glanced in the direction of the woman. "Aye. That I will."

The door to the dungeon slammed shut. Finnegan looked toward it. Each day was becoming more difficult than the last. He would like nothing better than to only concern himself with the raising and selling of his birds, but he had made a promise to the dying MacCloud.

Finnegan had vowed to stay and watch over Simon. He wondered for the hundredth time what would be the damage to his immortal soul if he broke his vow. His faith was strong, but of late it faltered.

He glanced in the direction of the woman and knew he was about to break one of God's commandments. The woman's name was Bridget. However, once the woman entered the dungeon Simon never again referred to them by name. Finnegan rubbed his eyes; he remembered them all.

In the beginning he felt Simon was justified in ridding Inverness of those who were accused of an allegiance with the devil, but that was before Fiona. In the end the women's only crime was that they refused to sleep with Simon. Finnegan came to realize that after watching them undergo relentless torture. A person would say anything to stop the pain.

The woman on the stone floor moaned in a merciless sleep. She had succumbed to her pain and was unconscious. It was unfortunate she still lived. When she awoke, Finnegan knew Simon had planned a new horror for her. Finnegan had not the power or strength of will to stop Simon, he could only do what he could to spare the women in his care when opportunity presented itself. As it did now.

He withdrew from under his wool shirt a pillow filled with down and placed it over the woman's face.

The angel of death had arrived.

10

Gray clouds moved across the morning sky like thin sheets of gauze and a breeze, laced with frost, stirred the tall grass. Eilan lay on the cold, damp ground and shivered. A forest of velvet green trees marked the perimeter of the meadow and the lone cry of an eagle echoed through her. She shivered again and tried to block out her growing panic.

Moments before she had been standing in the antiques shop. The instant she placed the gold band on her finger and told Conor she would help him, the ring had felt warm and somehow familiar. Now it was as cold as the air around her and as foreign as her surroundings.

Her head throbbed as though she had fallen and it looked like silver glitter showered down from the sky. She sat up and rubbed her fingers against her forehead. Out of the corner of her eye she saw Conor. He stood as tall as the standing stone that loomed behind him and seemed just as mysterious.

She wondered what he would look like if he smiled. She rubbed her eyes. The constant, annoying sound in her ears combined with the pain in her head must have eaten a path to her brain. Conor was probably incapable of smiling. Good thing too, as she guessed he would be gorgeous. She amended the assessment, more gorgeous.

Conor knelt down beside her. He was frowning more than usual. He reached out to brush a strand of hair from her forehead. His touch was warm on her skin. It surprised her. She thought it would be as cold as his facial expression.

He cleared his throat. "Ye look as though ye are in pain. Magdah warned that ye might have some discomfort."

"Not so loud. This is more than a little 'discomfort.' My head feels as though it's about to explode." She pulled her knees against her chest and held her head in her hands. "What's happening to me?"

She reached for the leather satchel she had packed and rummaged around for her bottle of ibuprofen. She opened the lid and shook two pills into the palm of her hand and then popped them into her mouth. She wished she thought to bring the large economy size, but this would have to do. Without water the pills caught in her throat. She swallowed them down.

Conor lowered his voice and sat down beside her

and placed the shawl she had brought with her around her shoulders. "Magdah said that if ye had not used your powers overmuch, the journey would cause ye pain."

"You neglected to mention that small detail."

"I should have realized this would happen when I noticed your hair was still so dark."

She pulled the black-and-blue plaid wool fabric over her shoulders. Last night her mother's shawl fit Eilan's attempt at a costume, but now it was like a connection home. She hoped this plan of Conor's worked. It was her last chance. The doctors had all given her a few months. Conor was the only one who said he knew what was wrong. By not using her powers to their full extent, she was dying.

The more she used her empathic abilities, the whiter her hair would become and the ringing in her ears would disappear, along with the tumor. She wondered if, along with the white hair, her body would age as well. She shuddered. Well, she didn't really have a choice. Besides, there was always hair dye and cosmetic surgery.

She squinted at him and shielded her eyes against the glittering lights. She knew both efforts on her part were futile since the problem with her sight was not a result of outside factors, but internal pain. "Did Magdah happen to mention how long the pain in my head would last?"

He shook his head.

"Great." She pushed herself to a standing position on the damp grass. Her legs felt like overcooked spinach. She swayed on her feet.

Conor stood and put his arm around her waist to steady her. She leaned against his chest and felt the warmth of his skin and the rock hard muscles beneath his clothes. Heat rose to her neck and face. She swallowed. She nodded her thanks and pushed away from him. The last thing she needed right now was to fall for a tall, dark and serious.

The lights faded somewhat and all that remained was a dull headache. Her vision cleared slowly. The pills she'd taken must have kicked in sooner than normal. Maybe they were supercharged by their time travel experience.

Eilan took a deep breath and looked around. She was at the crest of a hill next to a grove of birch trees. A standing stone punched through the ground. Just as Conor had told her, there was a large circle etched into its surface. Its corners were rounded and weathered with time and the elements. She remembered her mother telling her that Stonehenge was reported to have been built around 2800 B.C. Maybe the one that stood before her could be that age or older. It was hard to imagine something men and women had placed here had endured for so long. It gave you hope that we really belonged in this world.

A village lay at the bottom of the hill and a river,

reflecting the gray sky, meandered through the center of the town. It was the sort of setting that would make any tourist reach for his camera.

A castle stood to the north and a gray church to the south. Even at this distance she could see horse-drawn carts and sheep wandering through the cobblestone streets. She sucked in her breath. They'd really done it. They were back in the fourteenth century.

She felt light-headed again. This was not possible. It was something straight out of a science fiction movie. Her legs buckled beneath her and she slumped to the ground. She tried to think clearly. An eagle soared overhead and she wondered if it was the same one she'd heard moments before.

The bird's appearance hadn't changed in hundreds of years. She doubted the eagle even cared what century she lived in as long as there was an ample food source and a place to raise her young. People often said humans were the most adaptable in the animal kingdom. She had no idea where these people obtained their information; she only hoped it was accurate.

Conor stood next to her in silence. He was probably waiting for her to adjust to her new surroundings, or maybe he was waiting for her to become hysterical. She wished she were the screaming type. It might help. At least he understood what she was going through. In her case she had the benefit of history books; he must have felt he'd landed on another planet when he'd arrived in the twenty-first century.

She stood and willed her legs to hold her weight. She glanced down the hill again at the town. Eilan remembered seeing an old movie with her mom called *Brigadoon* on a late night movie channel. It was her mother's favorite and starred Gene Kelly. The story was about an enchanted village in Scotland where time had slowed to the point of one day equaling a hundred years. The spell made it seem that time in the village stood still. The town below resembled the one she had seen in the movie. A miracle had made it possible for the hero to return to the woman he loved. It was sentimental and romantic and Eilan had loved every minute of the story. She wished real life could feel as good.

A cool breeze rustled the crimson colored leaves on the grass around her feet. She shivered and twisted the ring on her finger. Her words were more for herself than for Conor. "You were telling the truth."

"Always. I know of no other way."

Conor's matter-of-fact statement warmed her. He was a man of his word. Maybe it was okay if he didn't smile. She had met men who smiled while they lied through their teeth. This was better. Besides, he probably had his reasons for being so serious all the time.

Eilan suspected there were battles he felt the need to fight alone. The one brief glimpse she had seen and the scars on his back had convinced her he had reason to build barriers around his heart. His guard had been down when he was unconscious, perhaps he would release it again when he fully trusted her.

He looked down the hill and then toward the edge of the meadow. "We should be on our way. We have a long journey ahead." He picked up the leather satchel she had packed and slung it over his shoulder. "Have ye recovered?"

She smiled. "That depends on your definition." She rubbed the back of her neck. Eilan already felt as though she had gone on a ten-mile hike. More walking was not what she had in mind. She wanted a nap or a long soak in a bubble bath. "Why can't we just go in to the town?"

" 'Tis too dangerous." He headed in the direction of the forest. "My brother, and those few who are still loyal to us, are hidden in the depths of the wood in an area my uncle fears."

"How far is it?"

He either hadn't heard her or chose to ignore her question. This was not a good beginning. If he reverted back to some Neanderthal creature, she would tell him he could find another Peacemaker.

His long strides were increasing the distance separating them. She jogged in order to catch him. His head turned slightly toward her as though checking to make sure she was still there.

She stepped over a mound of suspicious looking mud. "Don't worry. I can keep up with you. No need to slow down on my account."

Eilan ducked under a low hanging branch as she entered the dark green shadows of the forest. Conor had completely missed her sarcasm.

It began to rain. Not the soft mist type that often fell in Seattle, but the serious kind. The type that made you feel as though you had stood in a shower with your clothes on. She pulled the shawl over her head. The smell of wet wool surrounded her. She rubbed her nose and vowed to wear only cotton when she returned to her own time.

Conor's pace never slowed. He seemed oblivious to the weather. He was as steady as that bunny on the commercials with the battery stuck to its back. She thought about nicknaming him Bugs, but doubted he would see the humor. He would just stare at her as though she had rocks for brains.

The branches of the trees offered little protection from the sheets of rain pouring from the sky. She remembered her closet filled with waterproof hiking gear. She'd underestimated the weather in Scotland. The next time someone asked her to go time traveling through the centuries, she would tell them she couldn't go without her stuff. She knew it was a ridiculous thought, but so was walking in the rain and getting soaked to the bone.

Fat raindrops replaced the downpour. The ground was as slippery as a frozen pond. Her hair and clothes were plastered to her skin and still they pressed on. The afternoon had faded into the gray light that would herald the night. She shivered. There was a bite to the air. Perfect. She wished she had taken the time for a flu shot.

"Are we almost there?"

He paused. "Aye." For a brief moment she thought she saw the flicker of a smile brighten his normally somber expression. It must have been a trick of the light and shadows. Conor pointed in the direction of a bank that dropped off into a deep ravine. "Come, Dragon's Lair Castle is on the other side."

She pulled the sopping wet shawl closer around her and peered into the shadows, hoping to see a campfire. "I can't see anyone."

"We are still a long way from our destination, but the journey is shorter if we go through the castle grounds."

Eilan wiped her hair from her face and walked over rain-soaked ivy and plump mushrooms toward the place Conor indicated. She paused at the edge of a cliff. It was hard to estimate how steep it was because the bottom was filled with a thick blanket of mist.

Conor pointed to the other side. A cool breeze

swirled in the air and the mist thinned, exposing the ruins of a medieval fortress. It sat on a ridge and looked like an image from a fairy tale.

He brushed a low hanging tree branch out of the way. "This was where I was born. The castle was once a mighty stronghold for the MacCloud clan." His voice was only a whisper. "That was another lifetime ago."

She smiled. "From the size of the towers still standing, it must have been magnificent."

He nodded. "Aye, all of that and more." Conor slowly released the branch.

It sprayed water droplets in the air as he walked along the perimeter, close to the cliff edge. She heard a lot of pain in his voice when he spoke of Dragon's Lair Castle. She wanted to ask him what troubled him, but sensed he would tell her in his own time. Not being able to read a person's thoughts really had its disadvantages, especially in moments such as this.

Eilan slipped on wet leaves that had accumulated on the path. She grabbed the trunk of a tree to steady herself. Her pulse raced as she peered over the side. She had better pay more attention. It was a long way down. She glanced toward Conor's back. He was so engrossed in his thoughts he hadn't even noticed she'd lost her balance. Perfect. She was on her own.

She followed Conor but kept a safer distance between herself and the edge of the cliff. The footing looked stable enough, but there had been a lot of rain.

Eilan knew from her experience as a tour guide in Colorado you couldn't rely on appearances. Mother Nature was not to be trusted. Weather conditions could undermine even the most stable terrain.

Loose rocks skidded from the ledge toward the bottom. However, Conor didn't seem aware he had caused the disturbance.

She raised her voice. "Conor, you're too close to the edge."

He glanced over his shoulder and nodded.

The air was still and a deafening silence pressed in on her. All she heard was the beating of her own heart. This was not good. It was too quiet. It was as though all the animals had disappeared.

The ground trembled.

Eilan froze. She looked toward Conor. He stood as though rooted in place. Her heart hammered against her chest. Were there earthquakes in Scotland?

Without further warning the ground broke off beneath Conor's feet, carrying him downward on a wall of mud.

Conor disappeared from sight.

Another curtain of mud followed. A loud crack as a tree was uprooted.

Conor would be buried alive.

The ground trembled again. It was more like a sigh. Mother Nature could be just catching her breath. Eilan had to find him.

She put her weight on her right foot. The ground seemed stable. She walked cautiously toward the spot she'd last seen him. The cliff was ragged and looked as though it had been scooped out with a giant spoon.

She laid down flat and peered over the side. Wet mud oozed slowly down the hill. It was hard to see. Her pulse quickened.

She raised her voice. "Conor, are you all right?"

A branch snapped and she heard a muffled oath. "Aye, I am intact."

He sounded nearby.

"Conor, where are you?"

"Below ye."

She scanned the darkness, but couldn't see him. The clouds moved away from the crescent moon. Its light only deepened the shadows below.

"Eilan, I can see your face."

The wet mud soaked her to the skin. She crept closer to the edge and peered down in the direction she'd heard his voice. It might have been wishful thinking, but she thought she saw a dark form to her left. It appeared he was clinging to the root of the fallen tree. She didn't know how long before it would give way. Climbing back up the hill would be impossible. There weren't any solid footholds.

She needed something Conor could grab on to and pull himself up the side of the cliff. If this were a movie she would have thought to pack a fifty-foot rope. Of course Conor was carrying her bag so even if she had been the perfect Girl Scout, the rope would now be buried in the mud.

She brushed her shawl off her head and looked around. Think. What could she use? Branches. She shook her head. She'd forgotten to pack a hatchet. This was nuts. There must be something. Conor couldn't hold on much longer and Mother Nature might be gearing up for round two. She removed the shawl. She stared at the sopping wet cloth. Of course. She picked up an end of the wool fabric. It just might work.

She could dangle it over the side, Conor would grab it and she would pull him up. However, she would need a bigger piece. Her shawl wasn't long enough the way it was now.

"Eilan." Conor's voice sounded strained. "I am sorry."

She took the fabric in both hands and yanked. "This is not your fault." Nothing happened. The fabric was still in one piece. And then she remembered some random piece of trivia from the History Channel. Cloth becomes stronger when wet. Great.

"Eilan, if I canna climb back to ye, promise me ye will return to your own time."

She suppressed the impulse to scream. Why did

men always do that? He was turning heroic on her by telling her to save herself. It blurred her thoughts at a time when her mind had to be crystal clear. Now what was she going to do? She edged closer. "I'm not going anywhere. Not yet, anyway."

She reached for a rock. Maybe she could cut the blasted wool. After several tries, she gave up. Her shawl must be spun with steel. She would just have to use it as it was. With any luck, it would be long enough.

She raised her voice. "I'm going to lower my shawl and you can pull yourself up."

" 'Tis a good plan."

Eilan muttered to herself. "It will have to be. I can't think of anything else to do."

She tried to estimate the distance that separated her from Conor and even without a measuring tape it was obvious the shawl would not be long enough. Besides, who was she trying to kid? There was no way she could pull him up this bank. He was not double her weight, but it was close.

Eilan dropped the end of the shawl over the edge. She hoped she would get a strong dose of that superhuman strength people talked about in times of a crisis.

The ground trembled again.

"Ah, oh. This can't be good."

11

Eilan scrambled to her feet. In the next breath, the ground dropped away. The force threw her back. She was propelled downward over a path of wet underbrush. Air rushed out of her lungs; leaves and twigs whipped against her skin. Mud choked her as she was tossed from side to side.

A grove of birch trees loomed ahead.

Her pulse raced. She was heading straight for them. She couldn't stop. Like bugs on a windshield. Yuck. That was not the image she wanted as her last thoughts on earth. She screamed for help. Her voice thundered in her ears. She shut her eyes and threw her arms across her face. She couldn't watch.

Someone grabbed her around her waist and pulled her out of harm's way.

It was Conor.

She rolled on top of him and down another incline.

She was airborne.

Eilan landed facedown in a pool of water and clinging ivy. She gasped for breath and struggled to stand. It was no use. The vines pulled against her, keeping her from breaking free.

Conor rose from the water and rushed over to her. "Are ye injured?"

"No, nothing seems to be broken." She tried to yank free. "Wait. I need your help. I can't get away from these blasted things."

"Eilan, dinna struggle, it only tightens their hold."

Panic set in. Her breathing came in gulps. "Get them off." Terrific, she'd landed in a vine-eating world. His fingers brushed her chest and grabbed hold. "Conor, watch what you're doing. That breast is attached."

He paused and glanced toward her. "I was just trying to free ye. They are wrapped around ye. Forgive me. I will be more mindful . . . of where the vines are on your body."

He took the knife from the scabbard at his belt and cautiously cut the ivy away from her body.

She nodded. "Just be careful."

Eilan smiled to herself. Well, I'll be darned. Conor was blushing.

As the last of the ivy dropped to the ground, Conor picked her up in his arms as though she were as light as air. That was a complete rush. He set her down on solid footing. It had stopped raining and the air smelled fresh and clean. She inhaled the sweet fragrance and had the overwhelming impulse to pretend to slip and lean against him. She'd tilt her head back and wait for him to kiss her. She paused. Or, maybe not. She thought better of the idea. She had never been the type to manipulate situations and she wasn't about to start now. No matter how tempting the circumstance.

Eilan decided it was her brush with death that had addled her brain. Or perhaps the fact that the guy who had saved her, even covered in mud, was a hunk.

Conor looked toward the cliff. "Would you like to slide down the mountain again?"

"I beg your pardon?"

She couldn't believe what he had just said. He'd almost been buried alive in mud and she'd missed having her bones shattered by inches. If he hadn't pulled her out of the way, she'd be plastered against the trunk of a tree. She looked toward him. His face and clothes were caked in mud. Leaves and twigs stuck out of his hair in all directions. And he was grinning.

She was stunned. She was still shaking from the near death experience and he wanted to do it again. That confirmed it. He was crazy.

He turned toward her and grinned. "Well?

"In the first place, that was not a mountain, just a very large hill and in the second place, no, absolutely not."

His eyebrows scrunched together. "Ye dinna find it exciting?"

She put her hands on her hips. "We almost died."

"But we did not."

"You're nuts." She headed in the direction of a clearing she hoped was not a figment of her imagination.

He raised his voice. "Where is it that ye go?"

She stopped. This was frustrating. "Actually, I have no clue."

He stepped in front of her. "Admit it. You had as much fun as I did."

The change in Conor caught her off guard. It was as though their experience had transformed him. Or was it the forest? It was hard to figure out what had made the difference. Whatever the cause, she liked the new Conor MacCloud.

However, that didn't mean she wanted another trip down the mountain. If she'd known he was such a thrill seeker, she would have insisted they take a white water rafting trip. That would get his blood pumping.

She walked around him. "You must have hit your head when you landed. How could you possibly think that I enjoyed careening off that cliff?"

He caught up with her. "Ye were smiling."

She stopped. "I was not."

He nodded. " 'Tis true. Why can't ye admit it?" He brushed a wisp of hair behind her ear. "A strand of your hair has turned white."

"I'm not surprised. I was scared out of my wits." His touch sent warm sparks racing through her.

She crossed her hands over her chest. "I admit this experience was sort of like a water slide I'd been on once. If it were possible to take away the fear of death thing, it might be worth it. However, I survived once, I don't want to tempt fate by trying it again." She paused. "What's wrong? You're smiling. Well, that's not exactly a smile . . . more like a grin. Are you okay?"

"Ye are most appealing covered in mud." He kissed the tip of her nose. "And tasty."

His smile was infectious. Darn him. She had been right all along. He was only grinning and her heart was doing Olympic Gold Medal flips. If he ever smiled, she'd be lost. It was hard to stay mad. And why did he have to kiss her? The butterflies were back. She felt her face warm beneath his stare.

She tried to keep her voice steady. "You look as though you've taken a mud bath as well. Any chance there is an inn nearby?" A room at the inn meant beds. Good grief, her thoughts were wandering into dangerous territory. That confirmed it. She was the one, not Conor, who had landed on her head.

He picked a leaf out of his hair. "Nay, there is not an inn, but if it is a bath ye desire, there used to be a spring near the castle. It gave the inhabitants a supply of fresh water. 'Tis not far from here."

"That's great. I packed some soap in my satchel. We will be squeaky clean in no time at all." She felt vindicated. She'd forgotten the rope, but right now getting rid of the muck that covered her from head to toe was a priority.

The mud on her face was drying and pulling against her skin. The sooner they made it to that spring the better. She had always wanted to treat herself to one of those Swedish-type spas. However, if she ever had the chance, she decided she'd eliminate the mud bath part.

"Which way to the water?"

Conor motioned in the direction on his right. He seemed preoccupied and was staring in the direction of the wall of mud they'd just come down.

"Is something wrong?"

He turned toward her. "Ye know the satchel I was carrying for ye?"

Eilan had a sinking feeling in the pit of her stomach. "Yes?"

He rubbed the back of his neck and then pointed in the direction of the cliff. " 'Tis there, somewhere. Do ye want me to find it for ye?"

She glanced at the mudslide and then toward Conor. It could be anywhere and was probably buried under tons of mud. She remembered the thought process and the time that had gone into her packing. Rose scented bars of soap, because she'd read that the type used in the Middle Ages was hard on your skin and smelled bad. Toothpaste and mouthwash, because the thought of using twigs and mint leaves sounded gross. And, of course, her bottle of ibuprofen.

Eilan smiled. It turned into a laugh. She doubled over and held her sides. She had packed as though she were going on a vacation. The only real loss was the pills.

Conor put his hands on her shoulders and turned her toward him. "Are ye all right?"

"No." She laughed. "I mean yes." She tried to bring her laughing under control, but it turned into giggles. "I'm fine. Let's go find that spring."

"Are ye sure?"

"Positive."

And she was. He had saved her life, but that was not what made her feel so lighthearted. Somehow just knowing he would not have rested until he'd found her satchel was all that mattered. He reached for her hand, as though it were the most natural thing in the world, and led her toward a winding path. It meandered up the hill through the dense underbrush. She looked over her shoulder toward the cliff and smiled. Conor was right. The ride down the mountain was worth the danger.

The afternoon sun was high over the horizon as the spring came into view. A waterfall cascaded down a wall of rock and splashed into a sapphire blue pool. It looked inviting.

Eilan held Conor's hand as he led her up the tree-lined path. Her heart hammered in her chest. She didn't even mind that her clothes were plastered to her skin; her shoes were so wet they sloshed as she walked, and mud had dried on her skin.

Lush ferns framed the shore and a plump squirrel skittered up the trunk of a tree, seemingly unconcerned with their presence. Behind the rain-kissed firs a dark eyed deer gazed in her direction. It was as though this glen was shut off from the harsh realities of the world, keeping out fear and distrust.

She turned toward him. "Want to go for a swim?"

He arched an eyebrow. She interpreted that as a no.

Well, maybe he could stand to be coated in mud, but her skin was beginning to itch. If she were a true free spirit, she'd strip down and run naked into the pond. She opted to leave her clothes on.

She removed her socks and shoes. Twigs and leaves tickled her feet as she walked toward the water and waded in. She jumped back on shore and shivered. "It's freezing."

He grinned. "Aye. I could have told ye as much."

She put her hands on her hips. "And why didn't you?"

"Would it have made a difference?"

She mumbled under her breath. "No."

His grin widened.

That did it. She wasn't going to let a little thing like subzero temperatures deter her from washing off this blasted mud. After all, she was used to swimming in Lake Washington. She gritted her teeth, clenched her fists and marched toward the water. The waves lapped against her feet.

She sucked in her breath and shivered. She heard laughter and looked over her shoulder. Conor was enjoying this moment entirely too much. A thought swam around in her head that just might make it all worthwhile.

Eilan turned toward the water, took a deep breath, arched her back, and dove for the center of the water. The cold temperature shuddered through her and her clothing weighed her down. It felt as though she'd plunged into a bathtub filled with ice cubes. She rose quickly to the surface. Her body adjusted. It wasn't so bad. She just had to get over the first shock. It was actually a little warmer than Lake Washington.

She tread water and looked toward shore. Conor was pacing back and forth, a worried look on his face. He probably hadn't counted on her diving in and thought she couldn't swim. Maybe she should have told him she had a drawer full of medals from high school. Nah. It served him right for laughing. Now for her plan. She'd fake she was drowning and then when he was sufficiently concerned, she'd swim back to him.

Eilan screamed for help, flapped her arms like some demented bird, and sank beneath the surface. She held her breath until her lungs burned and then surfaced. She scanned the shore. He was nowhere in sight. Where did he go? She knew he couldn't swim. The books in her mother's library said the people in the Middle Ages were afraid of the water. That's why they didn't bathe.

Then she saw him paddling a few feet from her. His arms churned the water and his head bobbed from side to side. It wasn't pretty, but he was swimming toward her.

"What are you doing?"

He gasped for air. "I have come to save ye."

She laughed. "My hero." She put the heel of her hand in the water and sprayed him.

He blinked, and his eyes widened as light dawned. His mouth curled up in a smile. "Ye were not drowning."

She shook her head. "I swim like a fish."

He swam until he was within inches of her. Before she could react he pushed her under.

Eilan sputtered to the surface and smiled. "So, you want to play?"

She rose above the surface and tried to dunk him. He moved slightly. She slammed against his bare chest and thighs.

She disentangled herself from his arms and legs. "Oh my God. You're naked."

"Aye. I dinna want to get my clothes wet."

The water around her suddenly seemed to be boiling. She pushed away from him and swam for the shore. This was the second time she'd dissolved in a puddle when she'd seen him naked. Of course, she hadn't exactly seen him. Rather she'd felt him. She groaned as she stood and walked onto solid footing.

She saw his plaid lying on the ground. She paused and then leaned down, picked it up, then walked over to the side of the spring.

She heard Conor yell for her to stop.

Eilan smiled and dropped his kilt into the water. She dusted off her hands. *Good, now we're even and we can continue our journey to the castle.*

She looked toward him and swallowed.

Conor had almost reached the shore. He stood in the shallow end and walked toward her. The water lapped around his waist as he moved forward. She should turn around. Yes, that would be the right thing to do. Now why should she do that? There was no reason to run. He would retrieve his kilt, wind it around his body, and attach it however it was that the thing was attached. And all would be well. There was no reason to retreat.

Conor walked past the plaid floating on the surface and advanced toward her.

She focused on his face. He had a chiseled jawbone, intense blue eyes. His lips parted. She cleared her throat. He was still coming toward her. Her heart beat against her chest. She couldn't move.

He reached out and put his hand behind her head and pulled her gently toward him. She felt his breath on her lips.

"Eilan."

She was melting now. She leaned into him, resting the palms of her hands on his bare chest. Her fingers tingled from the contact. She felt the pressure of his mouth on hers. Her lips parted as he deepened the kiss. Conor wrapped his arm around the small of her back and pulled her closer still. She was dizzy. Her body warmed under his touch.

He pulled away and kissed her on the tip of the nose. "I have been wanting to do that for a very long time."

She didn't trust her voice. She nodded and hoped it sounded steadier then she felt. "Me too."

He winked. "Well, maybe we should be going."

She took a deep breath. "Yes, that sounds like a good idea."

He turned, walked over to the water and retrieved his plaid. When he bent over to pick up his clothes her body's temperature shot up at least twenty degrees. She swallowed. Muscles flexed over his shoulders and arms as he adjusted the kilt around his waist. Her pulse raced and it was hard to catch her breath. She wiped perspiration from her brow with the back of her wet sleeve. The cool cloth seemed to help. Actually another swim would be the best tonic.

Conor finished dressing, and reached for her hand. He smiled and pointed to an area above the waterfall. " 'Tis my home, Dragon's Lair Castle." He smiled and kissed her lightly on the lips. "I want ye to see it more than ever."

A warm glow wove around her as she looked where he had indicated. The mist had cleared and the towers were in plain view. She shielded her eyes from the sun. "That's odd. On the edge of the cliff the castle looked as though it were in ruins, however, from this angle it appears intact."

He was silent as they rounded the corner of the water and headed in the direction of the falls.

He raised his voice to be heard over the roar of the water. "Aye. It has always been thus. The mist that covers this valley is said to be under a spell. One moment the walls of Dragon's Lair appear whole and in the next they look crumbled with age. Superstition and fear kept all but the MacCloud clan away."

"You were not afraid?"

Conor shook his head and looked over his shoulder. "It was in our family since the beginning. We had nothing to fear, until Simon came to live with us."

He paused at the base of the falls and turned to pull her onto the first of the stone stairs cut into the side of the hill. A shadow crossed over his expression. "But all that changed."

She put her hand on his shoulder as she joined him on the step. They were so close she could feel his warm breath on her skin. She swallowed. "What happened?"

He took a deep breath and continued up the stairs. "My sister, Elizabeth, jumped to her death from the tower. Rowan and my father declared the place must be cursed and fled to Castle MacCloud."

Her heart felt the blow. She pressed her hand on her stomach as she kept pace with him up the side of the hill. The tragedy and death in his life kept building. No wonder he felt no joy. "Did you agree with them?"

"Nay, Elizabeth would not have killed herself, but I was never able to prove who was near her at the time."

"You must miss her very much. What was she like?"

They reached the top of the waterfall. Eilan looked down at the trees. They draped over the water like an emerald green lace curtain. A robin chirped in an oak tree nearby as though in greeting.

He had not answered her question. She wondered if it was too painful a memory for him. She would not ask again. Eilan would enjoy the peaceful time they had together. She suspected that when she reached their true destination, things would not be the same. The tone in Conor's voice when he spoke of Simon told her that much.

Conor stood behind Eilan and put his hand on her shoulder. "No one has ever asked me about my sister before. They know how much I grieved for Elizabeth when she died and perhaps thought the memories would be too painful for me. But when ye asked about her I found it eased my heart. For that I thank ye."

He pulled her against him. "Elizabeth was sixteen when she died. She rode better than Rowan or myself and would often best us in a race. Her aim with a bow and arrow was true as well. She had planned to join us on our journey to fight in the Crusades."

She felt his warmth surround her as he held her close. She leaned against him and felt as though she had known him for years instead of days. "You would have let her go with you?"

He grinned. "We could not have dissuaded her once her mind was decided." He turned Eilan toward him. "Ye are much like her in that regard."

She smiled. The day seemed warmer somehow. "Are you saying you like stubborn women?"

He shook his head. "Nay, not stubborn, but women who value their own advice."

She wondered if he could be more perfect and chided herself for sounding like a greeting card slogan. Time had shifted to a place where there was no clear indication of the century, only the meeting of two hearts. Eilan didn't want this moment to end.

He kissed her at the base of the neck. "When ye are able to bring peace to these lands, all will know joy once again." He turned her toward him and reached for a strand of her hair and twirled it between his fingers. "When I first saw ye, I doubted Magdah's wisdom."

Her breath caught in her throat. The strand of hair he held was stark white. Conor had mentioned something earlier, but she had not taken it seriously. She pulled it out of his grasp. It might not be new. It was hard to tell without looking at herself in the mirror. Was that the reason for Conor's change? No, that couldn't be right. She had not had any mind connection with him. His thoughts were closed.

He lifted her chin. "Ye are far away, Eilan Dougan."

She bit down on her lower lip. "Sorry, I was just thinking. What were you saying?"

He grinned. "Only that I am anxious to see how ye will bring about peace to the villagers' hearts."

She forced a smile on her lips and pressed against him. "So am I."

12

Stars dusted the night sky as Eilan walked beside Conor into his home. Emerald green ivy covered the stone walls of Dragon's Lair Castle and maple trees, their leaves, crimson and burnt orange, formed an archway into what looked as though it had once been the Great Hall.

Eilan had walked around the castle grounds for the last couple of hours, exchanging memories with Conor and gathering wood for the fire. He had showed her where the stables had once been, and the place where he had first learned to use a sword. She told him about Colorado and her parents. He'd even caught a fish for their dinner. Camping had never been so much fun.

She had kept from him the nagging feeling that her empathic ability had somehow been the cause of his transformation. It was impossible, she kept telling herself. Yet, the idea wouldn't go away.

There were even times this afternoon when she

had forgotten the reason she was here. She wondered if it was the same for Conor.

A crisp autumn breeze stirred the leaves as rain drizzled down through the branches. She shivered. Her clothes had not dried completely.

Conor put his arm around her shoulder. "Ye are cold. We will warm ourselves by the fire."

"That sounds perfect."

His voice had sounded hollow as though he had been as lost in his thoughts as she was in hers.

Conor stopped beside the west tower. It was one of the few that remained and its walls offered the most protection from the growing storm. This was where they had built the fire.

He nodded toward a stream that flowed nearby. It seemed to disappear under the wall. He smiled. "Come, there is something I wish to show ye."

He walked past the fire that crackled cheerily. She felt the warmth of the flames as she ducked under a latticework archway into the chamber beyond. The walls were covered with tiles the color of translucent opals. They glistened in the firelight.

Eilan glanced around the room and rubbed her hands together. "This is beautiful. What was it used for?"

He smiled and nodded toward what at one time might have been a stone pond. There were steps leading to the bottom and a shelf-like structure about halfway down the sides that ran around the perimeter.

He bowed and made a lavish sweep with his arm. “Milady, this is the MacClouds’ bathing chamber. When filled with water, it may suit ye more than the icy spring below.”

She kissed him on the cheek. “It wasn’t that cold.”

He winked. “Aye, I thought so as well.”

Eilan laughed. She liked the change that had come over Conor. He was more relaxed and easy-going here than he was in her world. The lines around his eyes had softened as though the years he’d spent in the Crusades were forgotten. She hoped it would last. She would just have to make sure it did.

Eilan turned her attention to the bath Conor had indicated. She couldn’t believe her eyes as she walked over and knelt beside it. A few of the stones had broken away, indicating years of neglect, but it held distinct possibilities.

She turned to Conor. “This is amazing. How is it possible? All the books I’ve ever read said the Middle Ages shouldn’t have anything this advanced.”

He knelt down beside her. “Ye also dinna expect me to know how to swim.”

“How did you know?”

He shrugged. “ ’Twas the look on your face. We may not have all the fine inventions of your world, but we are not as backward as ye would think. Admit it. Ye were not expecting to find something like this here."

"You're right. And I am sorry for trying to trick you earlier today."

He cupped her face in his hand. "I am glad ye did. Your blush gave me the courage to kiss ye. To receive such a gift was well worth the price of plunging into icy waters. Now, lass, have ye heard of the Roman baths?"

She leaned her head on his shoulder and laced her arm through his. "Of course."

He placed his hand over hers. "The story goes that they were the original occupants of this castle. It was they who built this place. There is a system of passageways underneath that keep the water flowing in and out." He frowned. "They must be clogged. It should be a small task to return them to working order." He shrugged. "However, the one thing they neglected to install was a way to heat it. I never appreciated that until I encountered one of the Roman baths on my journey."

"Warm was it?" Eilan smiled to herself. She had heard about the reputation of the Roman baths on the numerous TV specials she'd seen on the History Channel. A lot went on there that had nothing to do with bathing.

The color on his face deepened. He glanced toward her. "Aye, the water was warm."

Eilan smiled. "Just checking to see if you blush as easily as I."

"Ye know that I do."

She laughed, remembering the ivy he had cut away from her body when they landed at the bottom of the ravine.

He stood. "Are ye hungry?"

"Starving."

He reached for her hand, pulled her to her feet and put his arm around her waist.

The closer to the fire they walked the warmer she felt. And it had nothing to do with the flames that rolled around the wood. It was his hand on the small of her back that was causing all the heat.

Earlier in the afternoon Conor had pulled a tapestry from one of the walls and together they had cleaned it as best they could and dragged it near the fire. The colors were muted with age, but it was still breathtaking in its beauty. Woven into the fabric was a picture of Dragon's Lair. Unicorns grazed on a pasture nearby. She smiled. It lay on the ground beside the fire.

She glanced over at the flames. The trout roasted on a stick and the rich aroma floated in the air and combined with the warmth of the fire. A golden glow settled over the room. She could stay here forever. She sat down on the tapestry and pulled the fish off the stick and rested it beside the coals to keep warm.

Conor knelt down beside her and put his arm around her. "This was a section of the castle that was the hardest hit during the clan wars. My family had taken residence in the west wing and abandoned this section. I used to come here when I wanted to be alone." He laughed and pointed to a pile of rubble overgrown with thistles and dandelions. "In my youth I would pretend that this area was inhabited by a green dragon named Rufus. I spent many hours fighting mock battles to save a golden princess or defeat the black knight."

Eilan smiled. The memories of Conor's childhood softened his expression. The dark cloud that seemed to follow him was lighter in this place, as though the darker side of life was left outside these crumbling walls. She leaned against him and her thoughts conjured an image of a winged beast as tall as the walls of the castle, with eyes as dark as the sky during a thunderstorm. She sensed she was seeing the same image as Conor. Odd that a childhood memory would be the thought they shared. She felt as though a window was opening to her.

She felt closer to him than ever before. "Tell me about the dragon. Did you ever succeed in defeating him?"

He tucked a strand of hair behind her ear and kissed her neck.

It sent delicious shivers through her. What was

he doing? This was very distracting. She didn't want it to end.

His words came out slowly as though he felt the same way. "Rufus was very clever. At times I believed I had driven him from his lair only to discover he was just hiding in another part of the castle. He led me on a wild chase for many years." Conor lay back and put his arm over his eyes.

"Well, don't stop there. What happened next?"

He shrugged. "It was time to shed the carefree life of my youth and become a warrior."

Eilan saw a shadow cross his face as though a cloud had drifted over the path of the sun. She had been so close and now it would end. Eilan grabbed a fistful of the dandelions growing out from a crack in the stone and sprinkled them on his head.

Conor swatted them away and smiled. He leaned on his elbow and glanced in her direction. "Is that your way of telling me I have once again grown too serious?"

She leaned toward him and kissed him lightly on the mouth. "Aye, my crazy Scotsman. I want to know more about this dragon. What he looked like, if he was the fire-breathing kind or just went around crushing people with his tail."

Conor cupped the side of her face in his hand and traced the line of her mouth with his thumb. His touch sent warm shivers through her.

His eyes crinkled at the corners and his smile

broadened. "Rufus dinna breathe fire. He was clumsy, but it was more likely he would crush trees and heather beneath his wide feet than any of the townsfolk. The great beast was in truth more a friend to me than an enemy."

Eilan brushed his hair off his forehead. "I'll be darned. You had an imaginary playmate."

He kissed her on her lips. "Indeed. Rufus was not real, but just the image of light and shadows." He kissed the base of her throat. "However, ye are very real to me."

She could feel him against the length of her and her body warmed. She moved closer still. She whispered. "You're changing the subject."

"With every fiber of my being."

"Aren't you hungry?"

He whispered against her ear. "Aye."

His touch sent warm shivers up her spine. "It's burning."

"Aye."

It was hard for her to breathe with him so near. "I meant the fish. I left it too close to the flames."

The trout was singed as black as coal.

Conor laughed as he pulled it farther away from the flames. "I had something else on my mind."

"I just figured that out."

He smiled as he turned toward her. His voice was deep and echoed through her. "Your clothes are still wet."

She swallowed. "So are yours. We could dry them by the fire." She couldn't believe she'd just said that.

He winked and a smile spread across his face. "A very sensible plan."

She laughed and leaned on her elbow. "Do you want me to help?"

Conor shook his head as he unfastened his belt and placed his weapons on the floor. They clattered on the stones. His kilt fell away and he pulled his shirt off as well. "Done."

"That was fast."

She could feel the heat on her neck spread over her face and felt the steady rise and fall of her chest. The firelight flickered over his body, casting it in a bronze glow.

He smiled and moved toward her slowly. His fingers grazed her breasts as he unbuttoned her blouse. "The rest will be slow."

She groaned as he covered his mouth over hers and spread the tartan over them.

Eilan felt his hand against her thigh and his touch ignited the flame within her. He kissed her full on the mouth as she wrapped her arms around his neck. Her clothes fell off her body and the contact of bare skin took her breath away.

This is my first time, she said over and over to herself. He touched every part of her, sending her emotions on an ever-ascending journey of pleasure.

Yet she could not read his thoughts. She didn't need to. His gentle touch told her more completely than words. The message was clear. He cared for her. He kissed and caressed her as though time stood still. Indeed, she felt as though she were floating on an endless sea.

He entered her and then hesitated. He whispered against her ear. "I am the first?"

She nodded.

He brushed hair from her forehead. "Eilan, are ye sure?"

She pulled him closer to her. "I have never been more sure of anything in my life."

13

A robin chirped outside the castle walls and the morning sunlight spread across Eilan's face. She lay on the tapestry with Conor's plaid as their only blanket and rested her face against his bare chest. She snuggled in the embrace of his arms, feeling the warmth of his body surrounding her. In all her dreams and all her imaginings she never would have envisioned that the first time she made love it would be this wonderful.

Conor pulled his plaid over her shoulders and kissed her on the forehead. He whispered. "Are ye awake?"

She snuggled closer. "That depends. What did you have in mind?"

He laughed. "Do ye want to help me hunt for our morning meal?"

"I think I'll pass."

He winked and kissed her on the base of her throat. "Make love?"

She rose up on her elbow. "I thought you'd never ask."

"Did ye sleep well?"

She smiled and gazed into his intense eyes. "The best."

Conor held her close. "Ye have made me feel alive again, Eilan Dougan." He cupped her face in his hand and kissed her. His touch warmed her to the tips of her toes.

"Hmmm." She smiled against his mouth. "This is a better way to wake up than hearing the sound of an alarm clock."

He laughed. "I think those blasted contraptions are still ringing in my ears." He smiled. "I have something else in mind besides talking about clocks."

She traced the contours of his lips with the tip of her finger. "And what might that be?"

He kissed her on the tip of her nose. "That is for ye to guess."

His mouth covered hers and the gentle pressure sent warm currents through her. She pressed against the length of him as he put his hand on the small of her back and drew her nearer still.

The ground vibrated beneath her.

Her pulse quickened. Her immediate thoughts were forged together in a combination of "not again" and "lousy timing." "What was that?"

Conor sat up abruptly. "Ye felt it as well?"

"Yes. What do you think it is?"

He turned toward her and rested his hands on her shoulder. "I am not sure, but it could be a rider. One of the great advantages of Dragon's Lair was that we could feel the approach of an army long before they attacked. In the end, however, it was not enough. There were too many of them." He paused. "Ye should get dressed."

She smiled. "Well, at least it's not another mud-slide."

His face was turned away from her. "I wish that it were."

He wrapped his plaid around his waist and belted it in place as he walked over to the opening of the enclosure. Time seemed to stand still as he looked around.

Eilan had heard the urgency in his voice. She scrambled to her feet and grabbed her clothes. Last night she had draped them on a rock over the fire. They were stiff and smelled of smoke, but at least they were dry. Her hands shook as she pulled on her clothes.

Conor turned and rushed back to her side. " 'Tis as I thought. A rider approaches from the north. 'Tis the only unprotected side of the castle."

"Do you think it's Simon?" Eilan sat on the ground, pulled on her socks and tied her shoes. She had never met Conor's uncle, yet fear raced through her nonetheless.

Conor shook his head as he laced up his leather

boots. "He is afraid of this place. Besides, he would not travel without his guards. He may possess a dark soul, but he is not without intelligence. He knows he is hated and many would risk their own life to end his. However, it could be that he has sent one of his scouts here in search of me."

"Great."

He leaned toward her and tilted her chin toward him. "Ye havena seen me fight. One man is no match for me. 'Tis a waste of my time. I prefer to fight two or three at once."

She smiled in spite of her fear. It was hard not to in the face of so much confidence. He almost looked eager. As ridiculous as it seemed, his comment had actually made her feel better. Now was not the time for her to find out that the guy she'd traveled with back in time didn't like to fight. She'd be willing to bet that his testosterone level was off the charts. His courage had the desired effect. She started to relax.

Conor kissed her quickly on the mouth. "Promise me ye will stay hidden."

"Maybe I can help. I'm not some shrinking violet type that needs to be wrapped in cotton and hidden away. I know you think you're this incredibly strong warrior, but two against one is better odds in any century."

He put his hands on her shoulders. "Can ye wield a sword?"

She crossed her arms over her chest. "Of course not."

"Then please stay here. I willna be long."

Again with the overconfidence. After the first flush of feeling all warm and fuzzy that a big strong man was going to protect her, annoyance set in. She was not helpless and she wanted to prove it to him.

Eilan watched as he disappeared outside. She rushed over to the far wall on the north side of the room. Maybe she could see what was happening. This was aggravating. His over confidence just might get him killed. If there were more than just one, she could warn Conor. She might not be able to use a sword, but she could scream loud enough to wake the dead. At least that was what her mother used to say.

Clumps of dirt and grass flew from the horses' hooves as the lone rider approached. Her heart beat in tune to the trembling ground. A man on a chestnut brown horse led two mounts behind him. The man leaned forward and turned in her direction as though he knew she was watching him.

She backed away from the opening. If the man knew she was here, she couldn't help Conor if he needed her. She looked around and picked up a chunk of stone and weighed it in her hand. This would do. She felt a little like David, except without the slingshot.

She looked again. The rider reined in his mount and jumped to the ground. Even from this distance she could see an angry scar that ran down the length of his face. It marked him as a warrior who was used to surviving. Eilan held the rock in her hand. The man was not as tall as Conor, but was about the same build. She was becoming more apprehensive by the minute. She gripped the jagged stone and felt it cut into the palm of her hand. She couldn't see Conor from where she stood. This situation kept getting worse.

The man's words tumbled out in a thick Scottish burr and his voice carried over to her. "Welcome back, brother." He pulled Conor into a hasty embrace. "I have missed ye."

She heard Conor's deep voice. " 'Tis good to be home, Rowan."

It was Conor's brother. Relief was so sudden she felt as though the ground beneath her was moving. She braced herself against the stone wall and took a long slow breath of air. She dropped the stone, dusted off her hands and hurried to join Conor.

Rowan stood beside his horse. Now that she wasn't as worried, she could see the family resemblance. Rowan was clean-shaven, his shoulder-length hair pulled back at the nape of his neck. He wore the same plaid pattern as Conor and it was in the same state of disrepair. The marked difference between the two brothers was in the eyes. Rowan's were a light shade of gray and crinkled with mischief, while Conor's were dark blue and intense.

Rowan smiled and then nodded toward Eilan. His voice was so low she almost missed the words. "So, this is the woman Magdah foretold ye would find."

Conor smiled. "Aye. Her name is Eilan Dougan."

Rowan's smile spread across his face. She guessed he was in his late twenties. He bowed lower. "Ye are welcome, Lady Dougan."

She smiled and decided she liked him. He was trying to make her feel at ease and it was working.

Rowan's expression grew serious as he looked over his shoulder. "We have little time to dwell here. Simon's men could come upon us at any time. And this castle, in its present state, would not be easy to defend. Just yesterday I saw a company of men in the area. Fortunately they dinna see me."

Conor clasped Rowan on the shoulder. "How did ye know where to find us?"

Rowan shrugged. "Magdah predicted I would find ye both here."

A crisp breeze rustled the long meadow grass. Eilan stuffed her hands into her pockets. "Magdah must be a real help to you. I've never met someone who could foretell the future. How did she do it?"

Rowan laughed. "She shakes stones on the ground. But she is wrong more than she is right."

Conor reached for the reins of a black horse. "Yet she told ye we would be here."

Rowan scratched his head. "She said ye would return within the cycle of a full moon. I knew that if ye did, ye would have to travel through Dragon's Lair Castle. I have been searching each day since ye left."

Eilan felt the tension in the air. It was as though a cloud had passed over the morning sun. She shivered again.

Conor reached behind the saddle of his horse and unwrapped a wool blanket. He draped it over her shoulders. Her teeth clattered together. She knew it was not from the cold.

He reached for the knife at his belt and handed it to her. "I want ye to have this. 'Tis not good that ye dinna have a weapon."

She drew back. She liked the idea of a rock much better. "I can't use a knife."

Conor reached for her hand and placed the hilt of the blade in her palm. "I have brought ye to a dangerous land. All who dwell here are armed."

Rowan mounted his horse. "There is a price on all of our heads. He wants us dead. We must make haste. I brought a horse for Lady Dougan as well."

Eilan tucked the knife in the belt of her jeans, hoping she wouldn't regret accepting the weapon. The leather creaked as she reached for the reins and settled in the saddle. She adjusted the knife so it didn't press against her leg. She didn't like weapons. She was here as the Peacemaker. Besides, she had no idea if she could even use it if they were attacked. "Is this Simon person open to negotiation?"

Conor took a deep breath. "I hope so."

The silence was so thick Eilan could have cut through it with a knife.

Rowan's voice was even. "Have ye given thought to what should be done if Simon refuses a meeting?"

Conor shook his head. "We will lay siege to Castle MacCloud."

Eilan didn't like the sound of that. Well, the good news was that if it required a virgin sacrifice, as of last night, they were out of luck.

Rowan straightened in his saddle. "We should be on our way. Have ye ridden before, Lady Dougan?"

Eilan smiled. "Why don't you call me Eilan? And the answer to your question is, yes and no." She remembered guiding tourists on horseback to the campsite where they would begin their raft trips. No galloping was required, only a slow walk over a well trod path.

Eilan's horse flicked its ears as she scratched its nose. The horse turned her head toward Eilan, but other than that, the animal remained still. So far so good.

She stroked the horse on the neck. "What's her name?"

Rowan smiled. "Shadow. From the moment the mare entered this world, she followed us around as though she were our shadow. It seemed a fitting name."

Conor paused and glanced to the north. "Do ye think ye were followed? I believe I saw something."

Rowan looked over his shoulder. "I was careful, but I am not certain. 'Tis all the more reason to make haste. The best way to reach our camp is through Ferry Glen."

Conor mounted his horse. "Why use that route? 'Tis shorter to use the path on the west side of the Loch Ness. Besides, Ferry Glen is said to be haunted."

Rowan nodded. "True, and thus the safest path. I have heard it said that Simon is afraid to enter. They say it is the portal to the Underworld."

Eilan adjusted the blanket around her shoulders. "You're just kidding, right?"

A flock of birds flew from the nearby forest and soared toward the clouds. Something had disturbed their peace.

The horses whinnied and pawed at the ground. Eilan tightened her grip on her reins. Now what? A dark foreboding wove around her.

An arrow whizzed past Eilan, grazing Rowan's arm. His horse reared on its haunches. A war cry pierced the air. Armed men galloped toward them. They rode low over the necks of their horses. Fur capes billowed behind them like dark waves over an angry sea. Eilan's heart thundered in her chest.

Conor's horse whinnied and reared. He brought the animal under control and shouted, "We ride." He looked toward Eilan. "I will guard your back." He slapped her horse on the rump.

"Ride?" She screamed.

Eilan's horse lurched forward. She clung to the saddle.

Another arrow whizzed through the air, hitting a tree nearby. It vibrated on the trunk. Eilan rode toward the clump of trees, bouncing up and down in the saddle. She gritted her teeth and held on to the odd-looking saddle horn with all her strength. She repeated the words nuts, crazy, insane, out of your mind.

Another arrow sped by. Eilan crouched low over her horse's head and concentrated on surviving.

An hour passed and she was still alive. Every muscle in her body ached. The dark green forest enveloped her like a cloak and shut out the sun. Shadows merged together. The shouts of the warriors who chased them had faded as Eilan, Conor and his brother ventured deeper into the forest. Conor rode behind her in silence as Rowan led the way.

Right now she felt more isolated with two men than she had when it was just Conor. She supposed it was because now, with Rowan here, traveling back in time seemed more real. To make things worse, Conor had retreated once more into his sullen self. His facial features were as expressive as a chunk of granite. She was separated from all she knew and all that was familiar. They had escaped once, but those men didn't look like the kind who gave up easily.

Okay. Stop thinking. It was only making it worse.

She ducked under a low hanging birch tree and heard an owl hoot. She wondered if it was a greeting or a warning for her to turn back. Her river rafting and tour guide business had prepared her physically for the endurance part of this journey, but that was not what worried her. She should have taken the time to learn as much as she could about this century. Thumbing through a few books hardly qualified her in the mental survival skills she suspected she would need.

Her stomach rumbled. She shouldn't be hungry. Last night she and Conor had stuffed themselves full of trout. She smiled remembering the kisses in between each mouthful of fish. Eilan had hardly noticed it was burnt. She glanced over her shoulder. Conor hadn't spoken a word to her since they had begun their flight from the archers. Of course, in the beginning there wasn't time. However, after the danger had passed a "How are you?" or "Are you okay?" would have been acceptable.

She took a deep breath. Last night seemed more like a dream than a reality as well as a lifetime away. Her stomach rumbled again. It was a welcome distraction. She wondered if the food was safe to eat in this century. Her high school history teacher had liked to tell stories about how venison rotted out in the sun and then was brought in to the medieval kitchens, covered in thick, fatty gravy and served to unsuspecting victims. She shuddered. Maybe now would be a good time to become a vegetarian.

The bushes alongside the path rustled and Eilan turned in time to see a red-tailed deer dart out of sight. Startled, her horse broke into a trot down a slight incline in the path. It caught her unaware and she bounced hard in the saddle. She reined in her horse and vowed to pay more attention to what was going on around her. She could stress about the food in the Middle Ages later.

A cool breeze rustled through the trees and a fine mist of rain filtered down through the branches. She shivered, wishing she'd had the foresight to wear her down jacket. Maybe she should have brought gloves and a hat. The wool sweater and jeans were not going to offer that much protection if it started to pour.

Her horse snorted and tossed her head. Eilan bent down and patted the animal on the neck. It was as though her horse had read her thoughts. "Yes, you're one hundred percent correct. I am complaining too much. After all, we did escape from those archers. It was a good thing they were such bad shots."

Conor edged his horse alongside Eilan and put his hand over hers. "We need to keep our voices low. Did ye not hear it?"

Eilan straightened in the saddle and listened. There was only silence. "I don't know what you're talking about. It's peaceful and quiet."

"Precisely."

Conor reached behind him to the sword strapped to his back and drew his blade from its scabbard. Eilan glanced toward Rowan. He had done the same thing. It was as though the men had stopped breathing. Even the rain had ceased to fall.

A war cry pierced the silence and seemed to tear through the air.

Men, wearing fur cloaks, sprang from the shadows. The archers had returned. The men pressed in on them on the narrow path. Their swords glinted in the gray light.

The sound of metal striking metal rang in Eilan's ears as Conor and Rowan blocked the attack. She gripped the saddle horn. Her pulse raced.

A man with wild eyes and a patch over his eye swung his blade toward Conor. Conor blocked the attack and drove his sword into the man's chest. Blood flowed from the wound as the man fell off his horse into the mud.

Eilan shuddered. Bile rose to her throat. Another man raced toward Conor. She turned. The horror pressed in on her. Rowan fought as tirelessly as Conor. Blood flowed to the ground, turning the moss-covered path crimson.

Eilan's horse tossed her head, and her nostrils flared. The animal smelled the bloodlust and seemed as disoriented as Eilan. She tried to keep her horse under control.

Eilan felt someone grab her leg. When he touched her she was able to read his thoughts. Terror ripped through her. In the midst of all this madness and death, he meant to rape her.

She pulled free and kicked him in the face. Blood spurted from his nose. Another man joined him and together they dragged her from her horse. Both men meant to have her, right here, right now. She screamed out Conor's name.

The shorter of the two slung her over his shoulder. The force of landing on the man's shoulder caused her to lose her breath. She couldn't scream as she was carried into the dense forest. The man's thoughts were dark. He had raped before. In her mind's eye she saw the face of a young woman. She had pleaded for her life right up to the moment he had plunged a knife into her heart.

Eilan gulped for air and tried to yank free of his grasp. It was futile. He held her in an iron grip. She searched his mind for some hope of sanity and found none. His soul was as black as the dark forest he was running toward.

She would not be like all the others he had raped and mutilated. She would fight, right up to the end. Eilan pulled away from his thoughts with all her strength. They were clouding her ability to fight back. She concentrated on trying to wrench free of his grasp as the dark shadows of the forest closed in on her.

14

The clash of steel rang in the air as Conor blocked the attack. Eilan's cry for help tore through Conor. Out of the corner of his eye he saw her pulled from her horse. He had failed to keep her close. Red-hot fury coursed through his veins. Conor blocked his assailant's blade and shoved his knife into the man's throat. Blood spurted from the man's neck as he grasped the knife. Conor leapt from his horse and drove his blade through his assailant's heart. Conor had to reach Eilan before it was too late.

Another warrior took the place of his fallen comrade. Conor clenched his jaw. Terror gripped his attacker. The man's sword arm was weak. Simon's paid assassins were poorly trained.

Conor raised his sword and sliced through the man's chest. The man pressed his hand against the gaping wound and stepped back. He was dead. He just had not realized it as yet. Another assailant took the place of his fallen comrade. Conor feared for Eilan, but he could not reach her. Rowan was a mighty warrior, but with only one eye, he was at a disadvantage. Conor gripped the hilt of the sword and prayed for Eilan and his brother to hold on.

The lyrical notes of a bagpipe added to the sounds of battle. He recognized the tune, 'twas the MacIntosh clan. They ran toward him and Rowan and battled beside them to defeat Simon's men. The MacIntosh and MacClouds had been feuding with each other for over one hundred years. However, today they fought against a common enemy.

Conor nodded toward the clan's laird. They had matters well in hand. His brother was safe. Conor could now turn his attention to Eilan. He only hoped it would not be too late. He ran toward the last place he had seen her. The man who had taken her had two choices. He would die swiftly if Eilan were injured or harmed in any way. Her captor would be begging for a quick death.

Eilan's ribs felt as though they were being crushed against the man's shoulder as he ran through the forest. She swallowed her fear and continued to close off her mind to his thoughts. She knew Conor would come for her, if he were still alive. Tears threatened to blind her. She couldn't give up hope. She only prayed she was alive when he came for her.

The man smelled of stale beer and sweat. Her

stomach clenched. Fear combined with last night's dinner and the man's foul stench made bile rise to her throat. She retched down the man's back.

He stopped abruptly. "Bloody hell, woman. What have ye done to me?"

He swung her off his shoulder and dumped her on the ground. She landed with a thud. Pain jolted through her on the rock-strewn path. Her backside ached, and the knife at her belt pressed against her leg. Her mind reeled from the realization. She had a weapon. She glanced over at him. He wasn't paying any attention to her. He was too concerned with the mess she had made of his back and side.

She looked down at her leg. The blade had punctured her jeans. Blood seeped through the fabric. The wound wasn't deep. She should be able to stand, and then run. Eilan knew any sudden move would alert her kidnapper. She pulled the knife out of her belt and rose slowly.

The man seemed to come out of his daze and turned to face her. His eyes seemed to focus on her blade.

He laughed. "That's better. I like it when I have to fight for my pleasures." Eilan tightened her grip on the knife and held it out in front of her. She was not going to waste time talking to this creep. She backed away. The most she could hope for was to stall for time.

The sound of bagpipes pierced through the air.

The man straightened and turned toward the sound. When he glanced at her once again, a frown creased his face. "As much as I would like to have a dance with ye right here, it will have to wait." He held out his hand. "Come quiet like, and hand over the knife."

"Not a chance."

She watched him closely. For some reason the sound of the bagpipes had rattled him. Good. Maybe help was on its way.

Without warning, he lunged toward her. She jumped sideways out of his reach.

He growled and charged again, grabbing her wrist and the knife. She held on and struggled against him. She stumbled back and fell to the ground. He landed on top of her, crushing her beneath him. He wrenched the knife free from her grasp and held the blade against her throat. It pricked her skin.

He laughed. "Maybe we will have that dance after all."

"I dinna think so."

It was Conor.

The man was yanked off her in one swift motion. She scrambled to her feet. Conor waited for the man to draw his sword, but it was over almost before it had begun. The man lay on the ground. His lifeless eyes stared toward the sky.

"Conor."

He pulled her against him. His thoughts surrounded her as he held her close. She clung to him and felt the depth of his fear that she would be killed, that he would never see her again. Tears filled her eyes. She pressed closer to him.

Conor tilted her chin toward him and bent over her as he whispered her name. His lips were warm against her mouth as his thoughts merged into her own. The forest disappeared. They were together; that's all that mattered. His kiss deepened. She felt longing and hope within his embrace. It mirrored her own thoughts.

A twig snapped, followed by a thump and a loud oath.

He turned toward the sound. " 'Tis Rowan."

Eilan felt Conor's peace-filled thoughts replaced by dark shadows of guilt as he gazed toward his brother. She wondered the cause. His outward appearance to his brother did not match his thoughts. But just as she felt she was getting close to the answer, Conor's mind closed to her. It was like a heavy velvet curtain shutting down on the third and final act of a play.

Rowan limped toward her, rubbing his knee. "Blasted gopher hole. Dinna see it until it was too late." His words poured out in a rush. "And I see, brother, that ye have found the Peacemaker. Is she unharmed?"

"Aye, she is well. We were fortunate the MacIntosh clan appeared when they did."

Eilan looked from one brother to the other. "What happened?"

Conor's face was devoid of emotion. "All of those who attacked us are dead. The MacIntosh clan came to our rescue. It seems we share a mutual enemy." He turned to Rowan. "Do ye know if they hate Simon so much they would fight him?"

Rowan shook his head. "They have witnessed what happens when someone opposes our uncle. They fear for the welfare of their families." Rowan nodded toward Eilan. "However, that willna be necessary, now that ye have brought the Peacemaker to us."

Conor shook his head. "Rowan, she was almost killed because of our carelessness. Let her be. There is time enough in the morning to discuss this matter. Come, let us return to our horses."

Silence wove around her as they made their way back to where the battle had begun. The moment of truth had arrived. She would have to help these people. But she suspected they wanted a giant fix. As though she had a magic wand that she could just wave over Simon and he would be as gentle as a kitten. It didn't work that way. It was not so important that Simon had to change; rather, the people around him had to find their own path. They gave the power to behave as he did. Without their belief in him he would be powerless. She had to find a way for Conor's people to learn to live again and fight Simon.

The path widened and a group of approximately twenty men, women and children stood tending their horses. A woman with long red hair stood apart from the rest. A young boy of about eight or nine stood beside a woman in a faded plaid skirt and shawl.

Rowan pointed toward the group of people. "The MacIntosh clan. I recognized their plaid as well as the woman who rides with them." His voice lowered as though he were speaking to himself. "Margaret is as beautiful as I remember and I would venture her skills as a healer have improved as well. But there be bad blood between our clans."

Eilan noticed the woman looked in Rowan's direction and as she did so, pushed the young boy farther behind her.

Rowan nodded. "The MacClouds and the MacIntosh clans have been feuding for over one hundred years. I have never seen them so close to our lands before. A cow taken from time to time, on both sides, but never were they known to venture into these woods. However, today I am glad of their boldness."

"I agree, they have proved strong allies this day."

Rain misted down through the branches and a cool breeze rustled through the limbs of the trees.

Eilan blew on her hands to warm them and wondered how long it would be before someone spoke. The two clans stood facing each other. Each side waited for the other to make the first move. They had fought together, yet still they held their silence. If all these Scots were anything like Conor, they would stand their ground until the winter storms had run their course and the first flowers bloomed in the spring. In other words, until hell froze over.

She looked over at Conor and his brother. They were both stone silent. Conor's expression looked as though it were chiseled out of granite. Rowan rubbed the arm where the arrow had grazed his skin and stared in the direction of the woman. It didn't take an empath to see the sparks flying between these two. Their problem might not be too hard to solve if she was able to settle the differences between the MacCloud and MacIntosh clans. Eilan tucked a lock of hair behind her ear.

It would be a simple enough thing for a person with her gifts to find out. She was looking for a way to begin the peace; this would be a perfect place to start. The feud had lasted over one hundred years. That was long enough.

As Eilan headed toward the clearing, Conor reached out and put his hand on her shoulder. "Where are ye going?"

She smiled. "To thank our friends for saving us and to see if they would like to join us."

Rowan scowled. "They would never agree. There are too many differences between us."

She sensed that Rowan was not talking about the MacIntosh clan in general, but Margaret in particular. Eilan shrugged. "Well, let me try. Besides, don't you want to see the Peacemaker in action?"

Rowan's eyes widened as he nodded, but Conor's expression was as somber as ever. His eyebrows seemed to grow together. " 'Tis not necessary that we bury the bad blood between our clans, only that they agree to fight by our side to defeat Simon."

The wind whispered through the trees and rattled the branches. The words "not enough" echoed through her. She shivered. Arguing with Conor would do no good; his mind was set. She guessed he had spent a lifetime knowing only one way to defeat his enemy. It was ironic that he had been the one to ask for her help.

Maybe starting with the clan feud was too big a step for him to grasp. She would tackle the problem with Margaret and Rowan.

Conor watched Eilan as she walked toward the clearing that led down to the shore of Loch Ness. She was a remarkable woman. He admired her courage and boldness. However, he hoped it did not mean that she would take risks, especially with Simon. The man could not be trusted.

When he had seen her taken, white-hot rage had raced through his veins. He could not bear to see her come to harm. Conor had not realized the depth of his feelings for her until that moment. When he had at last held her in his arms he felt complete.

He closed his mind once again to thoughts of Eilan. She deserved better than he could offer her. He watched as she spoke with Margaret and a few of the men from her clan.

Eilan was not in any danger, of that he was assured. His clan and the MacIntosh may have been feuding for a long time, but there was never any violence between them. No one had ever come to harm. Magdah had said the woman he would find was a Peacemaker and he had gone in search of Eilan because of a promise he made to a dying friend. He wanted to believe Magdah's claim; maybe today he would find out if it were true.

Rowan stood beside Conor. "Why do ye think she speaks to Margaret and not the head of the clan? Ye should order her to stop at once."

Conor shook his head. "Ye are a wonder to me, lad. Ye have much to learn about a woman. A lass doesna like to be ordered about. More than not, she will say nay to ye, just for spite."

Rowan gently rubbed the wound on his arm. "Mayhaps, but seems an odd way to make the peace between our clans." He paused. "Eilan is small in stature. I thought she would be larger."

Conor looked toward Eilan. "It matters not her size."

A breeze blew through Eilan's hair. It floated on the air like spun silk. He remembered the feel of her bare skin and how she felt against him. She was perfect. He shook his head. "She is the right size."

Rowan rubbed his arm. " 'Tis only that if she were larger of frame, she would be more intimidating to those she wished to coax into peace. Have ye seen yet how she is able to turn men's hearts to peace?"

Conor shook his head. "We have only Magdah's word that it can be done."

"And if she is wrong?"

"We are lost." Conor raised his voice. He did not want to dwell on that outcome. "Prepare the dead. No matter that they tried to kill us, they deserve a decent burial."

Conor watched Eilan as she talked to Margaret and her son. For a time at Dragon's Lair, he had forgotten Eilan's purpose here, but Rowan and his men would not. They expected a Peacemaker. A person to solve their problems. Conor prayed Eilan was that person; he could not foretell their reaction if she failed.

Eilan tousled the boy's dark curls. The boy lifted his chin and smiled at her. There was a look about the child that was a puzzlement, but he could not place why the lad's features were so familiar to him.

Margaret motioned for the boy to stay with a member of her clan as she walked with Eilan in Conor's direction. They talked together as though they had known each other for a very long time, but then Eilan had that effect on people. She was the sort of person that just being around her made the sun shine brighter.

Eilan smiled as she drew near. "I would like you all to meet Margaret MacIntosh. She has agreed to take care of Rowan's wound."

Rowan was uncharacteristically quiet. Without being asked, he slipped his shirt over his head and walked over to Margaret. Dried blood was smeared over his upper arm. However, the wound did not look deep.

Margaret examined it and told Rowan to follow her to the shore. Together they knelt beside the water. She tore a strip of linen from her undergarment and cleaned his wound.

Conor had seen enough wounds in battle to know his brother's was not fatal. For that he was grateful. The only fear now would be from infection. He had heard of Margaret's healing powers before. Her reputation was sound.

Conor lowered his voice as he turned to Eilan. "I thank ye for asking Margaret to tend to my brother, but I am surprised that the head of her clan would agree."

Eilan shrugged. "I didn't ask him."

Conor arched an eyebrow. "That is odd that Margaret would not have asked his permission."

Eilan smiled. "Not really. I just told her Rowan was wounded and there was a chance he could die from the infection."

"True enough. But I still dinna see why she would be concerned about a MacCloud."

She smiled. "This is not the first time Rowan and Margaret have met."

Conor glanced once more in his brother's direction. "They do appear to be comfortable in each other's company."

"Yes, that would be a very good way to put it." Eilan paused. "Margaret's son's name is Angus and he is about eight or nine years old. How long did you say you and your brother were fighting in the Crusades?"

"It was about that same length of time. But what would the boy's age have to do with how long we were away?" He could not understand Eilan's interest in the child. This was odd indeed.

Eilan laced her hands in front of her. "Look closely at the boy. Don't you see a resemblance?"

Conor looked over at Angus. The lad's body was long and lean, and strong enough for him to begin training as a warrior. "He looks healthy enough."

Eilan took a deep breath. "Look closer."

Conor did as she asked. Angus's eyes were the

color of storm clouds, which was unusual for either a MacIntosh or a MacCloud. Conor had seen its like on only one other person: Rowan.

Conor straightened. Of course. Why had he not seen it before? The boy and Rowan both had the same color eyes. It must be a coincidence. Rowan had never mentioned Margaret. Still . . .

He leaned toward Eilan. "Do ye believe Angus to be Rowan's son?"

Eilan glanced in Angus's direction. The boy smiled. She waved to him. "Bingo."

Conor straightened. "Is that a word for son in your world?"

"Sorry. It's sort of a word that tells the person they answered the question correctly."

Conor tried to remember if Rowan had mentioned the MacIntosh woman, but knew the answer. Although women were drawn to Rowan in every city they had passed through, his younger brother was never one to speak of them. Conor had often wondered if Rowan and he had more in common than a shared heritage. They each seemed to build barriers around their hearts.

Eilan cleared her throat. "You are deep in thought. Would you like me to share with you what else I've learned?"

She had been in his world only a short time, yet it seemed like she had always been here. He wished she had known him before he had gone away to fight in the Crusades. He was a different man. Perhaps if she had, he would never have gone away. He shook the regret away. It would serve no purpose to dwell on that now.

Conor glanced over at Eilan. "There is more?"

She blew on her fingers to warm them. "This is not so much about Rowan and Margaret, but about her clan. They are the only ones left after Simon raided their village a short distance from here. That is why they hate him. I suggested to them that we join forces."

He raised an eyebrow. "Are ye talking about raising an army? All other attempts to capture Castle MacCloud have failed."

"Not exactly. I do want you and the MacIntosh clan to join forces. You can start with burying the dead. However, there is more. If all of the people around Inverness can be persuaded to join us, Simon will have no one to rule over."

"That is ambitious."

She placed her hands on his shoulders, stood on tiptoes and kissed him on the cheek. "And then there is the matter of the second thing. Margaret would like to marry Rowan."

"Did she say as much?"

"Not exactly."

Conor looked over at Rowan and Margaret. "Does my brother intend to ask her?"

Eilan smiled and turned toward the couple. "Not yet, but he will."

15

Rain soaked through Eilan's clothes. They were plastered to her body and branches brushed against her skin. She shivered in the night air and clung to the saddle horn. Everyone rode single file down a narrow path. Conor led the way this time. The MacIntosh clan was all behind her and Rowan guarded the rear. Margaret and her son rode directly behind her in silence. Everyone was lost in their own thoughts or else, like her, were too tired to make the effort at conversation.

It seemed as though they had been traveling for hours. She had lost track of the time. Each minute that passed made her more apprehensive. What had made her think she could be the one to make a difference in the world? She rubbed the tired muscles in her neck.

She couldn't read Conor's mind on any consistent basis and although the thoughts of the man who'd pulled her off her horse were clear, she'd not been able to find a way to turn his thoughts toward peace. This was not a good start. Maybe the full power of her "gift" as her mother liked to call her empathic ability, was limited to the twenty-first century.

She hunched over the saddle. She'd really made a mess of it this time. Conor was counting on her and she didn't know if she could deliver. And to make matters worse, she'd complicated the situation by sleeping with him. She sighed. There was probably some rule in the legend, written of course in fine print, or better yet, invisible ink, regarding fraternizing with the main warrior guy.

She didn't even want to think about how she felt about Conor. She didn't have to. He was this warrior god and she was the lowly peasant girl. She groaned. Her mind was drifting off into fantasyland. It must be the lack of food, extreme exhaustion and fear of death that had rendered her to the damsel in distress mode. Yuck. And of course she had no idea where they were going. It seemed a fitting scenario that both the location and her feeling for Conor should be plunged into uncertainty. As far as she could tell, she was following Conor and company into the center of the earth. Well, that probably wasn't true, because if it were, it should be getting warmer. Instead, it felt like the coming of the next Ice Age.

She sneezed and wiped her nose against her

sleeve. Her mother would be horrified that she had not used a Kleenex or handkerchief, but Eilan was past caring. Besides, she didn't have either one. Her fingers were numb and her hair was a tangled mass of leaves and twigs from the limbs she'd brushed against. She sneezed again. She was probably catching pneumonia. Perfect. Death would be a way out of this mess she'd allowed herself to be pulled into.

Conor held up his hand and shouted for them to halt. She wiped the rain from her eyes and tried to see why he had stopped. Maybe he had found a cozy inn with a warm bed and a cheery fire, or the portal back to the antiques shop. She sneezed again and decided she'd settle for anything that would protect her from the cold.

The path had widened into a clearing in the forest. A fire spat and crackled under the protection of the ruins of a stone arch. Whatever dwelling it was connected to had long ago been destroyed. She remembered Rowan saying that this place was thought to be the portal to the Underworld. She understood how it had received its name. Small thatched roof cottages and hastily made lean-tos dotted the perimeter. It must have been later than she thought because the place was deserted. Light shone from only one of the cottages. It was set apart from the rest.

In the dim light Eilan saw an old woman hobble over to Conor's horse. She wore a dark purple cape over a bright yellow and red silk dress. The wind blew her waist length white hair around her face. Her cheeks had circles of red rouge and the makeup around her eyes resembled the style worn by Cleopatra in pictures Eilan had seen. The old woman wore a ring on every finger of both her hands. This person seemed completely out of place and time. She was a composite of cultures. Eilan wondered if she was as interesting as her appearance. Eilan hoped so. She had never known her grandmother, but she had heard she was as eccentric as this woman looked.

Conor leaned down toward the old woman, but whatever conversation they were exchanging was lost on the breeze that rustled through the trees.

Margaret edged her horse alongside Eilan's and whispered. "I know of this woman. Her name is Magdah." She paused. "There are many who fear her."

Eilan didn't doubt it. The old woman's appearance was odd to say the least and most people, no matter the century, felt uncomfortable around people who either looked or behaved differently.

Eilan rubbed her hands together. She didn't think she'd ever be warm again. "Why are people so afraid of her?"

Margaret glanced in the old woman's direction. "It is hard to choose just one thing. She and her sister, Fiona, were the midwives who helped my mother bring me into the world. I remember their door was always open for the hungry traveler or curious child."

"She sounds like a good person." Eilan wrapped the soaking blanket around her shoulders. The wet wool was probably making her feel colder.

Margaret hesitated. "Not all would agree. Magdah was like a mother to me when my own died, but she clings to the old ways of the Goddess and for that she was forced into the forest around Loch Ness." She paused. "Her sister, Fiona, was arrested and burned as a witch."

Eilan felt a rush of emotion so strong her eyes brimmed with tears and shivers racked her body. In her mind's eye she envisioned a woman tied to the stake begging for her life as flames leapt at her bare feet. She shuddered. "I don't understand. What did Fiona do that was so terrible?"

Margaret shrugged. "No one knows. 'Twas Simon who brought the charges against her. But he did not accomplish all that he wanted. Fiona's husband and children escaped. However, Simon MacCloud would like nothing better than to see Magdah dead as well. But he canna catch her." She paused and looked toward her son, Angus, who slept slumped over in the saddle. "I fear Magdah will bring Simon's men down on us all."

Eilan reached over and put her hand over Margaret's. The woman was terrified, not for herself, but for her son. Eilan squeezed Margaret's hand. "I'm sure Conor can protect us."

Margaret bit down gently on her lower lip. "I hope ye are right. Thank ye for all of your kindness. It has been a long while since I have been able to speak freely to someone without fear of what they might say or do. But ye are different."

Eilan smiled. "Thank you." She didn't think it wise to explain to Margaret just how "different" she was. Margaret thought Magdah and Fiona a threat because their belief systems were different. Margaret would really freak if she knew Eilan was an empath, or for that matter, a person from the twenty-first century.

Eilan noticed Magdah glance in her direction, turn and walk toward her. The old woman's face resembled the full moon, round and translucent. She smiled and paused beside Margaret. "It gladdens my old heart to see ye so well, and Angus, how fares he?"

"He is well. And your health?"

Magdah winked. "Each day on this earth is a blessing." Her expression grew serious as she turned and walked toward Eilan. Magdah reached up and gently took Eilan's hand in hers.

Eilan was taken off guard. She braced herself for the onslaught of emotions she expected would flood her senses. Instead, the vision of a warm sun, a white heather-covered hillside and a crystal castle loomed in her mind's eye.

She let out the breath she was holding. It was a reminder that there were people in this world who often had pleasant thoughts. It wasn't all doom and gloom. She laughed to herself. Her mother often said there was more good in this world than evil. It was just that evil received most of the press.

Magdah smiled. "Ye are freezing, child. Ye will catch your death. Come, warm soup and a hearth awaits in the clearing just a short walk from here."

The old woman released Eilan's hand and with it the vision disappeared. Magdah motioned for Margaret, Angus, and Eilan to join her as she turned and headed in the direction where she had first appeared.

For some reason Eilan wasn't afraid. Maybe it was the pleasant vision she had seen, or maybe it was as basic as the offer of warm food and a chance to be close to a fire. However, the suspicious side of her nature cautioned that this scenario was much like the witch in the story of Hansel and Gretel. However, the opportunity to avoid freezing to death was worth the risk.

She looked in Conor's direction. He was busy seeing that the horses and his men were fed and cared for. He glanced toward her, but it was too dark to read his expression. He turned back and removed his horse's saddle.

Eilan dismounted, handed the reins of her horse silently to Rowan and followed Magdah. She was the first to admit she'd had very little experience with men. But she'd be willing to bet that Conor was trying to avoid her. Fine. What did she care? She was heading in the direction of food and shelter. What more could she need?

Magdah paused at a thatched roof dwelling on the edge of a stream. Moonlight shimmered over the water and smoke billowed from a hole in the roof. Eilan followed the woman inside. The smell of baked bread, chicken broth, and onions, filled the air. Ropes of garlic hung from the wood rafters, along with dried sprigs of rosemary, sage and dill. A fire crackled in the one-room dwelling. Cots hugged two of the walls and a table and three chairs were beneath the window on the left.

Eilan smiled. All this place needed was a big lap dog and gingham curtains to make it perfect. She changed her mind. No, what would be perfect was if she and Conor had it all to themselves. Eilan shook her head. What was happening to her? One night with Conor and she was ready to take up housekeeping. She'd probably set the feminist movement back a hundred years or so. She decided to focus on something else.

Magdah reached for a frayed wool shawl that hung on the back of a chair and placed it around Eilan's shoulders. "Come sit by the fire and warm yourself. Margaret, your son and ye are welcome to stay here as long as ye like. The men will find other accommodations under the stars. They like pretending they dinna mind the bad weather." She winked. "Being a delicate woman has its advantages."

Eilan smiled at the sarcasm. It eased her discomfort in the strange surroundings.

Margaret entered the cottage, with Angus close behind her. She walked over to the cot, tucked him in bed, and brushed waves of curls off Angus's forehead.

Eilan smiled at the tender exchange. Tucking a child in at night was the same in any century.

Margaret straightened and rubbed the small of her back. "Magdah, your soup smells delicious. What do ye call it?"

Magdah smiled. " 'Tis just a little of this and a pinch of that." She reached for two bowls on a shelf over the fireplace and ladled generous portions into each one. " 'Tis not wise to ask the cook what she has put in the pot."

Margaret laughed. "I forgot."

Eilan accepted the bowl of soup Magdah offered and watched as the old woman walked over and gave the other to Angus. He slurped down the contents, wiped his mouth on the sleeve of his shirt and yawned as he settled under the covers once again.

Margaret reached for his bowl and drew another blanket over him. It looked as though he fell asleep the minute he closed his eyes. She bent over and kissed him on his cheek.

Magdah whispered. "Now there's a warm sight.

He's a fine boy, Margaret, ye have done well." Magdah nodded toward the pot of simmering stew. "Eat as much as ye like. There is a matter I need to tend to before it grows too late. Consider this your home."

The old woman squeezed Margaret's hand before taking her leave. The candle on the table flickered as Magdah opened the door and disappeared into the night. It was as though she had taken the warmth of the room with her. Eilan pulled the shawl around her shoulders and looked over at Margaret, who ladled another portion of broth in her wooden bowl and settled down on a bench beside the fire.

Margaret sipped the broth and then rested it in her lap. Tears welled in her eyes and traveled down her cheeks. Eilan reached over and put her hand over Margaret's. The woman's mind was a jumbled mass of fear and uncertainty. However, at the center was the one fear that plagued her the most. Margaret was afraid Rowan no longer loved her. Eilan had seen the look Rowan and Margaret had exchanged. It would be a tragedy if their pride kept them from rediscovering true happiness.

Eilan smiled. "This is all so new to me. Why don't you tell me what you know about Inverness and the MacClouds?"

Margaret dried her tears and set her bowl on the

table. Eilan was not interested in the words, only that she remain connected to Margaret long enough to find if there was hope for Rowan and Margaret.

Magdah headed toward the water. She needed to speak with Conor and tomorrow might be too late. The moon and stars were blanketed with thick layers of clouds, slowing down her progress. A fire at the center of the clearing offered the only light. The men from the MacIntosh clan slumbered around the flames for warmth. Conor and Rowan were not among them. It was as dark as the belly of a dragon and twice over as cold, but there were words that needed to be said.

Through the flickering light of the fire she noticed Conor and Rowan under an awning of branches near the edge of the clearing. They were tending their horses. Conor and Rowan rubbing their animals down for the night with the remnants of an old blanket. Magdah glanced over at the men that slept by the fire. She knew exhaustion was not the only reason for their slumber. In sleep a man or woman could escape the harsh realities and fears that plagued their waking hours.

Magdah was aware that Conor MacCloud's dreams offered little solace. But that was not the reason she needed to talk with him this bleak night.

Conor turned toward her. "Magdah, I dinna hear ye approach."

Rowan smiled. "Some say she doesna walk on the ground, but glides over it."

Magdah frowned. "Dragon's teeth. Those that say such do so to hide the shame of having a mere woman come upon them unaware."

Rowan smiled. "Age has not softened the bite of your tongue."

Magdah patted Rowan on the side of the face. "It is not age that has caused my need to speak my mind, but the times in which we live. Now, be off with ye. I need to exchange words with your brother." She smiled. "Sleep well, for tomorrow ye will need a strong mind and sharp wits."

Rowan tightened the tether that secured his horse to the trunk of a nearby tree. "What do ye know of the future, old woman?"

"Only that if the future is aware ye know of its existence, it will change the path. Follow your heart and leave the rest to the powers greater than yourself." Her eyes narrowed as she poked him in the chest with her finger. "However, this much I do know to be true. If ye call me an 'old woman' again, I shall turn ye into a toad."

Rowan laughed, shook his head and headed in the direction of the fire.

Magdah smiled to herself as she watched Rowan do as she asked. He was a good lad and deserved the love and happiness that could be his if he opened his heart. His love had remained constant toward Margaret over the past eight years. Margaret should be well pleased with her choice. She need only cast adrift her fears and forgive the lad. Magdah sighed. If her sister were still alive, it would be a simple matter for her to nudge Rowan and Margaret together. But that was not to be. Hopefully they could find the path on their own.

She felt anger well within her at the loss to Inverness and to herself. Fiona should not have died. Her sister's death tugged at her still and hot tears stung her eyes.

Conor cleared his throat. "Ye wished to speak with me?"

Magdah turned toward the tall stoic man. He had stood silent while her mind drifted. One of the attributes he and Rowan shared was their patience. She wished Conor could have retained the humor and love of life as well.

It had not always been thus. There was a time when they were much alike. However, that was before their uncle Simon had come to live with them and before the death of Elizabeth. However, since Conor's return with the Peacemaker, she had noticed the shadows around his face had disappeared, especially when he gazed on Eilan. If what Magdah suspected was true, she was pleased for him. Love, even for a brief moment, was worth the price.

Magdah took a deep breath and turned to the problem at hand. "Perhaps your brother is right to refer to my age, as my mind ventures down paths of its own choosing, now more than ever before." She motioned for him to join her along a trail that wound around the water. "Come, I do not wish our conversation to be overheard."

When they were a safe distance from the clearing, Magdah turned to him. Her words were for Conor alone. She folded her arms across her chest and decided not to waste any more time. "Conor, who is this woman ye have brought here to me?"

Conor's eyes widened. "What are ye saying? Eilan is the Peacemaker. Your instructions were clear."

"Eilan is too young and inexperienced. She cannot possibly have the strength to defeat Simon. Even ye can see that she has not used her powers overmuch. My own sister's hair was as white as winter snow and still your uncle defeated her. We need someone closer to my age. Are ye sure she was the only one there when ye arrived?"

She walked to the water's edge. The cards had foretold the person Conor would encounter would be a worthy opponent to Simon's evil. However, Magdah had been so relieved to discover that Fiona's line had continued when she read her cards, that she did not take the time necessary to assure its success. She should have remembered the advice she gave to Rowan.

Tears welled in her eyes and this time she did not brush them away. The path had been altered and an inexperienced Peacemaker was thrust into the fire. She prayed that Eilan would not suffer the same fate as her dear sister.

Conor turned Magdah gently toward him. "Are ye saying that Eilan is not the Peacemaker?"

Magdah shrugged. "She is of the line, only not as experienced as is necessary. Given time, she might be able to accomplish the task. However, even that is not certain. Being born with the gift is not enough; she must have the heart and will to use it as well."

A shadow crept over Conor's face. "Ye have said that her time here is limited."

"Aye. Ye began your journey on the eve of a full moon. Eilan will return when it has made its cycle." Magdah rubbed her forehead. She could not tell him what she feared the most. Eilan might never be ready. She lifted her chin. "I will know how to answer ye in the morning."

He clenched his fist by his side. "Each day my uncle is in power more people die. If the Peacemaker canna help us, I must find a way to raise an army myself."

Conor stalked toward the clearing. Magdah did not blame him. She wrapped the cloak tighter around her and followed him. He had believed the Peacemaker would be a magic fix. Even if Eilan were a powerful empath, or if time was not against them, her success would still not be assured.

The forest thinned as Magdah approached her cottage. She opened the door and removed her cloak. The next few days would tell her what she needed to know. Again, she must follow her own advice and trust. She looked around the room. Margaret and Angus were asleep on one cot and Eilan stood near the hearth. The light from the fire cast a golden glow over the room and seemed to settle around Eilan.

Magdah looked closely at this strange young woman. This could not be. Wisps of white hair framed Eilan's face. Magdah was sure she had not noticed them before. Had Eilan already begun her Peacemaker task?

The embers glowed bright orange in the fireplace. Eilan stood and paced back and forth in front of the hearth. She had not been able to sleep. Magdah was bent over her caldron, stirring the broth. Eilan knew she should find a corner and curl up and try to go to sleep again. However, there were too many things on her mind and too many questions left unanswered.

She walked over to Magdah. "Aren't you tired?"

Magdah shook her head. "How can I sleep, lass, when I know ye are bubbling over with questions?"

Eilan looked at her. The woman had almost mirrored her thoughts. She suspected she should be courteous, but Conor had mentioned it was Magdah's idea that she was here. Besides, what was the worst thing that could happen? She thought of Fiona and shuddered.

Magdah smiled. "Do not worry so. What is it ye wish to ask?"

Eilan stared into the amber flames. "You had Conor find me?"

"Aye, and I am beginning to believe it was the right decision, after all."

Eilan glanced toward her. "What do you mean?"

Magdah stirred the thick broth in the black pot that hung on an iron rod in the fireplace. Steam rolled over the sides of the kettle. " 'Tis nothing, lass."

Eilan sank down on a bench beside the hearth. She might as well just blurt it out. "Conor brought me here to bring peace to his land. But I haven't the faintest idea how to start."

"Just follow your heart."

Eilan sensed that was another way of saying she was on her own. She decided to change the subject. She leaned toward the broth. "It smells great. What are you making?"

Magdah shrugged her shoulder. "I am not sure as yet. I keep adding a little bit of this and a pinch of that. I shall know it is done when the taste is right."

Eilan fought back the impulse to tell Magdah she was the strangest person she had ever met but

Eilan figured she would not be the first one to make that declaration.

Eilan clasped her knees against her chest. "You didn't answer my question."

Magdah reached for a rope of garlic that hung from the ceiling, plucked off a half dozen cloves, and removed the tough outer skins. She dropped the garlic into the broth. "Of course I did, lass."

Magdah paused and stared in the direction of a spider that dangled from a single silk-like thread by the window. She walked over and gathered the insect in the palm of her hand and brought it over to the fire, dangling it over the steaming broth. It wriggled and swayed in the steam. Eilan knew exactly how it felt. She was beginning to feel trapped herself.

Eilan stood so quickly the bench toppled over. "You're not going to put that insect in the soup, are you?"

Magdah cocked her head to the side. "Do ye think it will turn the broth sour?"

Eilan smothered a laugh. Magdah was serious. Eilan cleared her throat. "Yes, most definitely."

Magdah shrugged her shoulders. "Perhaps it was a good idea then that I dinna add the cockroach to the broth earlier. I saw a big fat one skitter across the floor just this morning."

Eilan couldn't believe she was having this conversation. No wonder the townspeople thought Magdah was a bit strange. Eilan took a deep breath. "Good choice."

Magdah returned the spider to the window ledge and wiped her hands on the folds of her skirt. "Now what were we discussing? Yes, now I remember. Although some things may not seem clear at the moment, ye need only to give it time." Magdah sat back down on her stool by the hearth. "Tell me why, at your age, your hair still holds its color? When Fiona was not yet one and twenty, her locks were completely white."

Eilan's stomach did giant flips. She didn't like the comparison. "What are you saying?"

"Only that Fiona was also a Peacemaker."

Eilan swallowed. "I heard how she died."

Magdah turned toward the fire. "I warned her." She paused and cleared her throat. "Ye will be more careful. Come, I will show ye how ye came to be here with us. 'Tis because of the ring ye wear."

Eilan glanced down at it. The soft blue aquamarine stone on the gold band sparkled in the firelight. It seemed a lifetime ago that she had placed it on her finger. She touched the smooth gem. "What do you mean I will have to be more careful?"

"Ye are not interested in the ring?"

"Will it keep me from being burned alive?"

Magdah shook her head.

Eilan pressed her hand against her stomach. "I don't know what to do."

Magdah reached for Eilan's hands and held

them with her own. A peace washed over Eilan like a warm spring rain.

Magdah smiled. "Change those who are willing to walk down the path of sunshine; the others leave for another time."

Eilan pulled her hands free from Magdah's grasp. "The times I tried it before my hair turned white." She paused. It was hard to voice her darkest fear. She straightened. "How much will it age me?" She hesitated. "I mean, if I do figure out how to do this, and I'm not even certain I can, will I grow old?"

Magdah patted Eilan's hand. "Of course not, lass." She gazed into the fire. "At least, I do not believe so."

"Swell."

Magdah turned toward her. "Interesting."

"What do you mean?"

"Only that ye did not know the full import of what would happen to ye and yet ye came here anyway. Why was that, lass?"

Eilan stood. "I don't really know myself. Maybe I thought I had to as it was my destiny." She smiled. "Or maybe I'm mad."

Magdah stood. "Ye are no more mad than I. Your doubts come from your fear. Let it go and ye will know exactly what needs to be done. But ye must understand all of it and the ring is intertwined in your destiny, as ye would call it."

Magdah walked over to a shelf beside the window. Clay bottles, wood and pewter bowls and a large sprig of dried basil all vied for space. Magdah reached for a container and returned to the fire. She set the bowl down and withdrew a folded red cloth and carefully unwrapped it on the bench.

Gold rings, each set with a single stone, reflected the flames of the fire. The stones varied from deep emerald green, black onyx, and red ruby to a lavender amethyst.

Magdah sat down beside the rings, reached for one and held it in the palm of her hand. The stone was lime green. She polished the gem against her sleeve. "When Conor came to me for help in finding a Peacemaker, I showed him these rings. The one ye wear represents his birth sign. I gave that to him to give to ye. He then chose one for himself."

She placed the ring back with the rest and smiled. "I had thought he would have chosen that one, but he surprised me. He chose the bloodstone."

Eilan looked at the ring on her little finger. Her mother had given it to her when she graduated from college. Her mother had done a lot of research and discovered the ancient stone for an Aries was not a diamond, as most people thought, but a bloodstone.

Magdah folded the rings back into the red cloth and hobbled back to the shelf by the window. She opened the wood shutters. The gray light of dawn spread over the small room. She should feel tired, but her mind raced at a dizzying pace.

Magdah continued. "Each ring represents a Peacemaker. Conor made his choice when he selected the bloodstone. Ye have the strength to defeat Simon and the darkness that coils around us like a snake."

Magdah's eyes were clear; her touch brought with it calmness and clarity as though Eilan sat beside a mountain-fed stream instead of in a small smoke-filled cottage. Eilan had only glimpsed a small measure of what these people had endured under Simon's rule.

Eilan lowered her voice. "How do I begin?"

Magdah kissed her on the top of her head. "Conor chose well. Many would not ask for advice. The first step on the path toward your goal is the ability to ask for help. Ye begin one person at a time."

Magdah rubbed her nose with her sleeve and glanced toward the cot where Margaret and Angus slept. "The little one and his mother will awake soon. Perhaps ye can begin by bringing peace to their hearts and reunite them with Angus's father."

Eilan looked over at the boy. He snuggled in his mother's arms. The brief contact she'd had with him told her how, despite his brave appearance, he felt emptiness not knowing who his father was.

Angus opened his eyes and rubbed them with his fists. He smiled as though he sensed she was thinking about him. She returned the smile and glanced toward Magdah. "I like your idea. I'll look for Rowan in the morning."

Magdah nodded. "A fine way to start."

16

Conor knew he was dreaming, but like all the other times, he felt powerless to wrench free from its hold. The nightmare had started out like all the others with the sounds of men screaming.

The Mediterranean Sea shone sapphire blue as the tide crashed against the shore and swords glinted in the afternoon sun. The sound of metal on metal echoed over the blood-soaked sand as his men fought to defeat the Moslems. He drove his sword into his opponent's chest as another warrior rose to take his place. This time Conor hoped the outcome would be different.

A war cry tore through him. Over the crest of the hill Conor saw the new terror that approached. The enemy's reinforcements had arrived. He and his men were surrounded. But this was not the end of his nightmare, it was only the beginning.

Screams wrenched through the morning air. Out

of the corner of his eye he saw the cause. Rowan was covered in his own blood.

Conor moved in slow motion as he drove his sword into his assailant, pushed him aside and tried to reach his brother. He felt as though he were walking through the currents of the ocean. The air was heavy and weighed him down. Red-hot fury sped through his veins. His brother must not die. He roared out his frustration as he reached Rowan and then turned on the man who fought his brother. Conor tightened his grip on his sword and brought his blade down and across, severing the man's head.

The sights and sounds of the battle merged together until all Conor could hear was the beating of his own heart. He turned to his brother and dropped to his knees. An angry gash sliced down the side of Rowan's face. Conor tried to stop the flow of blood with his hand. Panic tore through him. The clash of steel on steel surrounded him. The war raged on; it mattered not, his brother's life hung in the balance. Warm blood seeped between his fingers as his brother cried out in agony.

Someone screamed to Rowan to hang on to life. The sound vibrated through him. He recognized the voice. It was his.

Conor struggled to free himself from the nightmare. He did not want to relive the moment he had failed his brother. A dark void enveloped him, wiping out the sights and sounds of his dream as he fought for control. The darkness lifted and the image of a beautiful woman floated toward him. Her hair was dark, save for strands of white around her face. She brought him peace. He knew the woman's name. Eilan.

He heard someone call his name through the red haze of the nightmare.

It offered relief from the pain.

Conor awoke with a start and gasped for air. It was still dark. He felt disoriented and unable to understand what had happened. And then he remembered. He could almost taste the relief. He was back in Scotland and his brother was alive. And there was something else.

For the first time, since before leaving for the Crusades, he looked forward to the day. He glanced toward Magdah's cottage. Behind the stone walls Eilan slept. Her memory had pulled him through. He longed to wake her and hold her in his arms. Their time together was too short. Whether or not her task was completed, she would return to her world on the night of the next full moon.

He could not think of that now. Spending time with her would only make their parting more painful. The less contact they had with each other would be for the best.

The moon was low over the horizon. It would be dawn in a couple of hours. The fire had died down until only a faint glow was left from last night's warm blaze. However, the threads of the dream still lingered in his thoughts.

Rowan stood over him, shaking him. "Brother. Ye were having the same nightmare again."

Conor sat and rubbed his forehead as though to drive it out of his thoughts. This dream was always the same. It relived the last battle he and his brother had fought in the Crusades. The memory was so vivid he could smell the salt sea air and feel the merciless sun through the chain mail he had worn that day.

Rowan sat back on his haunches. "Ye must leave the past behind."

Conor looked toward his brother. A black patch covered Rowan's right eye, but it did not cover the jagged scar that cut the length of his cheek. His brother never mentioned the deformity, it was Conor who could not forget that if somehow he had stayed close to Rowan's side, it never would have happened.

Conor clenched his jaw. "I canna forget the day ye were injured."

Rowan put his hand on Conor's shoulder. "It was not your doing."

Conor grasped his brother's hand. "I know. However, I am unable to pull free from the guilt." He paused. "At times I feel the dreams are there to remind me to not give up our fight to regain control of Castle MacCloud. Perhaps then, the nightmares will be put to rest." He looked toward Magdah's cottage again, willing the dark memories to the corner of his mind. He needed to concern himself with the present. "If Eilan fails, I will take the castle by force."

Rowan stood and folded his arms across his chest. "I hope it willna come to that. We have neither the men nor the weapons to succeed. The Peacemaker may be our best option."

Conor took a deep breath, feeling the truth of the words wash over him. "Aye, I agree. We should send word to Simon that she has arrived. I would know his reaction before I allow Eilan an audience with him."

Rowan bent down and gathered a handful of dried moss from the trunk of the tree and tossed it on the fire. The embers crackled to life. "There is no need to inform our uncle. William was so convinced of your success that he rode to Castle MacCloud to inform Simon of Magdah's plan the day ye left. 'Tis fortunate that Simon is known for his fascination with myths and legends. I am sure our uncle will be eager to meet the Peacemaker. He had been searching for her and the Ring of Time all his life. He believes the two are connected."

Conor interrupted. "William went alone?" He felt as though the forest had closed in on him. What Rowan said of Simon was true, however, so was their uncle's fascination with death. He killed at will. "Who accompanied William?"

Rowan placed a log on the fire and warmed his hands over the flame. "There was no stopping him, and no one willing to journey with him. He blamed himself for Douglas's death. They had always vowed to watch each other's back and together survived the Crusades. William believed he had failed Douglas. I told him I would go with him to Inverness if he would wait until I escorted Magdah safely to this glen." Rowan stirred the embers with a stick. "William was gone when I returned."

Conor looked in the direction he knew to be Castle MacCloud. "How long has William been gone?"

Rowan scratched his head. "He left almost immediately after ye disappeared into the other realm. This morning would be five days hence."

" 'Tis too long a time. Our uncle cannot be trusted." Conor bent down, reached for his sword and strapped it to his back. "There may be little time left. I will see to William's return. If I learn our uncle is not interested in negotiating for peace, I will try to recruit warriors to our cause."

Rowan stood and dusted his hands off on his plaid. "There is little hope of that. All are as fearful as those huddled in this clearing."

Conor shook his head. "I will still attempt it. Ye must stay here and guard the camp."

"I am going with ye. Simon's guards willna allow ye entrance to the castle, let alone an audience with Simon. At least William would not have been recognized. Give him time, perhaps he stopped at one of the local taverns for a pint or two."

Conor did not believe either to be the case. William was present when they first encountered Simon after their return from the Crusades. His uncle would never have forgotten the men who attacked him that day. Conor headed over to his horse. It was tethered with the others and nibbling on blades of rain and dew-soaked grass.

He paused to stroke the animal's neck. "I hope William is safe as well. However, 'tis not like him to waste time when he knows the information he carries is important."

Rowan followed Conor to the horses and clasped his hand on his brother's shoulder. "And who will guard your back if ye discover William has been captured?"

"Trust that I will take care of myself."

Rowan's voice rose. "There is no shame in asking for help, brother."

"How can ye say such a thing to me? Was it not I who went to ask for the help of the Peacemaker?"

Rowan shrugged. "It was honor that drove ye to it. Ye promised to fulfill a dying man's last request. Even now, I doubt ye believe Eilan can accomplish the task. However, ye have little choice in the matter, since we dinna have the manpower to lay siege to Castle MacCloud."

Conor mounted his horse. "Do not worry."

"And what of Eilan? Do ye mean to bring her with ye?"

Conor shook his head. "She is safer here with ye. I must first find William and then learn if Simon will honor the safety of a negotiation. I dinna want her walking into a trap."

Rowan ground out his words. "Ye are determined to go alone?"

"Aye."

"Sometimes, I think ye have a death wish."

Conor ignored Rowan's comment as he urged his horse forward out of the clearing and turned him down the path toward Inverness. Conor could not comprehend Rowan's anger. He was doing this for them both. His brother did not understand. No one understood. Their land had been stolen from them and their people driven from their homes. It was all that remained of who they were. Without it, there was little purpose left in life.

An image of Eilan came unbidden to his thoughts. He knew in his heart that she would be enough for him. He would need no other time or place. However, that dream was even more painful than his nightmares. His dreams were based in reality, while being with Eilan was only a fantasy he did not deserve.

Conor spurred his horse to a gallop. He must occupy his mind with finding William and freeing Castle MacCloud. All else he must push aside.

*   *   *

Eilan shivered and pulled the blanket over her shoulders. She opened her eyes slowly. Light streamed into the one-room cottage through the cracks in the wood shutters. Flames rolled over the logs in the stone hearth and a kettle of steaming stew bubbled over onto the fire. The smell of basil and sage floated on the cool air.

She snuggled deeper under the covers. She was reluctant to leave the comfort and warmth of the bed and then felt guilty. The reason she was here was to make a difference. No, she corrected herself, she was here to save her own life. There was nothing noble about what she was doing. And because of that, she wondered if she really could be successful in bringing peace to these people.

The door to the cottage creaked open and the old woman lumbered in carrying an armful of dried twigs.

" 'Tis time to awake, lass. The child of the morning has grown to an adolescent. 'Tis well past midday."

Eilan felt something flutter against her leg. She scratched the place on her skin and yawned. She debated about how cold the floor might be and whether or not she should put her shoes on before she stepped down. Something fluttered against her arm. She scratched the area and than paused. Bugs!

She bolted to a sitting position, scrambled out of bed, and brushed herself off. Too late it hit her that the floor was as cold as a block of ice. Her toes curled. She grabbed her leather-hiking boots from under the bed, turned them upside down and shook them. Thankfully, nothing fell out. She shoved them on her feet, and then she heard it.

Magdah was laughing so hard she was doubled over. She straightened and wiped the tears from her eyes. "Well, lass, ye certainly know how to cheer a body. I havena laughed so hard in years."

Eilan saw nothing funny about the situation. She pointed toward the bed. "I think there're bugs crawling under the blankets."

Magdah shrugged. "Aye. Donna pay them any mind, ye'll get used to the little critters." She arched an eyebrow. "They make a tasty treat in the pot as well."

"Very funny."

Magdah laughed again and turned toward the fire. She reached for a long handled iron spoon that hung on a peg beside the hearth and stirred the broth. "Ye must wear the clothes I have laid out for ye. I fear the ones ye have would draw too much attention."

Eilan walked over to them. She hesitated. All the stories she had heard mentioned that the clothes in the Middle Ages and Renaissance were riddled with fleas. She remembered reading the explanation as to the reason the nobility carried around small dogs. It was in the hope that the insects would jump on the dogs instead of the humans. She cringed; wondering if being warm was worth sharing your bed with bugs.

Magdah laughed. "What are ye waiting for, lass? Ye look as though the clothes will bite ye. I saw to their mending and cleaning myself. They belonged to my sister. About your size she was." Magdah sniffed and rubbed her nose. "I still miss the lass and wonder if her two boys developed her skills."

Eilan reached out toward the soft brown wool tunic and faded blue long-sleeved sheath. These were Fiona's clothes. Instead of the idea making her feel uncomfortable, she felt as though they would help her become more connected to the people she was here to help. She sensed that would make her task easier.

Once committed, she brought the garments over to a corner of the room and began changing her clothes. After this was done, she'd have to deal with finding nature's bathroom. The years she had spent as a tour guide in Colorado had prepared her well. She slipped the layers of clothing over her head, finishing with a long tunic.

Eilan glanced down at her hair and noted the new strands of white streaks Conor had mentioned the morning after they had made love. Her fingers trembled as she tied her hair back with a leather thong.

She felt uneasy. She knew that each time she sought to guide a person to follow their heart her hair would lighten. Had her thoughts somehow penetrated Conor's mind? She could not deny her feeling for Conor, or that she was pleased with the change in him, but she was fearful that it would not last. The burden he carried with him was great. It might be easier for him to cast his feeling for her aside.

Eilan heard shouting. It broke through her troubled daydreams. Magdah seemed unaware of any disturbance and stood over the pot of stew. Eilan walked toward the window and opened the shutters. The camp had been transformed from the peace and tranquility of last night to chaos.

There was a chill on the morning air that had little to do with the weather. Women huddled around the open campfire and stirred an iron kettle. Their shrill voices reached Magdah's cottage. A group of men raised their voices and she heard the crack of fist on bone as a fight broke out. Dirt-smudged children wove around the adults, yelling and punching each other as they sped by her. They were dressed in tattered clothes, and chased a sheep through the camp. It bleated and darted around a fallen tree trunk. A fistfight broke out between two bearded men who landed in a heap on the ground. Men from the MacIntosh clan joined in the fray. A woman's shrieks broke through the shouting. She was encouraging them to kill one another.

Eilan gripped the window ledge. She felt like crawling back into bed and pulling the covers over her head. Bringing peace to this crowd was going to be a monumental job.

Magdah walked up beside her and make a *tsk, tsk* sound. "These people couldna work together if the reward was a purse filled with gold coin." She shook her head. " 'Tis Simon's doing. The distrust and despair is so thick they fear working together."

Eilan tightened her grip on the sill. The wood was damp and cold. The reason she was here was to try to change these people into a loving and cooperative group. She whispered. "I know you think I can change them, but there are so many. I have never attempted to reach this number before. I'm not sure my gift is strong enough."

"Fiddle-faddle. Ye are the Peacemaker. Your power is only limited by your desire to heal. If it was once in the person's heart to desire happiness, ye can show them the path once again. Fiona had the gift. It has been with us for thousands of years. In the beginning, many possessed it, but fear caused my people to reject the gift. At first my sister was reluctant as well to use her powers." Magdah hesitated. "Will this be your first time?"

Eilan remembered the bully on the playground when she was in third grade. The teacher thought the child had changed. No one, except her mother, realized that Eilan had been the cause. A vision of Conor crept into her mind. She quickly submerged the thought.

"No, it won't be the first."

Eilan did not speak the words out loud she most feared. With each successful effort to help people, she knew her hair would change and hopefully, the tumor that pressed against her brain. That, however, was not what bothered her. She wondered if her strength would diminish as well. If that were the case, would she still have the strength to confront Simon?

Margaret opened the door to the cottage and a blast of cold air followed her inside. She headed in the direction of the hearth. "Men. Their foolishness is beyond the limits of common sense. Do ye know what that man of yours plans now? He means to lay siege to the castle."

Conor was not hers, but Eilan decided it wasn't worth explaining. She blew on her hands. This might be a good time to watch and listen.

Magdah settled down by the fire on her stool. She cast a glance toward Eilan and held her gaze as she lowered her voice. "Margaret, was there any talk of trying to negotiate a peace?"

Eilan leaned against the wall by the window. She sensed Margaret didn't know everything.

Margaret plopped down opposite Magdah and leaned her elbows on her knees. "Aye, there was mention of it. That is the reason William left a few days ago. He was anxious to inform Simon of Conor's intention to reach a peaceful conclusion to the bloodshed." She took a deep breath. "However, if Simon refuses a meeting, that would leave them little choice but to attack."

Eilan shivered. She pushed away from the wall and walked to the fire. She knelt beside Margaret and took her hand in hers and felt the anguish. "Simon has to want peace."

Tears rolled from Margaret's eyes. "I hope he does."

Margaret glanced in the direction of the flames. "Their plans to lay siege to Simon's castle is so foolhardy. They have only about a half-dozen men who are willing to fight against Simon's army. Rowan believes his brother might be successful in gaining others willing to die for a lost cause." She took a deep breath. "Rowan survived the Crusades only to risk being killed trying to reclaim a worthless castle."

Magdah shut the door slowly and smiled. "Ye are correct. No one will fight Simon." She looked over at Eilan. "At least, not as yet." Magdah wagged her finger at Margaret. "But ye must support Rowan and his brother. They do what is right, for all of us."

Margaret sighed. "I know, but there are times when I wish that their fortress would disappear into a great dark void."

Eilan said out loud what she knew was in Margaret's heart. "You still love Rowan."

Margaret dabbed at her eyes with a corner of her shawl. "How could I not? He has returned from the

Crusades more handsome than when he left. The worst of it, however, is his reaction to Angus. I told Rowan this morning that Angus was his child, and he believed me. It would have been easier for me if he had not. I could have perhaps tried to hate him and thus protected my heart against possible rejection."

Eilan smiled. "Why wouldn't he believe you? It was the truth."

Margaret shoulders slumped forward. "I know, but there are men who may have doubted such a claim. It has been a long time."

Eilan gently squeezed Margaret's hand and felt the waves of confusion flow through her. "Rowan is not like most men."

Margaret nodded. "That is exactly what I have been saying all along." She turned toward Eilan. "Now do ye understand why the man frustrates me so?"

"Why don't you tell him how you feel?"

Margaret lowered her head and glanced toward the fire. She twisted a strand of her hair between her fingers. "I have grown so old. My hair is dull and my hands rough from digging the herbs for my medicines. He may favor Angus, but I canna blame him if he does not desire me anymore."

Magdah made a loud *humph* sound. "Old? Look on me and see what ye will look like and still I can turn a man's head if I've a mind. Ye are a bonnie lass, Margaret MacIntosh, and even if ye were not, the man loves ye. And therein lies the difference. I can see how he feels toward ye, reflected in his eyes. 'Tis a love that will endure and sees only what is inside a person, not the pretty package."

Eilan felt the wisdom of those words. Her parents were in their sixties and treated each other as though they were involved in their first blush of attraction.

The door to the cottage slammed open and Angus raced into the room. In between gulps of air he spat out his words. "Mother, can I go? Uncle Conor gave his blessing before he left."

Margaret stood and cupped Angus's face with the palm of her hand. "Slow down, child, and tell me where it is that ye wish to go?"

Eilan rose slowly to her feet. She said the words more to herself than to Angus. "Conor has left? Where did he go?"

Angus took large gulps of air and smiled. "Please, Mother, I want to go hunting with my father."

Eilan crossed her hands over her chest and tried to ignore the irritation rising within her. "Angus, do you know where Conor went?"

The boy nodded his head vigorously as he turned toward her. "Aye, Uncle Conor went to fetch William."

Eilan told herself it was probably nothing to worry about, but she had to ask. "Why do you think Conor wanted to find William?"

Angus shrugged his shoulders.

Margaret shook her head. "Rowan wishes to take a child of eight years of age on a hunt for dangerous animals."

The boy's mouth opened and closed but he remained silent.

Margaret reached for Angus's hand. "Come with me. We will discuss this matter with your father."

Eilan didn't envy Rowan at this moment. If he had never seen a lion defending the safety of her cub, he was about to experience it firsthand.

The door slammed behind Margaret. The sound echoed through the small cottage as though confirming her thoughts.

Eilan turned to Magdah. There were more important matters on her mind. "Do you know who William is?"

Magdah ladled a spoonful of broth and sipped the steaming brew. "Aye."

"Do you think Conor will be gone long?" It was of course, none of her business if his errand would take an hour or the whole day. She admitted to herself that she was a little miffed that he hadn't even taken the time to say good-bye.

"Hard to tell how long the lad will be gone."

Eilan grabbed her mother's shawl from the back of the wood chair. Obtaining an answer from Magdah when the woman was not interested in talking was only slightly more difficult than trying to punch a plastic straw into a square juice box. Maybe Rowan would have a better answer.

She walked out of the cottage and her shoes sank in the mud. There was a sucking sound as she pulled free and jumped to firmer ground. The history books said that people in this time period did not take baths. She decided that it was not that they were afraid of the water; it was just that with all this mud, they'd be washing several times a day.

As she focused on the clearing she noted the fight she had witnessed earlier had turned into a brawl. The only people not involved were Rowan, Margaret and Angus. Margaret was shaking her finger at Rowan and had him backed against a tree. Angus squatted on the ground and was drawing circles in the mud with a stick. Margaret shook her head, reached for Angus's hand and stomped off toward the opposite side of the clearing. Okay, so that had not gone well.

She glanced over at the screaming mass of arms and legs and started to prioritize. First she'd answer nature's call, then she'd find out where Conor had gone and last, but not least, she'd dive into the fray and bring peace and order to the clans. She knew she was in over her head. The job probably required a team of Peacemakers, not just one. However, all Magdah had sent for was her.

Eilan headed toward the edge of the wood. She glanced toward Rowan. He was staring in the direction Margaret and Angus had gone. Eilan guessed he was probably wishing he had left with Conor. She stepped over an exposed root and stomped on a clump of fallen leaves.

Conor had left without saying good-bye. It shouldn't bother her, but it did. Rowan had better have a good excuse ready when she returned. Like someone had been rushed to whatever passed for an emergency hospital in the Middle Ages.

17

Simon MacCloud dug his spurs into the sides of his horse and hastened to the meadow where he had last seen his hawk. His guards flanked him on either side as well as behind him. They rode in silence. He needed their protection, but not their conversation. The remains of the last guard to speak to him without permission still hung from the scaffolding in the courtyard of Castle MacCloud. His hawk would suffer the same fate if it did not return.

Of late the tiresome bird grew as lazy as his men. Black wings broke through the gray clouds. Simon held out his arm to the hunter. The thrill he had once experienced with hawking had lost its luster. Mayhaps it was the memories of a time when he would share this sport with Conor, Rowan and their sister, Elizabeth.

He clenched his jaw until his teeth ground together. He had thought of her every day since she had fallen to her death from the turrets of Dragon's

Lair Castle. He knew that Conor blamed him for her death, but it was not his fault. The little tease had smiled at him that afternoon and when he followed her to collect what was due him, she refused. She backed away from him, tripped and fell over the edge to her death. Pity, Elizabeth was such a pretty thing. However, much good came from it.

The hawk settled on his arm as Simon covered the bird's head with a leather hood and stroked his feathers. Elizabeth's death had changed everything. Simon's brother never fully recovered from his grief and died shortly after Conor and Rowan left for the Crusades, leaving Castle MacCloud in Simon's care. He smiled. Of course his fool brother made him promise to return the castle to his sons. It was a tactical error. There were no witnesses to the promise.

Simon shrugged. Besides, the Crusades had changed Conor and Rowan. Simon could see it in his nephews' eyes. They wanted peace at the very time when there was still much evil in the world, and more to come. Simon was sure of it. He nodded. Yes, it was better that Castle MacCloud remain with him. However, Simon could feel the unrest building around him since Conor's return. Each day it grew harder to maintain control. He must strengthen his resolve to find and kill Conor. With their leader dead, the rabble would be easier to manage.

He had spent much coin on assuring that his men were motivated to that end. Conor's feeble attempt to reclaim the castle had only resulted in the deaths of those foolish enough to fight by his side. Simon would relish the capture and slow deaths of Conor and Rowan. They deserved whatever befell them for challenging him.

He took a deep breath and watched the gray clouds pass across the sun.

Each day was like all the others. They merged together in an endless line of monotony. Even the attempt to reclaim the castle was little more than an annoyance. The witch trials had been both a welcome diversion as well as serving the purpose of gathering information. He enjoyed the responsibility of exposing the dark side of these women and personally supervised their questioning and their deaths. However, he had not found the information he sought. No one knew the whereabouts of the Ring of Time or the person who controlled its power. Simon fingered the amulet around his neck. The witch who called herself Fiona had given the lavender amethyst to him. He had met her when he first came to this godforsaken land.

Birds flew from the grove of alders at the edge of the meadow. The hawk grew restless as Simon straightened in his saddle. His horse whinnied and the guards beside him looked in his direction for guidance. It was forbidden for anyone to dwell within the shadows of Ferry Glen. All those who disobeyed his will were dead.

A predator may have caused the disturbance and the thought of the hunt, regardless if it were human or wild beast, caused Simon's blood to warm in his veins.

He uncovered the hood over his hawk's head and raised his arm. The bird spread its wings and soared toward the trees. "Mayhap the morning's entertainment has begun at last."

Simon kicked his horse in the sides with his spurs and motioned for his guards to follow him as he raced toward the forest. The overhanging branches seemed to weave together, forming a latticework ceiling. Simon tightened his grip on the reins of his horse, relishing the pursuit. He had conquered evil and proved to the town he was merciless in his pursuit of destroying all those whose beliefs were different than his own.

Through the limbs of the trees, he saw a woman kneeling on the ground, her arm outstretched toward a black squirrel. She held acorns in the palm of her hand and seemed to be talking to the creature. Streaks of white were laced through her shoulder length hair. Although the hair was darker than he remembered, the shape of her face was familiar.

Simon reined in his horse and felt the years fold back. He spurred his horse deeper into the forest and felt the blood pump through his veins. The resemblance was disturbing. Fiona had returned, just as she had promised.

The woman looked toward him. She rose slowly: the nuts she held dropped to the ground. He recognized the fear he saw reflected in her eyes. He had seen it before as women were dragged to the stake on top of a pile of wood and again when their flesh was burned from their bodies. He had enjoyed those triumphant moments when he knew he had conquered them. However, Fiona had been different somehow. She was not afraid. He shuddered at the memory.

The woman in the forest wrapped the shawl around her shoulders. Her gaze was steady as she lifted her chin. The fear he had seen reflected in their depths seemed to wash away. It was replaced by something he could not name. He gripped the amulet around his neck. It was foolish of him to have ventured into this wood. He was powerless against the evil of a witch. They were not of this world.

If it was true, and Fiona had returned, he did not want to meet her in this place. The wood was reported to be haunted. He should have stayed away. Perhaps she was not real. An icy breeze rustled the underbrush. He shivered. He feared she could draw him to the Otherworld to eat the flesh off his bones. One of the women he had questioned had spoken of such things. And he had believed every word.

Simon spun his horse around, pushing through his worthless guards as he headed down the path and out of the wood. He would send someone to find out who or what she was. If Fiona had returned, he would destroy her . . . again.

The heavy cloud cover of the night before had lifted and sunlight filtered through the limbs of the trees as Eilan walked back to the clearing. She had ventured farther than she'd anticipated, but it was such a great morning and it felt good to stretch her legs. However, it might have ended in disaster. Fortunately, the man she saw in the forest seemed as afraid of her as she was of him.

Eilan had been independent all her life and liked the solitude. However, this was not Kansas, and she was not in the Land of Oz, although it was beginning to feel as odd. And for that reason she should take a page from Dorothy's book and ask someone to join her the next time she felt adventurous.

Her encounter with the person in the wood was unsettling. At first when she saw him and the other men, she felt an overwhelming desire to run. In the beginning she thought it was because of the archers who had attacked them on the trail when she had first arrived in Conor's century. However, she sensed it was something more. She shrugged the uncomfortable feeling aside. Perhaps her imagination was just running amok.

As she rounded the bend she saw Rowan running straight for her. He skidded to a stop in front of her. "Where have ye been all this time? I am glad Conor was not here. He would have torn the forest apart looking for ye."

Guilt made her feel defensive. "If you must know, I had to take care of female type things."

He stepped back. "Oh."

Eilan smiled to herself. Mentioning the word "female" in that context always succeeded in ending the conversation with the male of the species. It was like shouting earthquake in a thirty-story building. The brain went numb for about five seconds and stopped functioning. However, hers had not.

She pulled the shawl tighter around her shoulders. "There were a group of men in the wood, but their leader rode off when he saw me."

Rowan's eyes widened. "That is odd. And they said nothing to ye?"

Eilan shook her head. "The leader had a hawk on his arm. Maybe he was in the wood to hunt."

Rowan combed his fingers through his hair. "Perhaps, ye are right, still, I will see to it that more men are on watch during the night."

A wood bowl sailed past Eilan's head, landing with a thud on the ground behind her. The squabbling amongst the people had accelerated since she'd left. She almost wished it would rain. At least that might drive some of them undercover. On second thought, that would not end the fighting, only bring it indoors. She sighed.

"I forgot to ask you. Who accompanied Conor to Inverness?"

Rowan seemed to ignore the chaos erupting around him. He shrugged his shoulder. "He went alone."

She put her hands on her hips. "Correct me if I'm wrong, but isn't that where this Simon person lives?"

"Aye."

"Why didn't you stop him?"

Rowan smiled. "Have ye ever succeeded in preventing Conor from changing his mind once he has set it in motion?"

She thought about the time they'd spent at Dragon's Lair Castle. She had relived it over and over in her mind. First to savor the emotions Conor had awakened in her and then to wonder if somehow her mind had nudged him into feeling something for her he didn't mean.

Conor's behavior had taken such a dramatic turn that she had a hard time trusting its origins. Regardless, he had ridden full tilt into the lion's den. Intellectually she knew it was to rescue William, but her heart was saying this was just an elaborate male avoidance plan.

Another bowl whizzed past her like some crazed, out of control Frisbee. It brought her back to the subject that concerned her.

She tapped her foot on the ground. "I'm not sure whether or not I've managed to talk Conor into something he didn't want to do." She felt a tug of guilt. "But that's beside the point. You need to send in an army to bring him back."

Rowan made a sweeping gesture of the camp. A new fight seemed to break out as soon as one ended. "And what army would ye wish I send?"

She glanced toward the squabbling men and women. The disputes seemed to grow worse by the minute. She heard someone accuse the other of stealing his cattle, followed by one man hitting the other in the jaw. The sound of bone cracking was overshadowed by shouts for vengeance. If she had heard correctly, this offense had taken place twenty years ago.

She rubbed her forehead. The headaches had returned. "Good point." She paused. "Okay, just head me in the right direction and I'll go. I'll meet Simon and . . ."

Rowan interrupted. "Conor forbid it."

Eilan doubled up her fist and then forced herself to remain calm. This adversarial environment was contagious. It was just the word "forbidden" that sent her into a tailspin. She needed to think like a fourteenth century male. She cringed and tried not to think too long on the "me Tarzan, you Jane" mentality. She understood Rowan's words as well as his tone of voice. The subject was closed. It was time for Plan B. She cleared her throat. "How about this idea? I will attempt to bring order to this camp and if I succeed, will you promise to rescue Conor?"

Rowan lifted his eyebrow. "My brother has never been in need of rescuing."

"That's not true. What about the time he was in prison?"

" 'Twas Conor who helped us to escape."

She was actually referring to the time he was in Seattle, but she figured Rowan would probably say that, given enough time, his brother would have found a way out by himself. Eilan had never had brothers or sisters, and seeing the loyalty between these two made her wish she had. However, despite Rowan's hero-worshiping of his brother, it didn't change the fact that Conor was not immortal.

Eilan paced back and forth in front of Rowan. She was losing patience and she feared each moment she wasted reduced the chance of finding Conor alive.

She ducked as a clay pitcher sailed past her and landed with a thud on the ground behind her. At this rate the people in the camp would have exhausted their supply of eating utensils. She hoped it was sooner, not later. "Well, do you promise?"

He looked over his shoulder. "Even if ye manage to prevent them from fighting with each other, they fear Simon and willna go against him."

"Let me worry about that detail. Plan to be ready this time tomorrow."

She sidestepped as a wooden plate sped past her. She took a deep breath. "It might take a little longer than twenty-four hours, but just remember our bargain."

Margaret walked toward them with Angus running along beside her. Rowan turned in her direction and the lines across his forehead deepened. Eilan decided there was no time like the present to begin. She reached over and touched his arm.

Rowan's mind was clouded with regret. The negative images repeated themselves, crowding out all hope. Eilan took three deep breaths and let them out slowly as she ventured deeper into Rowan's mind, past the present resolve and beyond the horror of the Crusades. His mind resembled shades of gossamer silk panels. The rainbow of colors ranged from the hues of a field of spring flowers to the deep shades of the ocean.

Eilan brushed aside each layer until she reached the memory she searched for. The moment he and Margaret fell in love.

Margaret was alone in a field of sweet smelling heather and was there to help a sheep give birth. Eilan felt Rowan's thoughts at the moment he saw her gentle touch and the soothing way she had with the animal. Without realizing it, he had dismounted and offered her aid after the successful delivery. Margaret and Rowan had spent the afternoon together.

Eilan took another deep breath and continued. She helped Rowan pull the memory and the emotions of that moment to the forefront of his thoughts. With that accomplished, she released her hold on his arm and stepped back. The lines around his forehead had diminished and a smile added a sparkle to his eyes as he greeted Margaret and their son.

Silently Rowan nodded toward Margaret. It gave Eilan courage as she watched the three of them disappear into the forest. The rest they would have to do themselves. The human race was a unique species. Hope and love was embedded inside their thoughts. It was as much a part of them as the need for food and shelter. At times Eilan believed it was more important. A body could endure without love, but their existence would lack color and texture. It would be like waking up one morning only to discover the world was painted beige. The grass, mountains, sun and flowers would all be the same shade.

She rolled up her sleeves and headed into the thick of the squabbling men and women. Margaret and Rowan were easy; this would be the real challenge.

Eilan reached the first group and ducked as a woman in her late twenties took a swing in her direction. She reached out toward her and rested her hand on the woman's shoulder. Waves of memory swept over Eilan. She had determined to search for a common thread within each person with whom she came in contact. She would take them back to a moment in time when they had performed an unselfish deed, no matter how small. The positive emotion would produce an overall feeling of goodwill that would hopefully transfer to those around them. Or at least, that was the plan. A negative feeling can tie a person's body in emotional knots, while a positive thought introduces peace.

She did not have to search long for the woman beside her. About two months before, Mary had baked an extra loaf of bread for a starving neighbor. Eilan smiled as she saw the transformation on Mary's face as the woman recalled the event.

Mary stepped away from the brawl and turned to her. She wiped her hands on her plaid skirt. "I am sorry. Did I hurt ye?"

Eilan shook her head.

Mary smiled. "I dinna know what came over me or the reason I tried to hit ye. These are challenging times. Ye should not be here, ye might be injured."

Eilan shook her head and hugged the woman to her. "This is exactly the right place for me."

She smiled again and turned toward a group of women who were screaming at each other. Eilan would have liked to find out how Margaret and Rowan were doing, but hopefully the memories she had pulled forth would help them to remember the reason that brought them together in the first place.

She hoped so, denying to your self the importance of the person you loved only brought unhappiness and unrest.

Margaret sat on a large flat stone on the rock-strewn shore. She pulled her shawl tighter around her shoulders as she watched Rowan and their son fish at the water's edge.

The shore dropped off to unknown depths. While it was too cold for a body to bathe in, its depths were teaming with fish.

Angus laughed at something Rowan said and she saw him tousle the boy's hair. Tears brimmed in her eyes. She quickly brushed them away. She reminded herself that her son had not lacked for attention these past eight years. Margaret had six brothers who treated Angus as their own. And the tears were not for her. Men only complicated a woman's life. She was better off without them. The wind must have coaxed the tears from her eyes. She had much to be thankful for and had successfully locked the memories of Rowan safely away, but seeing him after all these years had awakened them.

Rowan looked over his shoulder and smiled. Her heartbeat jumped. She clenched the shawl tighter and fought against returning the smile. They were not as they were before. She had grown into a woman and he a man. The time they had spent the day in a sweet smelling meadow was long past. She doubted if he remembered, however, she could not forget. She had known who he was the moment he had dismounted from his horse. The men of the MacCloud clan were well-known to her people. They were a powerful family who, while governing with a gentle hand, kept themselves apart from all the rest.

Of course the feud between her family and theirs strengthened the distance. The feud had plodded on for over one hundred years. Some say it started with the thieving of cattle, while Margaret believed the more popular view to be true.

The story told of a woman from the MacIntosh clan who fell in love with two men and could not decide between them. One of the men was from her clan and the other was a MacCloud. She could not choose between them and so swam out into the icy waters of Loch Ness and was never seen again.

Whatever the real cause, the feud had raged on and so Margaret was surprised that Rowan would help her in the birthing of the lamb. Yet, he had, and afterward they laughed while the wee thing took his first steps. It was so wonderful a day that there were times she thought she heard the lyrical music of the fairy folk who lived in the nearby glen.

Her son's laughter swept over her and pulled her from her daydreams. She stood. What could be the jest? Angus was not prone to such outbursts.

She pulled her shawl over her head and walked

toward Rowan and Angus. A cool breeze rustled over the waters of the Loch. They shimmered in the afternoon sun.

Rowan nodded as she approached. "We are pleased ye would join us."

Angus pointed to the center of the Loch. "Mother, did ye see him?"

Margaret gazed into the direction her son indicated. The water was smooth and clear. "What is it, Angus?"

"I saw the horse dragon that inhabits the Loch. Rowan said this is his favorite time of day."

Margaret turned toward Rowan. "So, ye have been filling the child's head with nonsense." Her words came out harsher than she had intended. She swallowed. It was hard for her to be so close to him.

Rowan smiled and leaned toward her. "Ye dinna think it so when we were young."

Margaret shook her head. "Ye forgot to add foolish."

Rowan reached for a strand of her hair that had blown free of the shawl. He gently twisted it beneath his fingers and whispered, "Margaret, forgive me."

He was so close she could feel his breath on her cheek. Reason told her she should pull away. But Angus might misinterpret either response. No matter her feelings for Rowan, this man was still her son's father.

She swallowed and her shawl dropped over her

shoulders. "Please keep your voice low. I have not told the boy all."

Rowan leaned within a heartbeat from her lips. "Have ye told him that I love his mother?"

"The words are easy to say, easier still to hear. But ye left me without a thought of what ye left behind."

He shook his head. "That is not true." Rowan straightened and rolled up the cuff of his sleeve. Straps of faded and tattered ribbons were woven around his wrist. "Do ye remember the day we said our farewells?"

A hot tear rolled down her cheek. Of course she remembered. The day was etched in her memory. That day she had longed to tell Rowan she carried his child, but she was afraid. If he knew and still left, it would break her heart. Better that he thought he was just saying farewell to her.

She swallowed. "I remember, but what . . ."

He interrupted and smiled. "That day I asked you to give me a remembrance. Ye took the ribbons from your hair." He paused. "They have been with me always."

His words warmed her soul. She put the palm of her hand on his chest and felt his heart vibrate through her. The shawl fell to the ground. "There was not one day that passed that I did not think of ye and pray ye would return to me."

He took a deep breath and the smile he always

wore faded as he touched the scar over his face. "I am not the man ye once knew."

She tilted her face toward him. "I am changed as well." She smiled against his lips. "We shall start anew."

Angus shouted. "I saw him again. He looked over at me."

Margaret turned toward the water. The calm waters had churned to life. Whitecaps formed over the surface. Toward the distant shore she thought she saw a massive fin slide beneath the dark waters.

Rowan put his arm around her shoulder. "It is just as before."

Margaret nodded and snuggled into his embrace. This moment was laced with magic as time folded back. If it were not for the age of their son, she would have believed only moments had passed, instead of years. Whatever the reason, she was thankful they had given themselves a second chance at love.

18

It had been a week since Conor had first ridden his horse into Inverness, and he was no closer to finding William than when he first arrived. All knew him here and feared Simon's wrath if they talked to him. It was time to try another plan. He must disguise his appearance.

Conor dismounted and unrolled the long dark cape and wrapped it around his shoulders. He brought the hood up over his head in the style of the clergy. It was a disguise that had allowed him and his men to pass freely through some of the towns on their return trip from the Crusades. Although the men under Conor's charge had not behaved thus, many of the king's soldiers had cut a bloody path of pain and destruction on their way to Spain and thus were not welcome.

An iron sign creaked back and forth over the tavern in the cool night air. He had avoided entering this establishment before as the owner and his father had been lifelong friends and thus Conor was well known here. The image of a boar's head was embossed in the metal and signified its name. Conor pushed open the door, bracing for the sight and sounds of a bawdy tavern. They never came.

A film of smoke from the endless fires in the hearth, coated the whitewashed walls, turning them gray. A staircase, in need of repair, hugged the wall. If possible, it seemed colder inside than out. The owner had once taken pride in his tavern. Much had changed.

The long trestle tables sat in rows across the center of the room. Candles dripped onto the polished surface. The place was deserted, unusual for this time of day.

A round-faced woman, her hair stuffed into a soiled linen cap, edged toward him. Conor recognized her. She and his sister, Elizabeth, had been friends. The years had not been kind to Sara. Sadness clung to her as tightly as her own shadow.

She approached, wringing her hands together. "Will ye be wanting a room, Father?"

Conor kept his head lowered so that the hood fell over his features. He adjusted his speech to reflect a man of the cloth. "Nay, I am passing through, my child. I seek only information. Do ye know if a man by the name of William Donovan has passed this way within the last fortnight?"

Her eyes widened. "What would ye want with the likes of him?"

Conor heard the fear laced through her words. "He is a friend."

She teetered as she stepped back and slammed into the table nearest to her. "We are a God-fearing town." She made a sweeping gesture with her hand. "Few come here for idleness, and them that do, tarry not."

Conor had not asked for an accounting of the morals of the town, but the woman had supplied them nonetheless. What was more, she deliberately avoided his question regarding William.

He did not want to alarm her, nor bring attention to himself by continuing. He needed to find William.

"Fear not. I need nothing from ye, save a warm meal and a tankard of ale."

She took a deep breath and smiled. "That I can do for ye and glad. Do ye favor rabbit stew?"

Conor nodded. "It is a favorite of mine."

Her head bobbled a yes and indicated a table and chair against the far wall.

"Make yourself comfortable. I shall be bringing ye a meal straightaway. Ye will be placing mouth to tankard before your thirst has a chance to grow further."

Sara turned and disappeared into an alcove toward the back of the tavern. In better times, the woman would have handed his order to a serving maid who would have brought his meal to him. It looked as though it had been a long while since such luxuries were in practice.

Conor walked over to where Sara indicated and sat down on the wood bench. He and Rowan had spent their last night, before leaving for the Crusades, at this tavern. The place was packed with both the regular clientele as well as those anticipating the defeat of the Moslems at the hands of the MacCloud clan. He had never known a time, day or night, when the Wild Boar Tavern was not filled to the rafters. This was odd indeed.

True to her word, Sara appeared from the back of the tavern, carrying a wooden tray. She set the tankard of ale in front of him, followed by a plate of brown bread and a steaming bowl of stew. "If ye need anything else . . ."

The door to the tavern slammed open, interrupting her as well as bringing in a blast of cold air and a half-dozen loudmouthed men. They shouted for the owner and pounded their fists on a table. The tallest of the bunch, picked up a chair and threw it across the room. It clattered to the floor. Conor rose from his seat and put his hand on the hilt of his blade. He had seen enough of this behavior to know it only grew worse if left unchecked. Frustration and inactivity over the past week had fueled his desire to teach these men manners.

Sara put her hand on his shoulder. He felt the gentle pressure as she tried to push him back down on the bench.

She leaned toward him and whispered. "This is none of your concern. These men are just itching for a fight and they care not if it be noble, serf or clergy."

He squeezed her hand. "Do not concern yourself. I have fought more than this number of men to a successful conclusion."

"What manner of priest are ye?"

One of the men turned in the direction of Conor and Sara. The belt around his tunic was encrusted with gemstones. He slammed his fist on the table. "Is there no one to serve me? Bring ale for my men and me. I demand to speak to the owner. He will suffer for such treatment."

Sara straightened. Her chin raised and her eyes narrowed as she whispered to Conor. "Heed what I said. Ye dinna want to fight their kind. My father tried to go against that devil, Simon, and paid the price with his life."

Conor tightened his grip on his blade. "I am sorry for your losses. He was a good man."

Her eyes clouded over with tears. "Many good men and woman have gone to their death. I dinna believe Simon will be satisfied until all of Inverness is buried beneath the ground."

The men's shouts vibrated in the tavern.

Sara took a deep breath, picked up her skirts and hurried to do their bidding.

Conor clenched his jaw. He was more determined than ever to end the fear that had plunged an entire town into despair.

The door opened once again. This time only one person entered.

The men turned toward the door and bowed. In as short a time as it took to take a breath, their manner changed from arrogant nobles to cowering servants.

The man with the gemstone belt bowed. "My lord, will this humble tavern be to your liking?"

From Conor's angle at the far side of the room he could not see who was being addressed. The sound of hollow laughter rang through him. It was familiar. Conor leaned forward.

It was his uncle, Simon MacCloud. This did not bode well.

Simon's laugh seemed to carry to the four corners of the room as he walked into the tavern and surveyed his surroundings like a king his court. A smile curled over his lips as Sara set the foaming tankards of ale on the table.

Simon walked over to her and tilted her chin toward him. "I had forgotten about you, until now."

She turned her face away and pulled from his grasp. "Will ye and your men be wanting anything else milord?"

The men erupted in laughter and pounded their tankards of ale on the table.

Simon nodded. "Calm yourselves, there is enough woman here for us all." He reached for Sara's arm.

Conor had seen enough. He stood so abruptly, the bench clattered to the floor. He was outnumbered, but it would not be the first time. He drew his sword and rushed to Sara's aid, pulling her out of Simon's grasp.

Conor pointed his blade at the base of Simon's throat. "Well, uncle, we meet again."

Simon's thin lips were drawn tightly across his face. "It seems so. I knew ye would come when I captured one of your men. He spoke of a foolish legend about a Peacemaker."

Conor tightened his grip on the sword and pressed the tip of the blade against Simon's skin. Rivulets of blood formed on the steel. Out of the corner of his eye he saw Simon's men circle around him. He and Sara were trapped. He would bide his time and wait for an opportunity. "Release William."

Simon shrugged. "Unlikely. I have not yet decided what to do with the lad. At first I was amused when he said you had gone on a quest to find the Peacemaker." He arched an eyebrow. "But I have lost interest."

"There was a time when ye believed in the legend."

Simon laughed. "I did and so I had her killed. Why would I want peace? Fear is a more effective form of control."

An icy shudder rippled through Conor. He should never have left Eilan. "Ye lie. She canna be dead."

Simon laughed again. "I lit the fire myself and saw to it that Fiona's ashes were scattered over Loch Ness."

Conor slowly let out his breath as relief washed over him. His uncle was referring to Magdah's sister, not Eilan. She was alive and would remain so as long as his heart still beat. He was foolish to think Simon would want peace; the man thrived on the chaos and fear he created. Conor would not risk losing Eilan. He must find a way to raise an army, but first he must escape.

It would be an easy matter to slit Simon's throat, but in the next instant the guards would cut him down. He had seen their like before in the Crusades. Their sort killed for pleasure. These mercenaries would no doubt ravage the land at will. They did not fear the forest as Simon did. No one would be safe.

Conor felt Simon's men edge closer. With a fluid motion, Conor withdrew his sword and pushed Simon toward them. Caught off guard, they struggled to catch Simon before he fell.

Sara reached for Conor's hand. "Come with me."

They rushed toward the back of the tavern, closed the door and slid the bar in place.

The next moment Simon's men banged and pounded against the door.

"Sara, is there another way out?"

"Aye." She hurried to the wall beside the hearth. She pushed against one of the wood panels, exposing a hidden passageway. Sara turned toward him. "Thank ye for saving me. 'Tis been a long time since someone has behaved in such a manner." She smiled and the lines in her face softened. "Your family was well loved."

The banging on the door increased and the metal hinges creaked under the strain.

Sara motioned for Conor to follow her. "We must hurry. There are those among us who would like to be rid of Simon. Perhaps ye can persuade them to fight. I will lead ye to them."

Conor followed Sara through the opening. She turned and silently closed the door behind them. The narrow winding staircase led to a dark chamber. However, the cold did not dampen his spirits. For the first time in days he felt a ray of hope.

The rain-soaked ground squished beneath Eilan's feet and the hem of her wool gown dragged in the mud as she headed toward the center of town. It had taken longer than anticipated to bring peace to the clans gathered around Magdah's cottage. One group of men was particularly stubborn. She had to venture into their childhood memories to find positive energy, but in the end, she had reached them all. What she had not been prepared for was the diminishing of her headaches and the ringing in her ears. She smiled, thinking the doctors would not know what to say when she returned and they learned her incurable tumor had disappeared.

The days were speeding by. Eilan paused and fought the wave of sadness that swept over her. Already almost two weeks had passed since she had first seen Conor. She would take the memory of him with her back to the twenty-first century, but she wanted more.

Eilan forced herself to continue toward the marketplace. The least she could do was finish her task and bring peace to Inverness. It would be her gift to him.

Rowan had kept his promise and escorted her to the outskirts of Inverness and was busy tending the horses. She had used the feminine shopping ploy this time to shake him.

The gray light of dawn still hung in the air, made darker by the two-story wood buildings lining the narrow street. Conor had told her his people were locked in despair. She wanted to view for herself the conditions of Inverness. Maybe she could help them as well.

There was a chill in the air that promised a harsh

winter. She wrapped her blue and red plaid shawl around her and looked toward the group of people who had gathered in town.

Booths were littered in the clearing and a number of tables were jammed with bolts of wool fabric. The muted colors reminded Eilan of the earth and sea. Other vendors offered ready-cooked foods, from sweetmeat pastries to dried salmon as well as live chickens and pigs. Men, women, and children, clad in patched and faded clothes, walked slowly through the street examining the vendors' wares. Thin, mangy dogs searched the ground for scraps of food. A low monotone hum of conversation hung in the still air.

Eilan reached the perimeter of the marketplace and paused beside a table lined with cages of gray pigeons. She looked over at the townspeople. Their voices were subdued, their actions orderly and controlled. Even the dogs moved silently through the market.

Eilan focused on a woman purchasing a live chicken. Her expression was passive as she handed a coin to the vendor and tucked the squawking bird under her arm.

She looked around, seeing the townspeople in a new light. They were like ducks on a pond. To the observer, they glided effortlessly, while under the surface of the water, their webfeet moved at a frantic pace.

The vendor of the pigeon booth tapped her on the shoulder.

Eilan jumped and the birds flapped and cooed their distress. She took a calming breath. She had startled them and herself as well.

The vendor scowled in her direction. He was stocky and his face weathered by time and the lessons of life. He shook a finger at her. "Move on, lass, or purchase one of me birds. I canna have ye scaring the little beasts to death, now, can I?"

She pulled away from the protection of the booth. His gloomy expression fit right in with the rest of the town. She pulled her shawl tighter around her shoulders. "I'm sorry if I've disturbed your pigeons. It won't happen again."

She remembered her reluctance the night before she had begun helping Conor's people. The result was positive and she had not encountered anyone who was living a secret life as a murderer. They were all good, hardworking folk.

The vendor might be the place to start. If she were to help, she would have to find the cause of so much despair. Eilan reached out and touched him on his arm. His thoughts slammed into her with so much force she felt as if she'd been struck with a bolt of lightning.

She shuddered as the faces of women she knew he had murdered floated toward her. The odd thing was that they did not accuse him, but considered him their angel of mercy. She forced herself to delve deeper, past the horror to a time of peace.

The vendor walked along the water's edge. His heart was filled with love and hope as he looked in the direction of his two young boys. He gathered a woman in his arms and kissed her. It was his wife. In this memory, Eilan could not see her face, but her hair hung past her waist and was a shimmering white.

Eilan had an odd sensation she knew who the woman was as she pulled the memory forward. She took a deep breath and broke contact.

Tears filled the man's eyes as he sank down on a bench behind the table.

She walked to the back of the booth and knelt beside him. She had searched for a pleasant thought; she had not meant to bring him pain. Eilan put her hand on his shoulder. Instead of pain, she felt happiness.

He smiled. "I dinna know what has come over me. I just remembered something I havna thought of in . . . well, a very long time." He reached toward her, but closed his fingers before he touched her. "It must be your hair. 'Tis not as white as hers, but it has the same look to it. What is your name?"

She smiled. "Eilan Dougan."

He returned her smile. "I am called Finnegan."

Eilan stood and leaned against the post of the booth. She was curious about the woman. "You said I reminded you of someone."

"Aye. She had a gentle way about her as well. Fiona was my strength. When she was killed, I nearly lost my mind. I saw to it that our sons were safely hidden and then I returned." Tears welled in his eyes and spilled over his face. "It was my intent to cut out the heart of the man who murdered her, but I was a coward. I lost my courage. It was then I vowed that, when possible, no one else would suffer as she had."

His wife's name rang over and over in her mind. She had white hair and her name was Fiona. The coincidence was too strong. The woman must be Magdah's sister and the Peacemaker murdered by Simon. Eilan felt her legs tremble. She gripped the post for support.

Finnegan rose to his feet. "Are ye all right, lass? Ye look as pale as down feathers."

She nodded, afraid to trust her voice as panic spread through her. Meeting Fiona's husband had made the woman's death seem even more real.

" 'Tis my fault. I dinna mean to tell ye such a sad story. And for a long time the sadness was all I could think of, but today a new memory surfaced. I thought of her last words to me before she died." He smiled and a peace seemed to wrap around him. "Fiona told me that love is a stronger power than hate."

Eilan smiled. If everyone in this village could reach the same conclusion as Finnegan, there would be no room for the fear Simon had introduced and nurtured. She straightened. This was going to be a long day.

Finnegan opened the birdcage nearest him, took out a pigeon and held it gently. He tossed it into the air and tilted his head toward the sky. The bird flew overhead. "I do not recognize the Dougan name. Are ye under the protection of another clan?"

She nodded and watched him free another pigeon. "The MacClouds."

He sucked in his breath and shook his head. "I know of them. Good lads. I was hopeful when they returned they would defeat their uncle, Simon." He tossed another bird toward the sky. "If they need help, let them know they can count on Finnegan."

"I will." She motioned toward the crowd of people lined up to purchase bolts of fabric. They all stood patiently in silence as though there was a NO TALKING sign posted over the vendor's booth. "Everyone seems to keep to themselves."

"Aye that we do. It was not always thus. Before Simon took control, we were a lively community, full of life and laughter. Not too much to celebrate these days. It takes all the strength a person has just to put food and drink on the table, clothe the wee ones and keep out of harm's way. Simon has seen to that."

She reached up and kissed him on the cheek. "Well, maybe things are about to change. I have a feeling your town will have to find their dancing shoes once again. Thank you for your offer to help Conor and his brother."

His face flushed and his smile spread from ear to ear. "Nay, lass, it is ye I have to thank. And I hope ye are right about them dancing shoes."

Eilan smiled, turned from the booth and walked to another closer to the center of the square. She knew the sun was still hidden behind a thick blanket of clouds, but somehow, it felt brighter. Well, by the time she was finished here, it would feel downright tropical in Inverness, Scotland. Last week she had helped people find peace and it had been some of the best moments of her life. For the first time she was thankful for her gift. However, as a child, she had not been able to understand what it meant.

Eilan remembered the day in first grade she had come home from school, feeling sad and overwhelmed by the feelings she had gleaned from the other students. She had been playing ring-around-the-rosy. All of the children held hands and danced in a circle. It was then that all of their thoughts flooded in on her at once.

A boy named David was angry because his parents were getting a divorce, and Judy's dog had died. It seemed as though everyone in her class was sad. She experienced each hurt as though it were her own. She had spent recess talking to each one of her classmates. Some welcomed the opportunity;

the majority called her names and told her to mind her own business.

She had been six years old and did not understand why the other students didn't want her help.

Her mother had gathered her in her arms and dried her tears. She told Eilan she was proud of her for trying to help, and that she had the unique ability of looking into a person's heart and feeling their pain or joy. Offering help to someone in pain was never wrong. However, her mother cautioned her to respect the private thoughts of others and train herself to concentrate only on the emotions. If Eilan sensed something was wrong, she should ask questions. If the person wanted help, they might be willing to share what was troubling them. It was then the healing could begin.

Her mother had made peanut butter cookies and sat Eilan beside her on the piano bench. They spent the entire afternoon playing the piano, singing songs, and laughing together. Eilan never forgot the time they spent together or the peace that came over her by sharing her thoughts with her mother. The next day at school Eilan put into practice what her mother suggested. On that day she decided to avoid human contact whenever possible as it hurt too much.

She stopped at a booth where bright-colored ribbons fluttered in the cool breeze. She decided she had wasted a lot of her life worrying about herself.

There was a risk involved in becoming close to people, but the rewards were worth any potential pain.

A woman holding the hand of a dirt-smudged child walked up to the booth and stood beside Eilan.

The ribbon vendor turned his attention to the potential customer. Eilan watched the exchange. Could the answer be as simple as the fact that Simon was living off the resources of the town, leaving little for the people? Or was there a deeper fear?

Eilan moved away from the booth and walked toward the center of the market. To the far side she saw a pile of charred wood and a post stuck in the center. An icy chill flushed through her body. She thought of the book *The Witch's Hammer*. Was Inverness in the midst of that type of madness?

The history books were filled to the brim with examples of women being tortured and killed. Each accusation was more ridiculous than the last, from turning milk sour to having a plant die under one's care. Midwives were accused of witchcraft if a woman died while giving birth. If the witch trials had hit Inverness, Eilan could understand why everyone kept to himself or herself. A misspoken word or deed could be misinterpreted. In normal circumstances, nothing would come of such an event. However, in the Middle Ages, it could mean torture and death.

Eilan shook the dark thoughts from her mind. She could not help these people if she was not focused.

Time was against him. It had been almost three weeks since he first arrived in Inverness. Conor pulled the hood over his head and walked to the center of town. It was the first time he had ventured out before dark, but his efforts in the local taverns had been successful and he was feeling lucky. He had discovered William's exact location and convinced a group of men to help him regain the castle. He would need more help, but it was a start.

The smell of baking bread floated on the morning air and a dusting of snowflakes covered the cobblestone streets. An outdoor market was the perfect place to disappear while he thought of a plan to free William. Besides, he was tired of a diet of ale, brown bread, rabbit stew, and salted venison. He remembered the food Eilan had introduced him to in her world. He had not enjoyed each experience, but the variety was to his liking, especially the item she had called pizza.

He walked down a narrow alleyway and headed in the direction of the booths, recalling news he had gathered while discovering the whereabouts of William. Sara had mentioned a woman with long white hair was here in the town. Wherever she went, peace followed. Was Magdah mistaken and a

Peacemaker had indeed survived Simon's mad witch-hunts? If so, that would mean Eilan was out of danger as there would be no reason to expose her to Simon when a more experienced person was here already.

Conor had learned William was being held in the dungeon at Castle MacCloud. Once freed, Conor would return to the glen where Eilan waited. He had wasted enough days away from her. At first he thought it would be better if they did not spend time together, making her departure that much more difficult. However, not being near her while she was still in his century was torture. He would return with William and spend every moment they had left together. The memories would sustain him when she was gone and the task of reclaiming Castle MacCloud would fill the void left by her absence.

Of course there was the matter of rescuing William. Conor had not worked out the details as yet, but he was close. All he had to do was sneak past approximately fifty guards, overpower the jailer and find the key to open William's cell. It should not be a problem. He hoped.

The lyrical sound of bagpipes floated toward him, combined with children's laughter.

Conor came to an abrupt stop. He could not believe what he heard. Just a short time ago this area was as somber as death. He slowed his pace and as he rounded the corner he straightened. He was not prepared for what greeted him.

The vendors' booths were in the same place as before, but there was a marked difference in the townspeople. Groups danced in the street, children laughed as they wove around their parents and each person he saw had a smile on their face. It was just as he remembered Inverness, before he and Rowan had left for the Crusades, and before Simon had taken power.

He rubbed the back of his neck. It must be the Peacemaker he had heard about. There could be no other explanation. Unless, of course, someone had managed to kill Simon. However, if that had occurred, Conor would have heard of it.

"Conor, 'tis good to see ye." Rowan waved a greeting as Margaret walked beside him. He reached for her hand and kissed it before turning toward Conor. "I have discovered William's location."

Conor's eyes narrowed. "I know where he is as well. He is in Castle MacCloud. Now answer me this question. What are ye doing here? I thought I told ye to stay and guard Eilan and the others."

Rowan shook his head. "There is no need. There are more than enough men in the glen by Magdah's cottage to defend it against Simon's guards." He shrugged. "Besides, I was not sure Eilan would be able to find ye right away, so I journeyed with her to offer my protection." He smiled. "However, she can take care of herself."

Conor clenched his fist by his side. He was losing control and Eilan was at the heart of the matter. He had a bad feeling. "Where is Eilan now?"

Rowan motioned with his head toward the center of the square. "She is over there talking with Finnegan."

Conor did not wait for further information or to find out who Finnegan was. He cared not. She had plunged herself into danger. Simon had not discovered she was here, but it would only be a matter of time. He pulled off his hood and looked where Rowan indicated. A woman stood with her back to him. Her hair was shoulder length and as white as winter snow. As she turned, Conor recognized her. Eilan.

She smiled and walked toward him. Her beauty stunned him. In his waking dreams he thought he remembered every curve, every angle of her face, but he had not. The white hair only enhanced her appeal and her face glowed with an inner peace.

Eilan stood before him. "I have been waiting for you."

He cupped her face in his hands. He should be furious with her, but all he could do was look into her eyes. He leaned forward and whispered against her mouth. "I have missed ye."

She smiled. "Then the time we spent apart was worth the wait."

He brushed her hair behind her ear. "Your hair."

Eilan combed her fingers through it. "I know. Each day it has become whiter. What do you think?"

He held her close to him and smiled. "Ye take my breath away."

She snuggled into his embrace. "A perfect answer."

Conor put his hand around her waist. He did not want this moment to end, but it was too dangerous for her. "We must leave before Simon discovers ye are here. Ye are no longer needed. There is another Peacemaker in Inverness."

Eilan reached up and kissed him on the lips. "I'm the only one here."

"That canna be true. It is said she has changed the town."

She cocked an eyebrow and made a sweeping gesture with her arm as she mimicked his Scottish burr. "Aye, laddie, it was I."

The sound of horses' hooves on cobblestone thundered through the streets. Conor put his arm around Eilan's shoulders. The lyrical notes of the bagpipes stopped as well as the laughter of the townspeople. It seemed as though everyone in the square held his or her breath.

It was too late to flee. They were surrounded.

Simon's guards descended on the marketplace and jumped from their horses, their swords raised as they ran toward Conor.

Conor tore off his robes, drew his blade and pulled Eilan behind him. She had worked hard to bring peace to these people and in the blink of an eye the fear had returned. The wave of men surged toward him, all with a single purpose in mind.

Kill.

19

Cries of pain and terror crashed around Eilan as Conor pulled her behind him. They were surrounded. The guards wore gleaming armor that covered them from head to toe. Their shields and swords formed a barrier, effectively cutting Eilan and Conor off from Rowan and the MacIntosh clan. Escape was impossible.

Arrows from the rooftop rained down upon them, striking the townspeople at random. A small boy cried out and grabbed his shoulder. His mother ran to his aid and covered him with her body as the unprovoked attack continued.

Eilan felt the muscles in Conor's back flex. "Simon," he roared. "'Tis me ye want." He tightened his hold on his sword. "Fight me, ye coward. These people are unarmed."

The archers pulled back and the nightmare ended as though controlled by a master puppeteer. Whimpers replaced the screams. Those still able to stand helped the wounded to safety. Out of the corner of her eye she saw Finnegan rush to help the woman and her child. An arrow pierced the mother's leg and arm, but she and her son were able to stand.

Tears welled in Eilan's eyes at the cruelty. Blood stained the cobblestone square and the smell of death closed in on her.

A trumpet blared. The shrill sound jolted her and she pressed closer to Conor. She could not sense what he felt as the barrier around his emotions was firmly in place. She now realized the value of such a barrier. Without it, the horror of battle would consume you.

The wall of guards parted as though from a silent command and a man on a black horse rode toward them. His guards flanked him on either side. Her stomach clenched. She felt a dark foreboding roll toward her like the slow building wall of water that heralded a tsunami.

She gripped Conor's arm. "I have seen this man before. Who is he?"

As she asked the question the answer wove to her from Conor's thoughts. The man before her was Simon MacCloud.

Simon reined in his horse and raised his arm as though signaling the world to halt while he took a breath of air. She could feel Conor tense.

He straightened and seemed to grow taller as his jaw clenched and his muscles flexed again. "Your rein of terror ends this day."

Simon laughed. "What army did ye bring to fight me this time? Would it be the sniveling varmint that crawled into the shadows, leaving you to fight me alone, or is there someone else?"

Conor reached behind him and pulled Eilan closer. At that moment she could read the fear in his thoughts for her safety.

He gripped the sword with both hands. "Fight me, coward."

Simon shrugged. "And why should I do something so foolish when there is nothing to gain and everything to lose? No, instead I will just take what I want after you are dead. This time I will make sure the woman with white hair remains dead. My spies tell me she has been at work again, undoing all that I have worked so hard to achieve." A smile turned up the corners of his mouth. "Her efforts were all for naught. As you can see, it did not take long to bend this town once more to my will."

Conor shook his head. "Ye are wrong, uncle. These people are tired of your evil and will rise against ye."

Simon laughed. "Even if that occurs, you will not live to see the day." He raised his arm again and a rain of arrows burst from the archers overhead. This time they had a target.

Conor.

The iron manacles rubbed against the soft flesh of Eilan's wrists as she struggled to pull free. Someone pushed her from behind and she stumbled down a winding stone staircase. She braced herself against the rough stones, reliving the last moments she had seen Conor alive.

Blood oozed from the wound in his chest. His face was ashen and his eyes glazed over in pain. Hot tears pooled in her eyes and traveled down her cheeks. She pulled once again at the restraints. Conor needed her. This century was not known for its medical advancement. A person had a better chance at survival if a physician didn't treat him. A wound, of any kind, was usually fatal. If one survived the injury, they had a good chance of dying from the treatment.

A guard placed his hand on her back. His thoughts merged into hers. She clenched her fists, expecting evil; instead she encountered a friend. It was Finnegan.

"Keep moving, witch." His words sounded harsh, but his thoughts reflected hope. Finnegan had a plan.

Eilan pushed away from the wall and clung to the chance of escape Finnegan offered as she walked slowly down the shadow-draped stairs. Even if she survived, without Conor, her life would be empty.

The red and gold flames in the torches on the walls of the Wild Boar Tavern spilled light over the empty room. The long trestle tables were littered with half-eaten haunches of venison, pewter trenchers, and spilled goblets of wine. The celebrations were forgotten when Simon had attacked the town. The people feared for their lives and had fled to the safety of their homes. Or at least, that was what Simon believed.

Conor struggled to a sitting position and pressed his hand against his side. Magdah had stopped the flow of blood, with strips of linen cloth and a foul-smelling poultice, but not the ache of both mind and body. He awaited a report from Finnegan concerning Eilan. She trusted the man and Conor would as well. However, if Finnegan proved false, well, that was another matter and the man would be dealt with.

Footsteps echoed over the wood plank floor. Conor did not have to turn to know who approached. Rowan and the men from the MacIntosh clan had returned, and Conor would wager they came empty-handed. Simon was too clever to allow himself to be captured easily.

Rowan paused in front of Conor. "How fare ye, brother?"

"I will live. What of Eilan?"

Rowan shook his head. "We were too late. Simon was able to imprison her before we could stop him." He lowered his voice and put his hand on Conor's shoulder. "We will rescue her, of that ye have my word. Our uncle was surprised with the swiftness of our attack and Finnegan reports that even Simon's guards are abandoning him. They did not approve of the order for the archers to assault the town. Many had family who were injured in the battle." He paused. "I will challenge Simon myself."

Conor shook his head and pushed himself from the bench. With the sudden movement he could feel warm blood ooze from his wounds. It mattered not. Eilan needed him.

He pressed his hand against the linen cloth that bound him. "The fight is mine, little brother. Simon's intent is to possess and control Eilan. He failed with Fiona and killed her because of it. I canna let the same fate befall the woman I love."

Rowan grasped Conor on the shoulder. "That may be true, but ye are in no condition to fight. Let me go in your stead. Ye are fortunate the archers became as disillusioned as the guards with Simon. I saw many aim their bows toward the sky rather than strike ye down."

"Aye. I owe them my life. But I will not be dissuaded. I plan to challenge Simon to the death, and fight him as long as my strength holds. This time he will agree."

Rowan combed his hand through his hair. "What has changed that he will fight ye?"

A spasm of pain shuddered through Conor. "Ye spoke the reason. His guards are deserting him. Many refuse to obey his orders and the townspeople are gathering to storm the castle walls. Simon may believe that if he kills me, his power will be restored. However, through Eilan's efforts as Peacemaker, the people have had a view of the brighter side of life. They have no intention of turning back. My death will only strengthen their resolve. While all are watching Simon and me fight, ye will have the opportunity to free Eilan and William."

Rowan took a deep breath. "And what of ye?"

"All will be well if Eilan lives."

Pewter and clay dishes clattered to the ground. Conor turned toward the sound. Magdah stood in the middle of broken and bent plates and goblets.

She put her hands on her hips as she ground out her words. "A noble and chivalrous act and worthy of a man who fought in the Crusades. To give your life, so that another would live, there is no truer gift, or so it is said."

"Do ye mock me, woman?"

"Aye, and more. I agree ye should fight Simon. He has given ye no other choice in the matter. But ye have the battle lost before it has begun. Are ye so willing to die?"

Her words hit their mark as true as any arrow. "Aye, if it would save my Eilan."

Magdah tucked wisps of hair into the rolled braid at the nape of her neck. "And why is it ye would give up so much for her?"

Conor paused. He loved and desired her. Of that

he had little doubt. However, there was more. Of late she had become his reason to take a breath of air. She made his blood boil like no other he had ever known, and her gentle ways soothed his tortured soul. He felt at peace with her as though she were a safe harbor after a black storm.

Magdah was within an arm's length of him. "Ye have not answered my question. Why is it that ye are willing to give your life to save this woman?"

The words came easily. "Because she is more important to me than my castle and all my belongings. She is my home and I love her without measure."

Magdah smiled. "That is the best of answers. And ye are her heart." She put her hand on his cheek. "Fight for her, lad, fight hard and long. Give all your strength to it and mayhaps the gods will see fit to give ye their strength to defeat Simon."

Conor believed Magdah's words held wisdom and strength, but not the message he most longed to hear. Time was running out. Whether he or Eilan desired it, the power of the Ring of Time would send her back to her own century. Life would lose all meaning without her.

Rain poured from the sky, soaking through the layers of clothes Conor wore all the way to his bare skin. An icy breeze wove around him. He clamped his teeth together to keep them from chattering and tightened his grip.

Simon stood before him; his eyes seemed to glow in the waning light. His lips curled in a smile. "So, it has come down to you and me."

Conor nodded. "That is how it should be. The fear you have locked the world in will end this day."

Simon sliced the air with his weapon. The blade glinted like newly forged steel. "All that will come to an end is your life. My only regret is that you will not witness the flesh being burned from that witch, Eilan. Prepare to die, nephew."

Conor circled Simon slowly, causing his enemy to turn toward him. Conor had learned this tactic on the battlefield. Another lesson was to strike without warning.

Conor lunged toward Simon. His enemy blocked the attack. Steel met steel and rang out through the streets of Inverness. Conor pushed Simon toward the water's edge. With each step Conor felt his confidence grow. Simon was an able adversary, but was already slowing his pace. Simon defended; he made no effort to attack.

Conor had never relished the game of cat and mouse. He would end it now and free Eilan.

A smile curled once more on Simon's face. "Did I mention that I moved Eilan's judgment day?"

Conor felt as though a clamp had been placed over his heart. He did not like the look in his uncle's eyes. "Speak your purpose."

A woman's scream tore though the rain soaked

air. Conor shuddered. It was Eilan. He stole a glance over his shoulder. Two of Simon's guards were dragging her to a pile of wood.

Out of the corner of his eye he caught the glint of metal. Simon raised his sword.

Conor turned. Simon's sword cut through the chain mail on Conor's arm to the flesh beneath. Hot searing pain rippled through him. Warm blood oozed from the new wound.

Simon laughed. "This will be easier than I had first thought. While you try to kill me, your witch will burn." He smiled. "Even if the impossible happens and you kill me, it will be too late for her."

Eilan was tied to the stake. Conor could see her look toward him. Her lips moved as she mouthed the words I love you.

Conor swallowed. One of the guards lit a torch. Conor did not have much time. "Simon, free Eilan and I will go willing in her place."

Simon's expression darkened. "We share the same bloodline and for that I will not lie to you. Know that the only choice I offer is to die at her side. She is a witch, and I will not tolerate her kind in Inverness as long as I breathe."

Only one option lay open to Conor. He must kill Simon. Conor raised his sword and drove his enemy toward the water.

A war cry echoed through the square, followed by shouting. Conor saw the townspeople descending on the guards overpowering them and freeing Eilan. They had kept their word. It was the end of Simon's rule.

Simon's eyes widened. He screamed. "No."

Conor drew strength from within and felt a swell of pride for his people and for the woman he loved. She was responsible.

Conor tightened his grip on his sword. He saw fear reflected in his uncle's eyes. Simon must know the fate that awaited him on the other side. "Prepare to meet your judgment." Conor drove his blade into Simon's heart.

Conor held Eilan in his arms as the moon rose over the horizon. The smell of smoke lingered in her hair. He shuddered and held her close. She was not meant for this time. She had survived today, but what of tomorrow? It was just as well she had to return. She was not safe in his world.

Eilan rested the side of her face against his chest and wrapped her arms around him. "I wish we had more time together."

"As do I."

Her kiss was feather soft. "Is it time?"

"Aye."

He reached for her hand and led her toward the standing stone overlooking Inverness. He traced his fingers over the circle etched on its surface. Conor felt Eilan's hand tremble.

He squeezed it gently. "Do not concern yourself. Magdah assures me the pain in your head is no more."

She leaned against him. "I know, it has been replaced by the one in my heart."

Conor turned her toward him and brushed the tears from her eyes. He leaned down and covered her mouth with his and opened his thoughts to her. He felt her love envelop him like a warm summer sun. He increased the pressure and pulled her closer, feeling her against the length of him.

The glow of the moon shone with such intensity it turned night into day. In the next instant, Eilan was gone.

Conor sank to his knees. It felt as if she had taken his heart with her.

20

A light dusting of snow covered Pioneer Square. It looked as though someone had sprinkled powdered sugar over the streets and sidewalks. Eilan opened the door of the antiques shop and inhaled the crisp winter air. She had been back for over two months, but instead of each day without Conor being easier, it grew harder.

A man in a gray suit hurried past her. He paused to smile, before heading in the direction of the business section of the city. Eilan smiled to herself as she noted the spring in his step. She closed the door and walked over to a wing chair by the counter. When it snowed in Seattle, strange things happened. People poured into the grocery stores to stock up on food, they stayed home from work, and threw a log on the fire. It was a magical time. If you talked about the rain in Seattle, you'd hear a grumble, but mention the word snow, and their eyes lit up.

Normally, Eilan reacted the same way, but when she had said good-bye to Conor, she felt as though the fire within her had been blown out.

The grandfather clock on the wall in the antiques shop bonged the hour. It was 9:00 A.M. Eilan curled up in the chair and reached for her latte. She thought keeping busy would help. But she had driven Dede nuts rearranging the shop, and then Eilan volunteered her time at the Woman's Center in Belltown. The days had gone by quickly and she felt she was making a difference in peoples lives, but her own seemed stuck in the Off position.

Her parents would be arriving home from their vacation tonight. She smiled, wondering what their reaction to her hair would be. It was completely white. Dede had offered to dye it back to its original color, but Eilan had told her friend that this was the shade she had always wanted. It had just taken a while to arrive at that conclusion.

With her parents back in town, she would be free to return to Colorado. She leaned back in her chair and sipped her coffee. Isolation had lost its appeal. Maybe she'd stay in Seattle a while longer. There was a lot more she could do here. Her experience with Conor in Inverness had changed her. She discovered that she enjoyed helping people find the sunshine in their lives.

She only wished a little of it would spill over to

hers. Arg. What was she doing? The wallowing in self-pity would have to stop. This wasn't like her. She was driving herself nuts. If she didn't halt this line of thinking, soon she would be referred to as the Mad Woman of Pioneer Square.

The grandfather clock bonged again.

Eilan leaned forward. What was that all about? Was it broken?

In the next instant every clock in the shop started chiming.

She jumped to her feet, spilling her coffee down the front of her blouse and jeans. Ow. That's hot. Great. She was a mess. She grabbed for the lace doily on the arm of the chair and dabbed at the stains. Her heart raced as her mind registered both the fact that she had probably ruined an antique doily and the chance that it was happening again. The rational side of her brain told her to calm down, the chances of Conor returning were slim and none. She pressed her hand against her stomach, afraid to move, afraid to hope.

A table crashed to the floor.

"Blast."

She screamed. Frozen to the wood floor. She never screamed. Well, almost never. She was nuts and hearing things as well.

"Eilan?"

It was Conor. She dropped the doily, turned and raced toward the sound of his voice, knocking over a lamp as she sped past. If this was being crazy, she welcomed it.

She stopped abruptly. He was standing next to a china hutch with a smile on his face that took her breath away.

She leapt into his arms.

He laughed and lifted her off the ground, holding her against him. "If I had known ye would be so pleased to see me, I would have come to ye sooner."

Her heart raced so fast she had to grasp for breath. She felt his love for her envelop her. "I don't understand. How?"

He smiled. "Magdah took pity on me. She said my sour disposition was undoing all the good ye had accomplished.

He was holding something from her. It was not like the barriers he had built in the past, but there was something he was trying to keep from her. Eilan pulled away from him and scrambled to the ground. "You are not telling me everything. Have you forgotten I am an empath?"

Conor shook his head and smiled. " 'Tis one of the things about ye I love the most. Magdah has sent me to ye. That is all that matters."

"Magdah knew all along you could return with me and said nothing?"

He reached for her and pulled her against him once again. He brushed a strand of hair behind her ear. "I like the color, it becomes ye."

"You're changing the subject."

"Aye."

He was being evasive. It overshadowed her joy. She must know. Was there a limit to the time he could stay with her? She had to know. She fought against the tears clouding her eyes. "Conor, tell me, how is it you are here with me?"

He combed his fingers through his hair. "Magdah was not sure if it was possible to send me to your world a second time. She believed there could be a risk."

"Risk? What kind of risk?"

He shrugged. "Nothing. A small matter compared with the reward." He smiled and reached for her.

She stepped back and put her hands on her hips. "I want to know. Am I going to wake up one morning and find that you have zapped back to the fourteenth century? I need to know how long we have together."

"The danger has passed. I will be with ye always."

She tried to ignore the way his last statement made her feel. It was as if the snow outside had melted, and in its place was a warm summer sun. She swallowed. But, he was holding something back from her. "What danger?"

He leaned toward her. "'Tis nothing. A small matter."

"How small?"

"Ye willna enjoy our being reunited until I tell ye?"

She nodded.

He kissed the tip of her nose. "Stubborn."

She smiled. "Aye."

He drew her close to him. "Magdah said no one, to her knowledge, had ever traveled twice to the same place and lived."

She leaned against him for support. Her legs did not feel strong enough to hold her weight. "That is not a 'small matter.' You risked your life for me."

"Of course. Magdah told me I had to catch a dragon and ask it for protection. It took longer than I thought. They are not easy to find."

Eilan searched his mind, but couldn't tell whether or not he was serious. "A dragon? You have to be joking. There are no such things as dragons."

He kissed her on the lips. " 'Tis a long story, and one that will take a lifetime to tell."

She liked the sound of that. She smiled. Well, if an imaginary dragon brought him luck, she didn't care. He was here. That was all that mattered.

He kissed the base of her throat. She felt time fold back to their first moment together at Dragon's Lair Castle. She reached up and put her hands on his shoulders. "What about your castle, your lands?"

His breath was warm against her lips. "I need only you."